OPEN

New York City, Summer/Fall 2001
Number Thirteen

Darling

poems

HONOR MOORE

Grove Press   Distributed by Publishers Group West

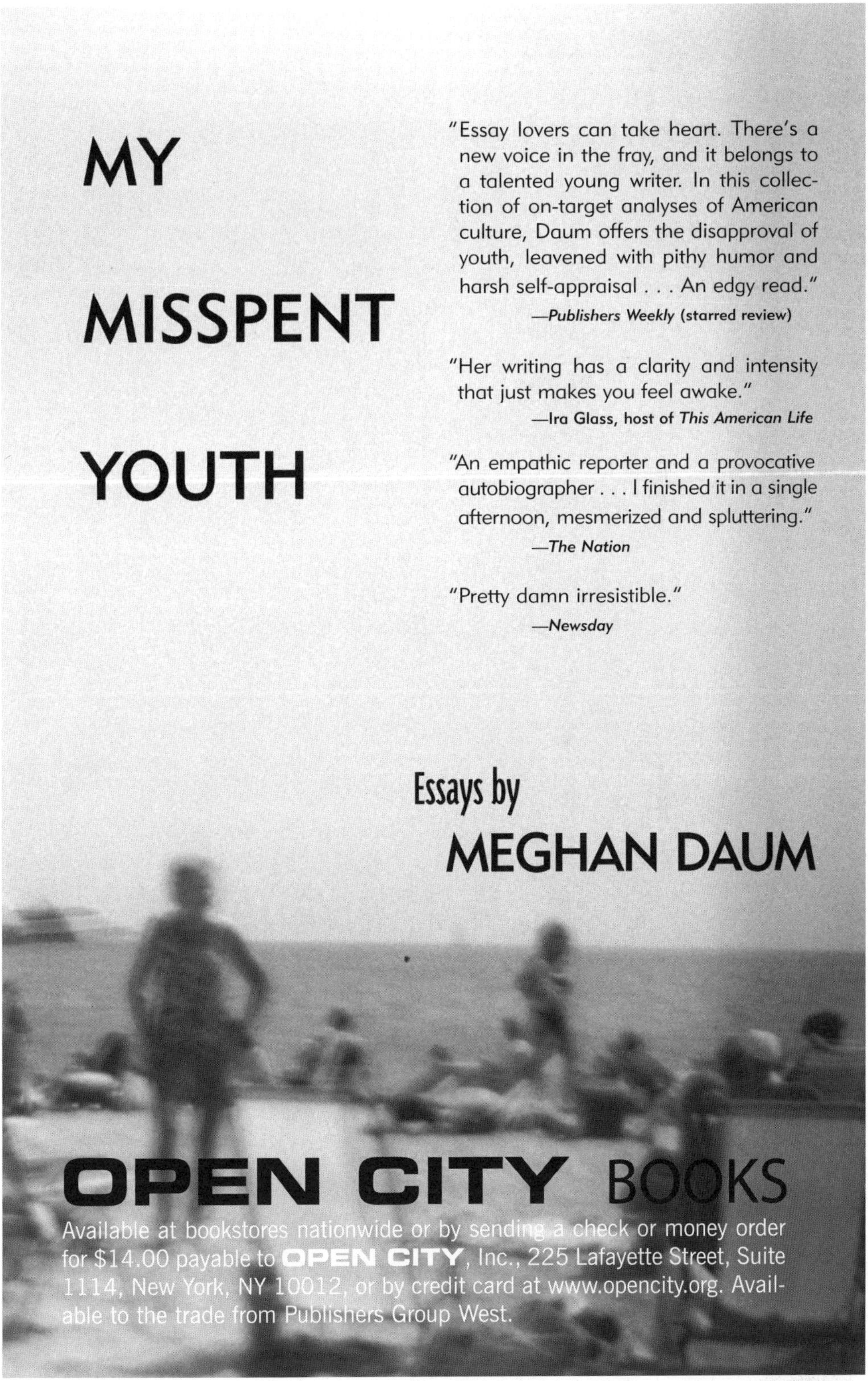
MY
MISSPENT
YOUTH
"Essay lovers can take heart. There's a new voice in the fray, and it belongs to a talented young writer. In this collection of on-target analyses of American culture, Daum offers the disapproval of youth, leavened with pithy humor and harsh self-appraisal . . . An edgy read."
—Publishers Weekly (starred review)
"Her writing has a clarity and intensity that just makes you feel awake."
—Ira Glass, host of This American Life
"An empathic reporter and a provocative autobiographer . . . I finished it in a single afternoon, mesmerized and spluttering."
—The Nation
"Pretty damn irresistible."
—Newsday
Essays by
MEGHAN DAUM
OPEN CITY BOOKS
Available at bookstores nationwide or by sending a check or money order for $14.00 payable to OPEN CITY, Inc., 225 Lafayette Street, Suite 1114, New York, NY 10012, or by credit card at www.opencity.org. Available to the trade from Publishers Group West.

OPEN CITY

*throughout

LINCOLN PLAZA CINEMAS

Six Screens

63rd Street & Broadway
opposite Lincoln Center
757-2280

PETER PINCHBECK

A Memorial Exhibition

July 18 to August 10, 2001

GREENE NAFTALI GALLERY 526 W 26TH STREET NYC 10001

in association with

Gary Snyder Fine Art 601 W 29th Street NYC 10001

ANNA
150 E. 3rd Street at Ave. A
212.358.0195

photo by Hellin Kay

OPEN CITY

EDITORS
Thomas Beller
Daniel Pinchbeck

MANAGING EDITOR
Joanna Yas

ART DIRECTOR
Nick Stone

EDITOR-AT-LARGE
Adrian Dannatt

CONTRIBUTING EDITORS
Sam Brumbaugh
Vanessa Chase
Amanda Gersh
Laura Hoffmann
Kip Kotzen
Sam Lipsyte
Jim Merlis
Parker Posey
Elizabeth Schmidt
Alexandra Tager
Jon Tower
Tony Torn
Lee Smith
Piotr Uklanski
Jocko Weyland

EDITORIAL ASSISTANT
Alicia Bergman

READERS
Gabriel Marc Delahaye
Jennifer Stroup
Susan Tepper

FOUNDING PUBLISHER
Robert Bingham

Open City *is published triannually by Open City, Inc., a not-for-profit corporation. Donations are tax-deductible to the extent allowed by the law. A one-year subscription (3 issues) is $30; a two-year subscription (6 issues) is $55. Make checks payable to: Open City, Inc., 225 Lafayette Street, Suite 1114, New York, NY 10012. For credit-card orders, see our Web site: www.opencity.org, E-mail: editors@opencity.org.*

Cover photograph by Julianne Swartz, "Beach with Car, Long Island," courtesy of Mixed Greens.
Front page drawing by Luisa Kazanas.

ISBN 1-890447-24-2
ISSN 1089-5523

CROWD

art poetry essays photos fiction

Submit

Subscribe

http://www.crowdmagazine.com

june – july 2001
paintings
(between text and textiles)

september 2001
*m*icrowave, three

Tel: 212 219 1482
Fax: 212 274 1726

www.123watts.com
gallery@tribecatech.com

123 Watts Street
New York, NY 10013

CONTRIBUTORS' NOTES

ERICA BAUM is an artist living in New York. She is represented by D'Amelio Terras.

STUART DAVID was born in Alexandria, Egypt, in 1969. He has published two novels, *Nalda Said* and *The Peacock Manifesto*, both released by I.M.P. Fiction in London. He is also the singer and songwriter with the band Looper, and was formerly a member of Belle & Sebastian. For more information, visit www.impbooks.com.

LORI ELLISON writes, "I showed these drawings to a musician/songwriter friend who was in the East Village in the early sixties when acid folk (The Fugs, Holy Modal Rounders) was coming into being. When I told him someone had said they looked like they were done on speed, he said he had done a few drawings with ballpoint pens on amphetamines. 'You always end up going over the same areas,' he said, showing me with his hand holding an imaginary pen, 'furiously, until you have a black (or blue) mass—and then you rip the paper.'"

WILL ENO is a Guggenheim Fellow in playwriting. He is also a Fellow of the Edward F. Albee Foundation and the Medway Writer's Retreat. His play *TRAGEDY: a tragedy* appeared at The Gate Theatre in London in April. The same play will be produced by BBC Radio Four for broadcast in November. He learned writing from Gordon Lish.

JULIANA FRANCIS is a New York actress and playwright. Plays she's written include *Go Go Go*, *Box*, *Saint Latrice*, and *George and Evelyn*. Her next acting gig is Richard Foreman's upcoming play *Maria del Bosco*.

SARAH GORHAM is the author of *Don't Go Back to Sleep* (1989) and *The Tension Zone* (1996), which was chosen by Heather McHugh as the winner of the Four Way Books Award in Poetry. New work appears in *The Paris Review, DoubleTake, Controlled Burn, Agni,* and *The Southern Review.* Gorham is editor in chief and cofounder of Sarabande Books.

LUISA KAZANAS lives and works in Brooklyn.

SAM LIPSYTE is the author of *Venus Drive*, a collection of stories published by Open City Books. "The Special Cases Lounge" is adapted from his novel, *The Subject Steve*, to be published by Broadway Books in September 2001. He lives in Queens.

MATT MARINOVICH lives in Greenpoint, Brooklyn. He has been published in *The Mississippi Review*, *Salon*, *The Quarterly*, *5_Trope*, and other magazines.

RICHARD MAXWELL, a native of West Fargo, North Dakota, is a playwright who now lives in Brooklyn.

HONOR MOORE's new collection of poems, *Darling*, will be published by Grove Press in September 2001. Her most recent book is *The White Blackbird, A Life of the Painter Margarett Sargent by Her Granddaughter*. She lives in New York.

VINCE PASSARO is a contributing editor of *Harper's Magazine*. His story, "Cathedral Parkway," appeared in *Open City #1*. This piece is taken from his novel, *Violence, Nudity, Adult Content*, which will be published in January 2002 by Simon and Schuster.

MELISSA HOLBROOK PIERSON is the author of *The Perfect Vehicle* and *Dark Horses and Black Beauties*. She has recently moved to an old farm, and needs $50,000 to fix the barn.

PETER PINCHBECK (1931–2000), moved to New York City from England in 1960, where he joined the second generation of Abstract Expressionists. His early works included wooden sculptures that referenced the utopian Modernism of the Russian Constructivists. In the 1970s, he returned to painting, limiting himself to a formal vocabulary of rectangles floating on colored fields. In the 1980s, his work became increasingly gestural and expressive, an evolution that continued throughout his life. "In the 1990s his colors heated up and his shapes became more playful, eventually evolving into buoyant, barbell volumes that appeared, paradoxically, to be continuous with the light-filled space they inhabited," according to Roberta Smith, in *The New York Times* obituary.

CARL HANCOCK RUX is a former resident artist of both Mabou Mines and The Ebenezor Experimental Theater in Lulea, Sweden, and one of this year's recipients of the NEA/TCG Playwright in Residence grant. He is developing two new plays: *Smoke, Lilies and Jade*, at The Joseph Papp Public Theater, and *Talk*, commissioned by The Foundry Theater, to be workshopped this summer at the Sundance Theater Lab.

PETER NOLAN SMITH is an underground punk legend of the 1970s East Village. He spent many years as a nightclub owner and doorman in New York, Paris, London, and Hamburg. More recently he has worked in the international diamond trade and the film industry. He is a constant traveler and has lived for long periods of time in Tibet and the Far East; he is currently based in Pattaya, Thailand. This is his first published work.

TERRY SOUTHERN (1924-1995) is the author of novels (including *Candy*, and *The Magic Christian*), essays, and works of short fiction. He won the O.

Henry Short Story Medal in 1963, and from 1964-1970, co-wrote the screen-plays *Dr. Strangelove*, *Easy Rider*, *Barbarella*, *The Cincinnati Kid*, *The Loved One*, and *End of the Road*. Recently found audio recordings of Southern (in French from the 1950s) have been remixed by his son Nile Southern as part of the ALT-X online sound project "Network Voices" (www.altx.com/mp3). The long-awaited anthology, *Now Dig This: The Unspeakable Writings of Terry Southern 1950-1995*, was recently published by Grove Press. Visit the Web site: www.terrysouthern.com.

JULIANNE SWARTZ is an artist who lives and works in New York. Her project, "Loci," appears courtesy of 123 Watts Gallery.

BILL TALEN is the author/actor who inhabits the anticonsumerist televange-list called Reverend Billy. He is grateful to Tony Torn for his editorial presence in this sermon.

TOBY TALBOT's books include *A Book About My Mother*, *Early Disorder*, *The World of the Child*, and several children's books. For many years she was the cultural editor of *El Diario de New York*. She runs the Lincoln Plaza Cinema with her husband, and teaches Spanish literature and translation at New York University, and film documentary at The New School. The following piece is an excerpt from *Gone*, a novel.

NICK TOSCHES's collection of poetry, *Chaldea*, was followed last year by *The Devil and Sonny Liston* and *The Nick Tosches Reader*. His latest book, *Where Dead Voices Gather*, will be published this summer by Little, Brown, who will simultaneously publish a new edition of his earliest novel, *Cut Numbers*. His new novel, *In the Hand of Dante*, will be published next year. He lives in New York City.

JACK WALLS is at work on a memoir from which "Hi-fi," in this issue, is culled. If you happen to see him when you're out at night, you are in the right place.

The PEN/Robert Bingham Fellowships for Writers

The Robert Bingham Fellowships will honor exceptionally talented fiction writers in the early stages of their careers whose debut work, in the form of a published first novel or collection of short stories, has represented distinguished literary achievement and suggested great promise.

Each winner will receive $35,000 per year for two consecutive years, a stipend intended to permit time to pursue a second work and other writing projects. Winners will also be required to undertake and complete a project of public literary service to be conducted under the auspices of PEN. These projects will be developed by the winners in discussion with PEN and are intended to support PEN's work, particularly those activities that bring authors and their works to disadvantaged communities outside the literary mainstream.

For Fellowships to be awarded in a given year, nominations from any source will be accepted until November 30, 2001, for writers whose first novel or short-story collection has been published in 2000 or 2001.

For more information, contact PEN at 212.334.1660.

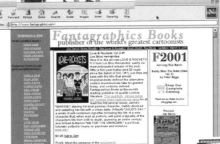

CANADA

359 Broadway (basement) NYC 212 925 4631
David Askevold Sarah Braman Aaron Brewer Karma Clarke-Davis
Robin Peck Jocelyn Shipley Anke Weyer Wallace Whitney

OPEN CITY

Arty, classy, hip, and edgy.
—NEW YORK PRESS

*An athletic balance of hipster glamour and
highbrow esoterica.*
—THE VILLAGE VOICE

Ambitiously highbrow.
— THE NEW YORK TIMES

*Takes the old literary format and revitalizes
it for a new generation's tastes.*
—LIBRARY JOURNAL

SUBSCRIBE

OPEN

Stories by Mary Gaitskill, Hubert Selby Jr., Vince Passaro. Art by Jeff Koons, Ken Schles, Devon Dikeou. (Vastly overpriced at $200, but fortunately we've had some takers. Only twenty-eight copies left.)

ISSUE # 1

Stories by Martha McPhee, Terry Southern, David Shields, Jaime Manrique, Kip Kotzen. Art by Paul Ramirez-Jonas, Kate Milford, Richard Serra. (Ken Schles found the negative of our cover girl on 13th St. and Avenue B. We're still looking for the girl. $100)

ISSUE # 2

Stories by Irvine Welsh, Richard Yates, Patrick McCabe. Art by Francesca Woodman, Jacqueline Humphries, Chip Kidd, Allen Ginsberg, Alix Lambert. Plus Alfred Chester's letters to Paul Bowles. (Our cover girl now has long brown hair. $150)

ISSUE # 3

Stories by Cyril Connolly, Thomas McGuane, Jim Thompson, Samantha Gillison, Michael Brownstein, Emily Carter. Art by Julianne Swartz and Peter Nadin. Poems by David Berman and Nick Tosches. Plus Denis Johnson in Somalia. (A monster issue, sales undercut by slightly rash choice of cover art by editors. Get it while you can! $15)

ISSUE # 4

CITY

back issues

Make an investment in your future...
In today's volatile marketplace
you could do worse.

Change or Die
Stories by David Foster Wallace, Siobhan Reagan, Irvine Welsh. Jerome Badanes's brilliant novella, Change or Die (film rights still available). Poems by David Berman and Vito Acconci. Plus Helen Thorpe on the murder of Ireland's most famous female journalist, and Delmore Schwartz on T. S. Eliot's squint. (A must-have at only $17!)

ISSUE #5

The Only Woman He's Ever Left
Stories by James Purdy, Jocko Weyland, Strawberry Saroyan. Michael Cunningham goes way uptown. Poems by Rick Moody, Deborah Garrison, Monica Lewinsky, Charlie Smith. Art by Matthew Ritchie, Ellen Harvey, Cindy Stefans. Rem Koolhaas Project. With a beautiful cover by Adam Fuss. (Only $10 for this blockbuster. Free to the first six people who request it.)

ISSUE #6

The Rubbed Away Girl
Stories by Mary Gaitskill, Bliss Broyard, and Sam Lipsyte. Art by Jimmy Raskin, Laura Larson, and Jeff Burton. Poems by David Berman, Elizabeth Macklin, Steve Malkmus, and Will Oldham. (A reader from Queens chastises us for our shameful synergistic moment with indie rock. $10)

ISSUE #7

Beautiful to Strangers
Stories by Caitlin O'Connor Creevy, Joyce Johnson, and Amine Zaitzeff. Poems by Harvey Shapiro, Jeffrey Skinner, and Daniil Kharms. Art by Piotr Uklanski, David Robbins, Liam Gillick, and Elliott Puckette. Look for Zaitzeff's *Westchester Burning* in stores soon. ($10)

ISSUE #8

Bewitched
Stories by Jonathan Ames, Said Shirazi, and Sam Lipsyte. Essays by Geoff Dyer and Alexander Chancellor, who hates rabbit. Poems by Chan Marshall and Edvard Munch on intimate and sensitive subjects. Art projects by Karen Kilimnick, Maurizio Cattelan, and M.I.M.E. (Oddly enough, our bestselling issue. $10)

Editors' Issue
Previously demure editors publish themselves. Enormous changes at the last minute. Stories by Robert Bingham, Thomas Beller, Daniel Pinchbeck, Joanna Yas, Adrian Dannatt, Kip Kotzen, Amanda Gersh, Jocko Weyland. Poems by Tony Torn. Art by Nick Stone, Meghan Gerety, and Alix Lambert. ($10)

Octo Ate Them All
Vestal McIntyre emerges from the slush pile like aphrodite with a brilliant story that corresponds to the tattoo that covers his entire back. Siobhan Reagan thinks about strangulation. Fiction by Melissa Pritchard and Bill Broun. Anthropologist Michael Taussig's Cocaine Museum. Gregor von Rezzori's meditation on solitude, sex, and raw meat. Art by Joanna Kirk, Sebastien de Ganay, and Ena Swansea.($10)

Equivocal Landscape
Sam Brumbaugh in Kenya, Daphne Beal and Swamiji, Paula Bomer sees red on a plane, Heather Larimer hits a dog, and Hunter Kennedy on the sexual possibilties of Charlottesville versus West Texas. Ford Madox Ford on the end of fun. Poetry by Jill Bialosky and Rachel Wetzsteon. Art by Miranda Lichtenstein and Pieter Schoolwerth; a love scene by Toru Hayashi. Mungo Thomson passes notes. ($10)

Please send a check or money order payable to Open City, Inc. Don't forget to specify the issue number and give us your address. Send checks to:

OPEN CITY
225 Lafayette Street, Suite 1114, New York, NY 10012

For credit-card orders, see www.opencity.org

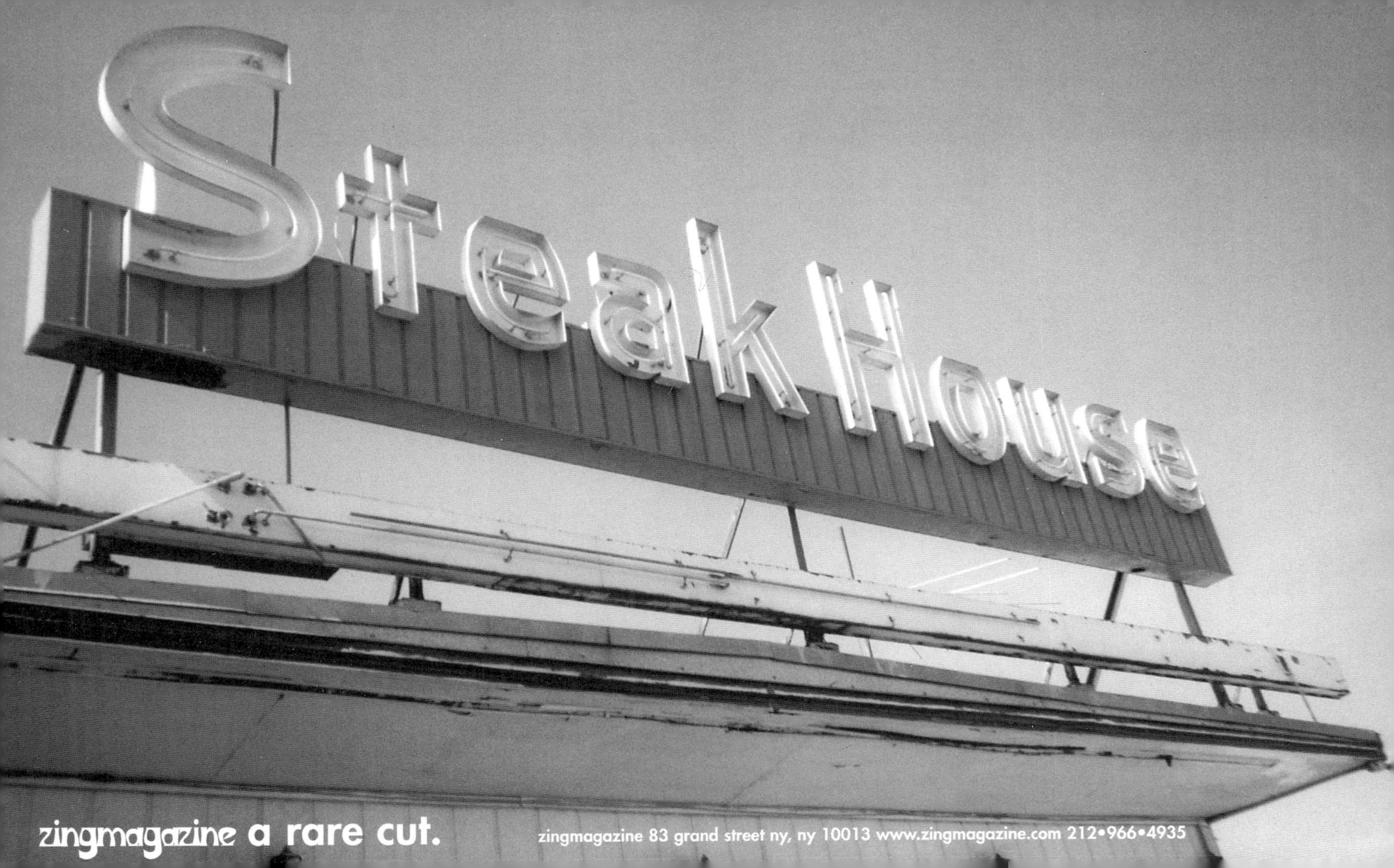
SteakHouse
zingmagazine a rare cut.
zingmagazine 83 grand street ny, ny 10013 www.zingmagazine.com 212•966•4935

Westcan
PRINTING GROUP

Our aim in business is very simple: to provide our customers with a top quality product and to always deliver what we have promised. To achieve this requires team effort – and over the years we have assembled one of the best teams in the industry – from administration through to production, our team of dedicated professionals genuinely care about each of the projects they undertake. We place the emphasis squarely where it belongs, upon the customer. We have long established the principle that our success depends on the success of our customers and therefore we will always do our utmost with each and every project.

We provide:

Competitive pricing, an efficient production schedule, exceptional quality and overall excellent value.

Proactive, knowledgable and friendly customer service from professionals who understand publishing and the needs of publishers.

A rewarding experience for all, we are passionate about what we do and are proud of the work we produce.

To learn more about us or to receive a quote on your next project, please call us toll free at 1+866.669.9914

84 Durand Road, Winnipeg, Manitoba, Canada R2J 3T2
Fax (204) 669-9920 • www.westcanpg.com

The official printing company of Open City

LITTLE ENGINES

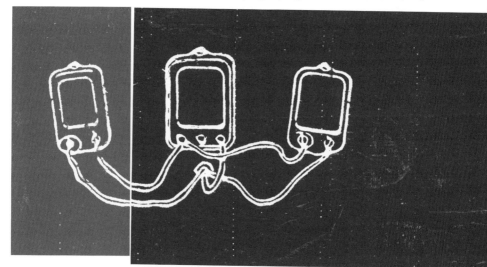

First issue includes fiction, comics and other surprises from:
JIM MUNROE, DAMIEN JURADO, AL BURIAN, ADAM VOITH,
ZAK SALLY, ANDY JENKINS and more

TNI TNI Books
2442 NW Market #357
Seattle WA 98107

ORDER ONLINE AT **TNIBOOKS.COM**
OR ASK YOUR FAVORITE BOOKSTORE/NEWSSTAND

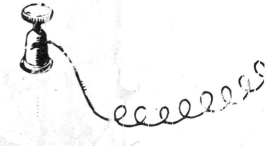

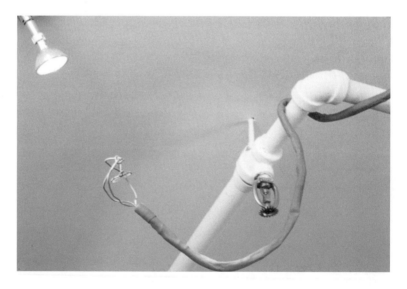

Loci
Julianne Swartz

The Special Cases Lounge

Sam Lipsyte

A CHECKUP, I WENT FOR A CHECKUP, A CHECK-THROUGH, A ticket-of-leave. I went to get vetted, poked, prodded, my chest thumped, my knees knocked, my arm in that armband, pressure's mourner. I went to get the speech, drop a few pounds, watch the vodka, the vodka tonics, the coffee, the cream.

The Philosopher was on the roster of my firm's new plan. He looked at my chart, my numbers, my counts. He stifled a chortle, gave out a tiny semi-philosophical sigh.

"I'll just be a jiff," he said.

He left me there on the checkup table, the paper sheet. I studied the pictures on his desk. He'd been to many beaches, stood in the shade of untold palm-tree stands. Jiff elapsed, the Philosopher returned with his colleague, the Mechanic. Together they reviewed the data from my chart.

Together, quite excitedly, they told me I was dying.

"Dying of what?" I said.

"We're working on that," said the Mechanic. "We'll have to get back to you on that."

They got back to me quite a bit.

We'd meet weekly in the Special Cases Lounge as I was such a Special Case. We sat on overstuffed sofas while a man in black surgical scrubs brought us tea and lemon cake.

"Can I get a drink around here?"

"Not officially," said the Philosopher, "but here."

He plucked a bronze flask from his coat.

"Brandy?" I said, sniffing it.

"Cognac," said the Philosopher. "With a dash of methamphetamine."

"Did you run those tests yet?" I said.

"Which tests would those be?" said the Mechanic.

"The ones you said you were going to run to get a better idea of how much time I had left."

"*Have* left," said the Mechanic. "You're not dead yet."

"Excuse me?" I said.

"Fascinating," said the Philosopher.

"We conducted the tests," said the Mechanic. "Frankly, they left us more baffled than before. Honestly, I can't tell you anything more than we've already told you. You're dying. You're dying quite quickly. The rest is a mystery better explored in our upcoming book."

"Your book," I said. "I don't give a rat's ass about your book. What about the cure?"

"Cure for what?" said the Mechanic.

"You know damn well it doesn't have a name," I said. "You're the ones who didn't name it."

"You see our problem," said the Philosopher. "Who's going to grant us the time, the money, the facilities to research a cure for a nameless ailment from which one person presently suffers? What are we going to do, mount gala events to raise funds for the Fight to Save Steve from Whatchamacallit? By the way, how's the hooch? The speed gives it a nice bite, right?"

"My name's not Steve," I said.

"Maybe not, but my point stands."

"We need more clients," said the Mechanic. "Or patients, if you prefer. Until then, I don't know what to tell you. We'll do what we can."

"What's in our powers."

"Our purview."

"Our ken."

When I phoned the clinic to confirm my next appointment the Mechanic took the call himself.

"We've got some exciting news," he said. "A breakthrough. I can't tell you over the phone, though."

The next day the nurse led me past the Special Cases Lounge and through a slim metallic door. We stepped into a bright amphitheater, a room like a grooved well. The Philosopher and the Mechanic stood down at the bottom of it behind a semitranslucent scrim. Dozens of others filled the raked seats. Some craned back to catch my eye, nod, enact hopeful semaphore with their thumbs. The Philosopher stepped out from behind the scrim. A lectern rose into his hands from some hushed hydraulics in the floor.

"Good morning," he said. "Shall we begin? Now, as some of you from the press may be unfamiliar with medical jargon, I'll try to stick to layman's terms. But first, a small caveat. While our tests can't be considered foolproof, the sheer quantity of data and the unequivocal agreement of it cannot be wished away. Since we have nothing comparable by which to judge the subject's condition, there is, to be quite candid, some element of faith involved, but I would by no means refer to it as a *leap* of faith. Consider it more on the order of a small hop. Or perhaps even a skip. Okay, then, on to the main presentation of our body, or rather, well, you know what I mean . . ."

There were giggles in the gallery. The lights dimmed. The Mechanic slid a videocassette into a dark notch in the wall. Out of speakers mounted in the ceiling came the whir and sputter of an old film projector. Nice touch, I thought, listened as a chime-y melody, familiar somehow, seeped into the room. It was American educational music, that old warped hope in major chords, and it bounced along to the vistas skating by on the screen: mountains and mountain valleys, jungles and jungle clears, lakes, rivers, streams, each yielding to the next in a bright ceremony of splice and dissolve.

Last was a light-filled forest, where all manner of creature began to stir, make their first nervous pokes from mound and burrow. I'd seen footage like this before, felt fourteen again, dozing in my snowboots, waiting for the afternoon bell. I remembered how much I'd always envied the tight life of voles. The hidey-hole was happiness.

No expectations down there.

Now the shot pulled out a bit. Here a stunted horse drank from a creek. There an odd bird jerked worms from the earth. Here came a rustle in the brush, a gentle tremoring that sent bugs the size of bullets to wing. Something huge burst into view, a shambling immensity I knew from coloring books, dioramas of yore. The woolly mammoth. Hairy-hided. Shovel-tusked. A great shaggy thingness. It looked about with what could have been innocence and not a little fear in its eyes. I wondered how much it cost to rent a toothless elephant, trick him out for another geological age. There wasn't much time to wonder. The music tripped into a darker key, some molester-on-the-carousel lilt. It was the end of innocence, or the end of something.

It was bum luck for the mammoth.

A band of humanoids lumbered up, a hunting party, crude men with crude spears in their tufted fists, loud language on their tongues. They whooped and hollered, circled the beast, rushed in and out and in again, stabbed until the mammoth's hide blew bright spouts of mammalian blood. The woolly fellow thumped to his knees, bellowing, bellowing, us thrust up now into the black pain of his mouth. His cries and the taunts of the hunters started to fade. There was darkness now, silence. There was darkness with a few faraway pricks of light. The universe. Universal shorthand for the universe.

We were moving through it now. We were gliding toward a greenish-bluish ball. Our ball, the home sphere. Sea and tree and all those organic shenanigans, all that fluke life. We were flying right smack into the middle of the fucker, flying and flying until it wasn't flying anymore, it was falling, and we were falling now through clouds and sky and down upon the body of a city, row-house bones and market hearts and veins of neighborhood, arterial concretions of highway and boulevard and side street, falling to a low float over pavement, a hover here in some lost alleyway, a superannuated little gland of a place, where a solitary figure walked with his hands stuck in his windbreaker. The figure began to glow, as though suddenly sensor-read, his organs swirls of grained color, his skull a glassy orb of dim pulses and firings, the lonely weak electrics of homo erectus. The man stooped for his shoelace. The picture froze at the beginnings of a bow knot. Through the speakers came the sound of gated film jumping its sprockets, the flutter of reel's end. The screen swiped to test bars. The music leaked away. The lights went up.

The Mechanic took the lectern, spoke into a thimble he'd slipped over his thumb.

"Any questions?"

There were questions.

"Should we assume the figure, the visible man, as it were, is the subject?" called a woman with a series of laminated cards clipped to her pantsuit.

"What's with the woolly mammoth?" said a kid with a video rig strapped parrot-like to his shoulder.

"Forget that," said an old man in a hunting vest. "What is the point of any of this? Is this some kind of gag?"

"I assure you," said the Philosopher, leaning into the Mechanic's amplified thumb, "this is no gag. Nor could it be construed as a bit. The visual aid is merely meant as a tool to help you better understand the scope of what we're about to tell you. Ladies and gentleman, the subject, who, as some of you may already have ascertained, is seated here among us, which I note as a precaution against insensitive comments regarding his condition, this subject is the first-known sufferer of what I believe will and should be referred to from now on as Goldfarb-Blackstone Preparatory Extinction Syndrome, named, I might add, for its discoverers, Dr. Blackstone and myself."

"Without being technical," said the kid with the parrot cam, "what exactly is the nature of PREXIS? PREXIS for short, right? I mean, what's the deal, nontechnically speaking? And why should we care, given all the diseases out there right now?"

"To put it bluntly," said the Mechanic, "those other diseases already have a name. And with it, a cause: viral infection, chemical compromise, cellular glitch, inheritance on the genetic level. This syndrome, though now named, still has no identifiable cause, which does not mitigate its unquestionable fatality. This man is going to die. But here's the kicker: he's going to die for no known reason. Maybe not today, maybe not tomorrow, but eventually, and irrevocably. He may show no signs of it yet, but he will, trust me. And though he may be the first, I assure you he is not alone. Like the beast in the film, and the prototypical bipeds who felled it, all of us here, too, will someday be extinct. Why? Who knows? Perhaps the cause is sheer purposelessness. At any rate, be advised, this subject, Steve, this mild-mannered thirty-seven-year-old adman, is but the first in line. Maybe you've been lucky enough to dodge everything else, the cancers, the coronaries, the aneurysms, but do not consider yourself blessed.

Goldfarb-Blackstone, or PREXIS, if you will, is guaranteed to claim us all."

"Aren't you just talking about death?" said the old man.

"Unfortunately, yes," said the Mechanic.

"But don't we already know about death?"

"What do we know? We know nothing. Now at least perhaps we have what little light the work of Dr. Goldfarb and myself can shed on it."

"I'm interested in what you mean by purposelessness," said the woman in the pantsuit. "Do you mean boredom? Do you mean to say this man is actually going to die of boredom?"

"That's one way of putting it, yes," said the Philosopher.

"Dynamite," said the woman, darted out of the room.

"Why didn't you tell me sooner?" I said, back in the Special Cases Lounge.

"We weren't sure."

"We couldn't be certain."

"All the data accounted for."

"All the numbers in."

"Sorted."

"Crunched."

"Mashed."

"Mealed."

"Until a granular quality obtained."

"Then checked and counterchecked against findings in our database."

"Adjusted for error."

"Baseline error."

"Human and otherwise."

"Human and counter-human."

"We had to be precision-orientated on this one. Or oriented."

"Either way."

"We had to be scientists about it."

"If we're not scientists, what are we?"

"If we're something else, who are the scientists?"

"So," I said, "how long have I got?"

My best friend Cudahy was waiting on the corner near my building. It looked like there'd been some sort of accident. News trucks and radio cars cordoned off the better part of the block. Cudahy threw a parka over my head, guided me over a hillock of root-ruptured pavement toward my door.

"Don't answer the vultures," said Cudahy.

"Which vultures?" I said.

Here they were upon us, pressing, pecking through my fuzzy sheath.

"How does it feel to be dying?"

"Do you believe you are bored to death?"

"Have you had any further contact with the mammoth?"

Cudahy shouted them all down. I felt his huge arms wrap around my head.

"Scum," said Cudahy, bolted the door behind us.

I let the parka slip to the floor.

"What's happening to me?" I said.

"Hell if I know," said Cudahy. "Why can't they let a man die in peace?"

"I'm in fine fettle," I said.

"Sure you are."

"All I did was go in for a checkup."

"That's how they get you," said Cudahy.

He cracked a bottle of beef-flavored vodka, turned on the TV. The woman in the pantsuit beamed up from my stoop. She fiddled with a coil of metal in her ear.

"Yes, Mike," she said, "he appears to be barricaded in this building you see behind me. And, truthfully, I can't say I blame him. Who wants to be the pace car in the race to oblivion? But there's another question, Mike, which I think you broached, or maybe breached, earlier. How do we know he's the only person on the planet with Goldfarb-Blackstone, or PREXIS, as it's so rapidly come to be known? It's hard to believe that this man, this so-called Subject Steve, is even the only victim of terminal ennui in this city. And if there are others, are they dying, too? Are we all, perhaps, dying? Have we, perhaps, always been dying? It's too early to tell."

"This is insane," said Cudahy. "A mass hallucination. I've read about this kind of thing. My life, there's a lot of downtime. I go to cafés. Some have free magazines. You get educated. History is full of this phenomenon. It'll blow over."

"I don't see it blowing over," I said.

"It's just started to blow, buddy. There's a whole blowing-over. Anyway, you've got more important things to think about. You're still, on a personal level, dying.

dying."

"But I'm in fine fettle," I said.

"Fettle is irrelevant," said Cudahy. "Science has proven that much."

Now a man I knew appeared on the screen. He sat at an office workstation, his thin hair blending with the fabric of the cube-wall weave.

"One thing I can tell you about the subject," said the man, "he always bought doughnuts for his team."

"Pastries!" I said. "Better than doughnuts!"

"It's okay," said Cudahy. "Calm down."

"It wasn't doughnuts."

"It's okay," said Cudahy.

"What are they talking about, boredom?" I said. "I've never been bored. Lonely, tired, depressed, of course. But not bored."

"I think they mean that as a euphemism," said Cudahy.

"A euphemism for what?"

"I'm not sure I follow," said Cudahy.

This was about the time I started to weep. This was the kind of weeping where after a while you're not quite sure it's you who's still weeping anymore. Some wet, heaving force evicts your other selves. Now you're just the buck and twitch, the tears. You fetal up and your thoughts are blows. Phrases drift through you. Rain of blows. Steady rain of blows. There's no relent. There's no relief. The hand of a comforting Cudahy is a hand of hot slag. The world is a slit through one bent strip of window blind. The noise of the city, the hum of the house, the hiss of the television, is wind.

I fell asleep, woke to a bowl rim at my lips.

My beautiful Fiona.

Dimly, men in Stetsons rode past boomtown façades and out on to a pixilated plain.

"I love this part," I heard Cudahy say, dimly.

"Fennel soup," said Fiona. "Drink, Daddy."

"They're doomed," said Cudahy. "They know they're doomed, and they also know their only shot at grace is precisely in that knowledge. There's an army of vicious Mexicans out there waiting to shoot them to pieces."

"I'd like to see the Mexican side of the story," said Fiona. "I'd like to read an oral history from the Mexican perspective."

"An oral history," said Cudahy. "I bet you would, honey."

"Gross."

"What's going on?" I said. I figured they needed a chance to adjust to my state, to their consideration of my state. My worry was I could sleep too much. A dying man sleeps too much, maybe his power slips away.

I needed all the power in my purview, my ken.

Cudahy muted the doomed hooves.

"Daddy," said Fiona.

"So," I said, "you heard. You came."

"PRAXIS," said Cudahy.

"PREXIS," said Fiona.

"You didn't seem so worried before," I said.

"I didn't know how serious it was. Daddy, I want you to know I'm going to be here for you. That part is settled. Don't argue. It's what I need to do now. For me."

"Thank you, baby," I said, and sang to her, weakly, the song about aardvarks I had sung to her in the days before she became disaffected, had to be boarded at the School for Disaffected Daughters for it.

Then I spit up some fennel shreds.

Cudahy came back with cabin food. Siege supplies. Soup cans and sandwich meats and bouillon cubes in silver foil. He pulled a newspaper from the grocery sack, folded to an item: "Doc's Prog for Our Kind: Game Over." Beneath my ex-wife's picture was a caption: "Ex-Hubby the New T. Rex."

"Where'd they get the photo?" I said.

"Eye in the sky, probably," said Cudahy. "Or the DMV."

"Mom gave it to them," said Fiona. "She left a message on my cell. She's getting calls from talk shows. She wants to know how you feel about her speaking publicly on the matter."

"You mean pimping my suffering."

"No, I mean sharing her experience, hope, and strength."

"Tell her she can do whatever the hell she wants."

"I knew you'd say that so I already said that."

"There's a guy out there," said Cudahy. "Says he can help."

"Reporter?" said Fiona.

"Don't think so," said Cudahy. "He told me to give this to you."

It was a mimeographed brochure, lettered in splotchy monastic script.

Have you been left for dead?

Do you number among the Infortunate—
shrugged off by family, friends, physicians, priests?

Have you been told you're beyond all hope?

Are you incorrigible, inoperable, degenerative, degenerate, terminal,
chronic, and/or doomed?

Are you lost, are you crazy, or just plain sick?

Maybe you should snuff it, friend.

Go ahead.

Pull the Trigger.

Turn up the Gas.

Do it.

Do it, coward.

Did you do it?

You didn't, did you?

Okay, don't do it.

You're not worth the
mess you'll make. Not yet.

Here's a better idea:

Call the Center for Nondenominational Recovery and Redemption and
deliver back unto yourself your dying body and your dead soul.

No malady, real or imagined, is too difficult to treat.

Forget the scientific phonies and the quacks of holistic boutiques.

Forget the false love of New Age shamans.

Forget the false touch of healing retreats.

Your health, your freedom, your salvation is a
toll-free call away.

Ask for Heinrich.

All major credit cards accepted.

Squeezed along the margin in fountain ink was this: "I have the cure—H."

I made of this inanity a nice coaster for my coffee mug.

"They'll really be coming out of the woodwork now," I said.

"What woodwork?" said Cudahy. "We're on an island of concrete."

Walking back to the clinic for my next appointment a few weeks later, I saw what Cudahy had meant. I'd lived in this city long enough to forget the absurdity of the place, all these surfaces refracting us in shatters, this tonnage that bore down on us with hysterical weight.

Someday sectors of this city would make the most astonishing ruins. No pyramid or sacrificial ziggurat would compare to these insurance towers, convention domes. Unnerved, of course, or stoned enough, you always could see it, tomorrow's ruins today, carcasses of steel teetered in a halt of death, half globes of granite buried like worlds under shards of street. Sometimes I pictured myself a futuristic sifter, some odd being bred for sexlessness, helmed in pulsing Lucite, stooping to examine an elevator panel, a perfectly preserved boutonniere.

I'd be the finder of something.

Now, walking along, I had only the sense of losing myself.

Yes, I could perambulate unpestered, unthronged. My saga was stale. There were fresh griefs upon us. A beloved lip-sync diva had choked to death on a sea-bass bone. The troops of our republic were poised on the border of a lawless fiefdom in Delaware. The Secretary of Agriculture had been exposed as a fervent collector of barnyard porn. Worse, he had yen for the young ones, the piglets, the foals. Bestiality was one thing, bellowed the ethics community, but these were babies. There were wars and rumors of war and leaks of covert ops. There were earthquakes, famines, droughts, floods. A certain movie star had made box-office magic once more.

The *National Journal of Medicine*'s scathing rebuke of the veracity of Goldfarb-Blackstone Syndrome, its excoriation of the ailment's namesakes as "freak show impresarios," had barely made the back pages, the spot after the break.

The air was out and I was glad of it. My fine fettle continued to obtain. Still, I somehow felt bound to these men, Goldfarb and Blackstone, the Philosopher and the Mechanic. They had shocked me into keener living. I was brimming with bad poetry and never reading the financials. I can't say I knew what counted in life but I was beginning to glimpse what didn't. I had Fiona back, and Cudahy, too.

I owed these doctors a courtesy visit.

The Philosopher was sniffing something from a vial of handblown glass. Dark powder dusted his nose.

"Want some?" he said. "It's a new synthetic."

"Cunt's out of control," said the Mechanic. "Making his own yay-yo, to hell with the world."

"Oh, piss off, Blackie," said the Philosopher. "Just a little pick-me-up."

These were not the dashing scientists of the amphitheater. The Philosopher was unshaven and looked long unwashed. His lab coat was covered with cobalt smears. The Mechanic had developed a tic of the eye which might have seemed lewd had the psychic deterioration which motored it not been so plain.

"Galileo," said the Philosopher through hinges of spit, "why have you forsaken me?"

"Cunt's dreaming of Pisa," said the Mechanic. "Can't see the truth of the situation. We got busted. We ran a scam and we got busted. I told him the mammoth bit was too much. Stupid. We could have had our own disease. Now we have squat. You can't patent death, I told him. You can't copyright a nonstate, let alone the extinction of a species. Especially ours. Didn't I say this? I said this."

"So, am I dying or not?" I said.

"God revealed it to me," said the Philosopher, "yet now I must defy God to appease the church. I shall perish from the hypocrisy . . ."

"That film, that idiotic film," said the Mechanic. "Somebody's cousin with an educational library. Dumb. Dumb, dumb, dumb. So now we have what? What do we have now? The answer is C: Squat. Squat is the correct answer. We had everything going for us. The two names, perfect. You need two names for a good disease. Goldfarb-Blackstone. A Jew and a white guy. What's not to trust? Can't be a conspiracy, right? I mean, sure it could be for some people, but we weren't planning on this being a black disease. They have no insurance, by and large. I mean, well, what I mean by that is by and large. I'm not a racist, you know."

"I didn't know that," I said.

"It's true."

"But what about me?" I said.

"What, you?"

"Yeah, me."

"Oh, you. No, you're dying. Sorry, kid. Hate to say it."

"Dying of what?"

"I don't know. We haven't figured it out yet. What did we call it? 'Whatchamacallit?' Good enough name as any, I guess."

"But you said it was a scam."

"The scam was everything else. See, we just wanted to stick out from the others. What's wrong with that? A brand, you know? Brand recognition. Brand—what's the word—leverage. You know, something for people to worry about on the drive to work. Something for the pharmaceuticals to jump on, the comedians to joke about. Lots of people die all the time from nameless, mysterious diseases. What, do we deal with even a fraction of the shit that goes on? The answer, by the way, is D: Less than a fraction of the shit. It's like all those murders. Most go unsolved."

"What murders?"

"Exactly."

"So, what am I going to do?"

"I don't know. Cry. Pray. Go see the castles of Scotland."

The Mechanic's eye began to spasm anew, as though straining to vomit some abominable vision. The Philosopher fondled himself on the sofa.

"Doctor, doctor," he sang, "gimme the news . . ."

"Consider yourself the luckiest guy in this room," said the Mechanic.

"But I'm dying," I said.

"But nothing, you fuck," said the Philosopher.

What part of yourself came from what part of someone else?
(Rux, page 189)

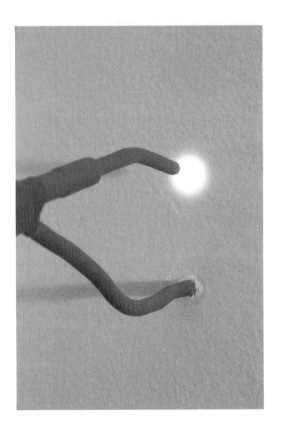

C'est Toi Alors
Scenario for Existing Props
and French Cat

Terry Southern

A SMALL APARTMENT IN LATE EVENING. A SENSITIVE-LOOKING young man sits at his desk scrutinizing the pages of a telephone directory. The sound track is military marches played very softly. The young man is wholly engrossed, but he suddenly starts up, as if at a knock at the door. He half faces the door, frowning with annoyance, and then returns quickly to his 'work' with the directory. After a few seconds he is startled again; then, with resolution, and a grim smile, he gets up from the desk, crosses the room, and dons a U.S. Army helmet, which he carefully adjusts. He takes up a machete (or bolo knife) which stands in the corner of the room, and a pistol from under the rug. He faces the direction of the door, holding the bolo knife in his right hand and making a narrow, menacing arc with it, while slowly taking aim with the pistol.

> YOUNG MAN
> *Entrez donc!*

His face grows tightly more resolute as he draws a bead, then expresses consternation, which gradually relaxes to mild annoyance, as if in recognizing a harmless but boring visitor. He lowers the pistol and half turns away (as if to say "So, it's you again, is it?"). It is a cat, entering the room at a trot, as on the way to food, but it sits down near the desk, to wait, and stare up expectantly at the young man—who, meanwhile, has crossed over to the desk again, where he doffs the helmet, placing it upside down on the desk. This is done quite casually, but as soon as it is done, he strikes an air of bravado and gives the helmet a spin with a flick of the bolo. A CLOSE SHOT reveals a large photograph of a cat inside the spinning helmet.

The young man glances disdainfully down at the cat on the floor; then, with an adroit movement of the bolo, he stops the spinning helmet, takes aim with the pistol, and fires into the helmet. He lifts out the photograph, examines with satisfaction the hole in the center of the cat's head, and with exaggerated nonchalance, tosses it aside. He lays the pistol and bolo on the desk, sits down, and resumes his 'work,' slowly turning the pages of the directory. He finds it difficult to concentrate, however, and it slowly dawns upon him that the cat—who continues to stare—*is up to something*. He starts suddenly as though the cat had addressed him; then, with a forced indifference, he turns and sits facing the cat in an attitude of listening—first expressing haughty amusement, then bland indifference, and finally, blatant disbelief, at which point he brings his finger to just below his eye and stretches it down in the classic French gesture of incredulity. This is done emphatically, however, so that his finger slips and gives him a nasty cut below the eye. He does not realize it at first, but after a moment of smugness, he begins to act as though the cat was laughing at him and was even calling his attention to the cut. He touches his face and looks at the blood on his hand.

YOUNG MAN (*demanding*)
Qui fait ça?

He turns and seizes a small mirror from the desk and examines his face minutely. He opens a drawer and takes out a Band-Aid which he sticks under his eye. Then he examines himself again, touching his hand to his hair and smiling mechanically in the glass to see his teeth. Now, in the realization of being watched, he slowly lowers the mirror, takes up the directory, and turns to face the cat—whom he regards with knowing suspicion. He resumes his scrutiny of the directory, which is now in his lap, glancing up from time to time to fix the cat with cold appraisal, exaggerated suspicion, and confidence (his eyes becoming mere slits past which the smoke of a cigarette rises). He turns a page and starts up mildly; there is a large photograph of a cat there. He picks it up gingerly and with a show of consternation, then holds it to the light. He is smugly pleased to see that it is the picture with the large hole in the cat's head.

> YOUNG MAN
> *Tiens!*

He attaches it with Band-Aids to the mirror, and with restrained mirth places the mirror before the cat. Then he doubles up with laughter, pointing in ridicule at the cat. The cat remains impassive. After a moment, the young man's mirth subsides, and he becomes livid with anger and frustration.

> YOUNG MAN (*in a hiss of rage*)
> *Je vous detéste!*

He turns back to his desk and quickly leafs over to the next page. He screams and recoils in horror, closing the page as he does as if to trap whatever is there inside, at the same time seizing the bolo and plunging it into the closed book. He slowly withdraws the bolo with the page on the end of the blade, holding it out like a writhing snake. CLOSE-UP reveals it to be another photograph of a cat, this one springing toward the camera. He crosses the room with it, quivering, holding it away from him, to the corner where he takes it off the bolo with his foot and slashes at it frantically. Visibly shaken, he slowly turns to face the cat on the floor.

> YOUNG MAN (*shouting*)
> *C'est toi alors!*

He leaps at the cat, holding the bolo like a dagger. The cat jumps aside, and the young man grovels on the floor, kicking his feet like a child and plunging the bayonet repeatedly against the floor, his face buried in the rug.

> YOUNG MAN (*shrieking insanely*)
> *C'est toi alors! C'est toi alors! C'est toi alors!*

CAMERA PULLS UP to show the cat sitting in the helmet which is slowly spinning on the desk. FADE TO BLACK.

FIN

L'uccisore e la Farfalla

Nick Tosches

Looking down that day,
the two old brothers who lived in the mountain woods
        saw it,
        and they told of it,
as did the woman,
        gathering rosemary
        from the scrub:

how Don Dario Cella,
temibilissimo e temutissimo,
        killer of men and
        killer of beasts,

walking the familiar narrow winding pass
beyond and high above Faraglione
        in the late calm afternoon

was startled,
        frightened,
        by a butterfly
fluttering
        softly,
        near his eye

and thus lost his ground,
and from the craggy pass
        fell,

screaming,
to his death
down the cliff to the black sea rocks below.

Ex Tenebris, Apricus

Nick Tosches

To have engraved in beauty, not with force as upon rock,
        or in cold delicate filigree,
but as holy breeze engraves its rippling, elusive but eternal,
        upon sea, or through the boughs of all seasons;
to have engraved such rippling upon the lake of the heart,
        within,
is to have been granted blessing to bear in that place
        that signature,
rippling and breeze and breath, of those gods without names who dwell therein,
        beneath, awaiting birth,
to rise in kind, in rippling, breeze, in breath, in turn.

To be reduced to a silence through which the leopard of all
        imagining and love and rhythm and power moves:
a silence that is serenity's one true bower,
        and that of wild illimitableness too,
and, too again, the one true sighing-place of whatever wisps of wisdom might come
        our way.

To have the Lord's day made holy after a lifetime of darkness
        —*ex tenebris, lux; ex tenebris, apricus*—
by a simple toss of a pale lovely neck, the toss of those nameless gods, those
        allotters, those dividers of destinies and days;
and to have that holiness lead the pulse
        to that place beyond all calendared days and time.

These are gifts for which there are no payment, no ledger-book, no thanking in
      words.
These are gifts that can be returned only by surrendering to them, and to their
      source and vessel:
to offer love that is of that rippling, that breeze, that breath,
      that frees and never tightens lung or heart or limb,
is all that can be done:
      to give over oneself perhaps to that thing called destiny,
but not to that vileness called will,
      and to neither make nor be master, mistress of either,
but to bow only to, and thereby rise with, those nameless gods themselves within,
and have them dance and mate in whatever manner gods
      may choose.

I'm in Love with Your Knees

Nick Tosches

Ain't gonna be no weddin', baby,
No vows beneath no trees.
Truth be told, little girl,
I'm in love just with your knees.

Gimme your knees,
Your knees is all I need.
Gimme your knees:
On thy patella shall I feed.

God gave you them knees
To give them unto me.
ἔρος λυσιμελής—
I will grease 'em and set you free.

Might work my way
Up or down a foot or so;
Just ain't no tellin'
Which way I'll go.

Take off them britches,
Set right in this chair;
Gonna finish this here cigarette,
Then, baby, I will be right there.

A Cigarette with God

Nick Tosches

The big terrace-gates of glass and heavy wrought iron are open,
and the delicate white curtains caress their outward parting in rhyme
      with the sweet chill breeze that comes and goes.

From where I lie, on my side, in bed, in the big vaulted room,
      looking out,
the shadows of the great domes and spires
      amid the soft, slow-stirring shadows of the midnight clouds
are like a suite of silent cellos whose movements
      are shadow and darkness themselves,
and all of the luxuriant melancholy that dwells therein.

My rectum does not hurt, as I had always believed it would.

Instead I feel there only a comfortable warmth,
      so strange, so new;
      and, yes, so pure.

A star appears amid the shadows of the clouds in the black of night.

Each star a soul, as Plato said;
      each star a soul.

I light a cigarette, not believing what has happened,
      but knowing that it has.

I breathe smoke toward the night,

the infinity,
the eternity that lies beyond the open window-gates,
transfixed by the lone distant star,
wondering whose soul it is.

—"Could I have one of those?"
He seems mildly amused that I smoke alternately, somewhat randomly,
        from two different packs,
        Rothman Blue and Camel regular.

—"Filter or non-filter?" I ask.
—"Non-filter," He says.
I turn to give Him the cigarette.
He places it between His lips,
        awaits the flame from my cheap plastic lighter.
—"Can I ask you a question?" I say.
His eyes close to the darkness,
        and His chest seems to move
        with a sort of tired and forlorn laughter.
—"It never fails," He says.
        "Seven thousand fucking years
        I've been trying to have one single cigarette in peace,
        and it never fails.
        Something, somebody: seven thousand fucking years
        and it never fails."

—"Seven thousand fucking years?
        They didn't have fucking cigarettes
        seven thousand fucking years ago."
—"Yeah, right," He says. "*They* didn't have fucking cigarettes
        seven thousand fucking years ago.
        I mean, look, I laid it all down here to
        bloom forth from the bosom of the earth.
        From garlic to saffron,

from opium poppies to tobacco:
I laid it all down.
I gotta tell ya, buddy,
you got some pretty slow movers in your crew."

He takes one deep drag,
and in that drag there seems to lie
more of fulfillment
than the sum of all dreams,

He flicks the long ash of this long drag into
the ashtray on the night-table at His side of the bed.

—"So what's the question?"

—"OK. There was Adam, and then there was Eve, right?"

He sighs. "Yeah, all right, metaphysically speaking: there was Adam,
then there was Eve."

—"Let's forget about this 'metaphysically speaking.' Just talk straight."

—"Oh, don't get me started on this genetic-code bullshit. Like I say,
ten thousand years to figure out a tobacco plant, then,
ten minutes later, these same fucking mo-mo's think they've
figured out the origin of life *and* the fucking universe in one
fell swoop. So, yeah, OK, there was Adam, then there was Eve."

—"Then you got mad. They wanted to taste wisdom,
and you got mad."

—"Taste wisdom? Give me a break.
Who ever got wisdom from eating a fucking apple?"

—"So why'd you get mad?"

He shoots me a look, a look that seems to say:
        watch it, pal. My love and my wrath are forever wed.

Then He gently speaks:
        "Why did I get mad? That's my fucking business."

—"But why was your anger eternal? Why have you doomed to death
        all who since have lived?"

—"Well," He says, still softly.
        "I am going to grant you a great blessing by not answering that.
        For your soul—no one's soul—could withstand
        the blow of the truth of that answer."

Then, almost consolingly, He speaks again:
        "Besides, let's look at it this way:
        Where would you all fit if you lived without end?
        You would not have room to breathe.
        I mean, this crew of yours can't really believe
        it's getting out of this joint;
        can't really believe it's going to—
        what's that phrase that's oh-so-dear to your little hearts?—
        colonize the universe?"

My rectum now begins to itch,
        begins to burn.

—"Let me try one of those Rothsteins."

I hand Him one, light it for Him.

—"Almighty," I hear myself mutter. "Creator of Heaven and Earth.

Can't even come up with His own smokes. He grubs."

—"I never carry," He says plainly.

—"Just one more question."

He takes the cigarette from His mouth, looks at it,
   and laughs as before,
   but with an undertone of low, daunting sound.

—"Shoot," He says;
   and there is in His voice at once
   a love that is supreme,
   an indulgence that is supreme,
   and an air of some vast and unknowable thing that is
   most supreme of all.

—"You are the God of vengeance."

He responds with a slow reflective nod
   that seems less a response to my words than a deepening
   entry into that unknowable thing that is most supreme of all:
   that unknowable thing that emanates from Him,
   that is Him, even as He enters into it.

—"So, then," I say, "why would the Almighty God of vengeance
   send down as the Incarnation of His only begotten Son
   a Lord of forgiveness and of love? I mean: 'I give unto you a
   new commandment: Love one another'?"

At this, the laughter in His gut and the sigh from His lips
   are of long-resigned forbearance;
   and He waves His hand slowly, tiredly before Him,
   in like manner, which might be,

or might be mistaken for,
a gesture of gentle disgust.

Once again He sighs,
and He slowly shakes His head,
as His hand completes its weary arc.

Then, with a murmur of laughter
in a voice as strong as the sea
and as tender as the dew of the first dawn that ever was:

—"Kids," He says. "Kids."

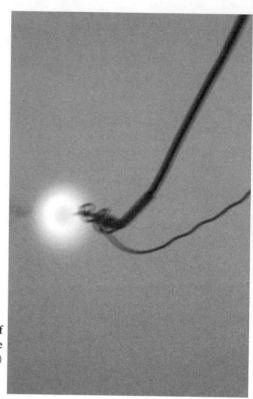

**following the whiff of
long-ago pleasure**
(Gorham, page 111)

Coffee Drawings

Lori Ellison

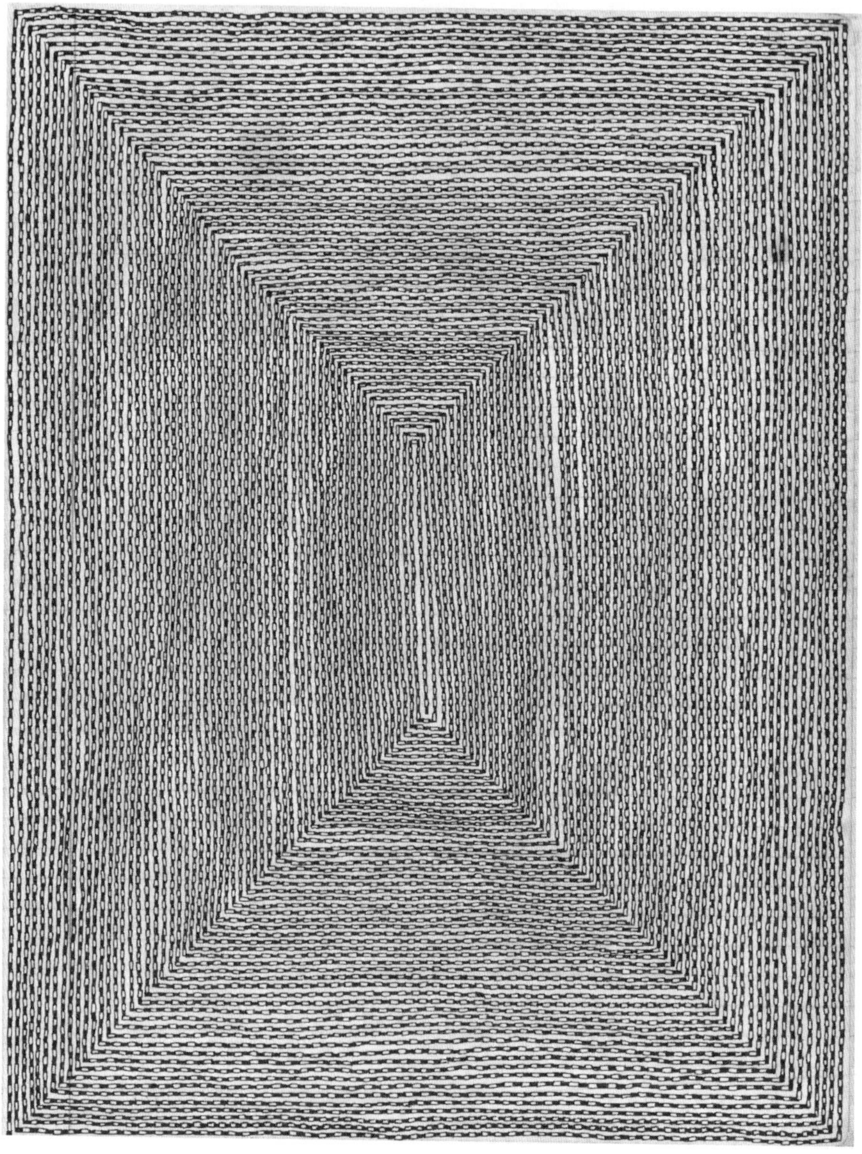

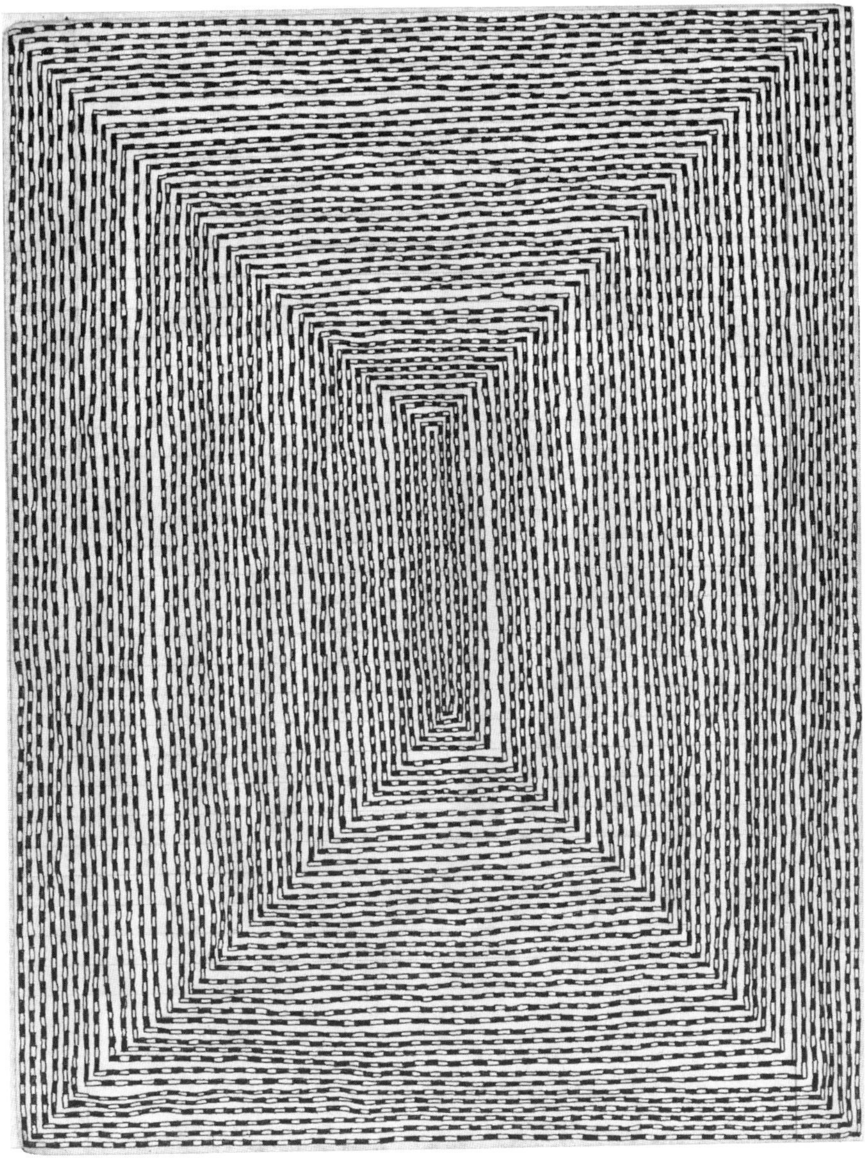

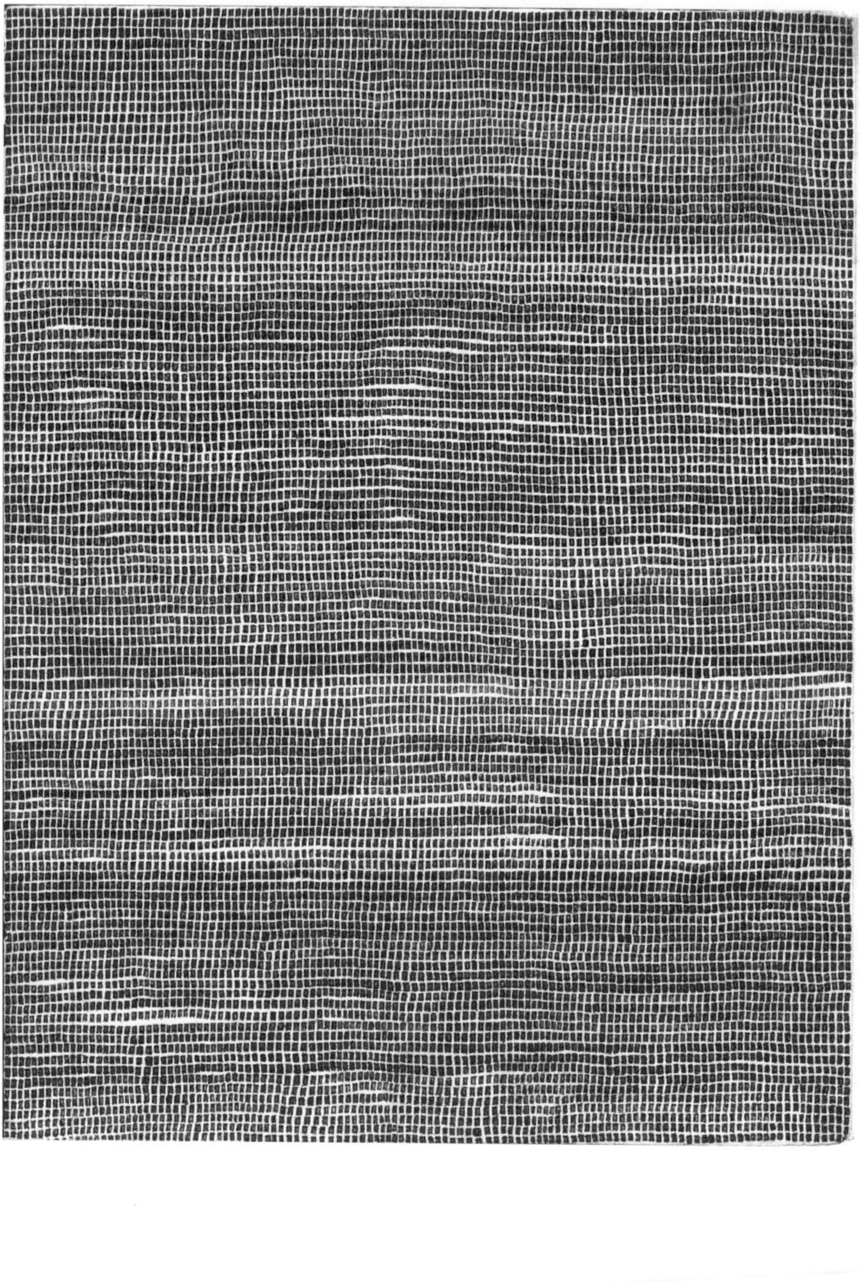

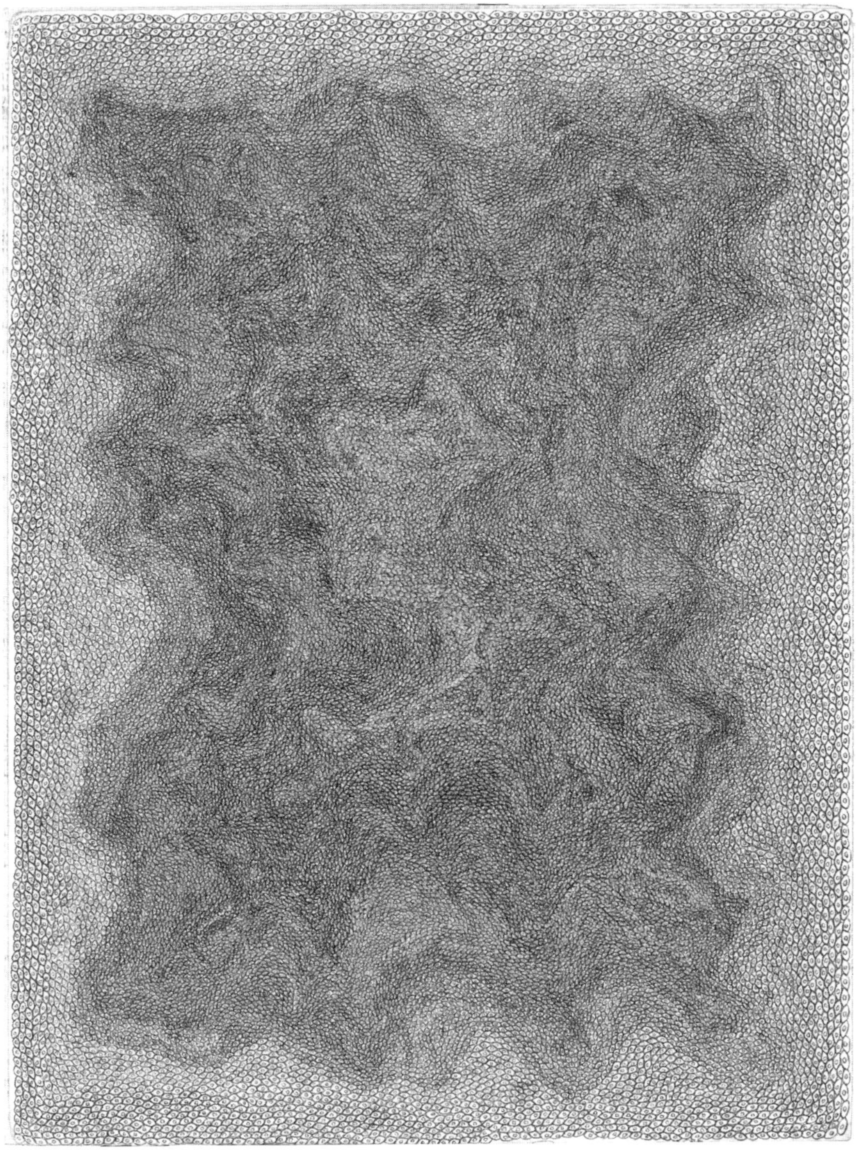

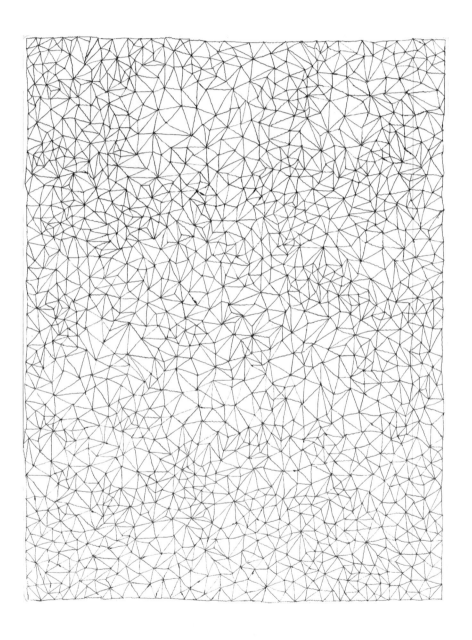

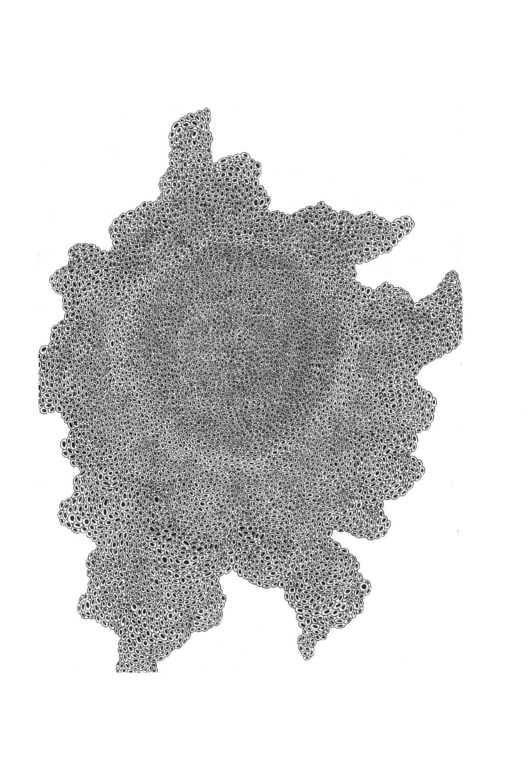

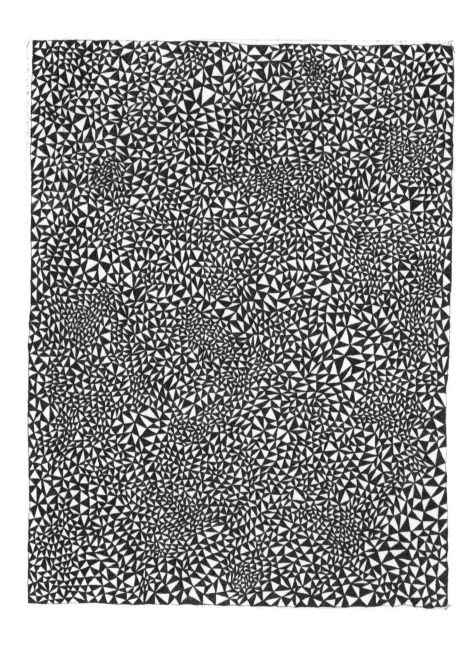

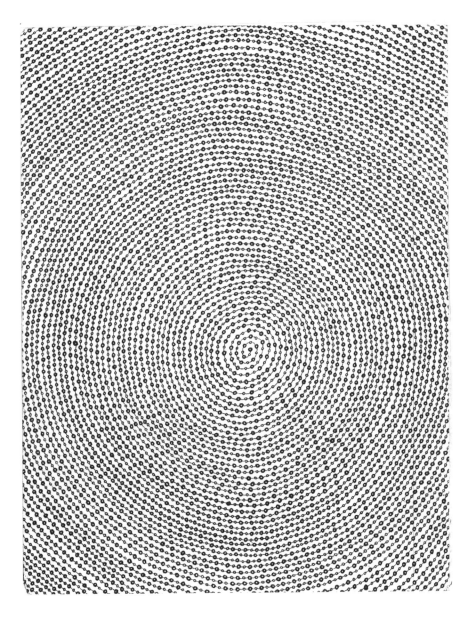

The change was determined by someone's *not* being here. (Smith, page 115)

My Public Places

Matt Marinovich

I AM A STUDENT OF PUBLIC PLACES. CRACKED WATER FOUNTAINS tucked in the overgrown corner of a public park. The dirt under a massive weeping willow trampled to a caked polish. An academy of bums teaching each other how to fall asleep on the steps of the public library.

I have my camera. I am standing outside the public library, waiting for the sun to split through the clouds. I have an album of photographs in my backpack. Italian piazzas. Roman coliseums. French amphitheatres. The Nazi "virtual" stadium designed by Speer. Columns of light thrown up by searchlights.

I have my textbook. I am sitting in class. Professor Leitz, who is an expert on the anthropological origins of all public places, has lost his place again. A student behind me coughs. There is an embarrassed shuffling of feet. I watch the professor trace a glossy page with his pale forefinger, a carpet of white hair bristling on the back of his hand. He looks up helplessly.

"Enjoy the long weekend," he says. Desks scrape on all sides of me. Velcro is pulled apart and sealed again.

After class, I follow Professor Leitz at a safe distance, watching him push the useless pedestrian buttons on stoplights. I want to talk to him about my term paper, a study of extraordinary events in city parks titled "Private Acts/Public Places." He turns and sees me coming.

"Beautiful night," he says automatically.

A boy in a hooded sweatshirt, riding low on a bicycle, nearly knocks us over. He glares at us as he goes by.

"This is a public sidewalk," I shout.

He waves his middle finger behind his head and peddles on, separating husbands from wives and startling strangers. They dance to the right and left and then pause angrily.

Professor Leitz is already a block away, stabbing at the groin of another stoplight. He looks at me suspiciously.

I wave sadly.

"Goodnight Professor," I yell.

His shoulders hunch with embarrassment.

A public goodbye.

I have my notebook. I have my pen. I am taking notes in the near dark. Inspired by the blue shadows that drift across this statue at the east end of the public garden. Three nymphs with outstretched arms and a dedication to the doctor who invented anesthesia. The lamps on the path have come on at once, light green halos spreading in random trees. A polluted underbelly of purple cloud and the last of the sunset. A few ripped condoms lying around. Someone's blue sweatpants. Two empty glassine packets. A dead squirrel, its remains being sucked from within. The man-made lake beyond the elms, three feet and five inches deep. In 1997, a man was arrested for wading there on a scorching July day. Imagine the cops clustered on the footpath, waving him in, the deranged man sloshing toward them, ripples traveling out to all the spectators. A slight breeze of applause as he is taken away, sweating profusely, his blue pants now wet and black. Barefoot. I have clipped the photograph.

Do you remember Hermann Duvoil?

He was the immigrant from Czechoslovakia who scaled the fence at the Central Park Zoo to join the polar bears. He scrambled up the man-made rocks in the middle of the night.

They lumbered toward him and sat on their haunches, campfire style. Two kids smoking pot nearby heard him talk to them in a loud voice about the political situation in his country.

"But what do you know?" he said to the bears, as if he suddenly realized where he was.

In the morning, his remains were removed by several humorless morgue technicians.

Or Edmund Allison? One of the most respected venture capitalists on the East Coast. His life was changed forever, just a few yards from where I'm sitting now. In April 1994, on a glassy spring day, he bumped into a man wearing an olive three-piece suit and was assaulted. Five punches later, he was on his knees. His hand pressed against his shattered nose, blood leaking from beneath his eyes, his voice gone hoarse from pure shock. A circle of Good Samaritans formed around him and touched his shoulders, his back, his hand.

Now half blind, he forgives all, and can be found on the bench near the south gate, spilling out his story at all hours. He cannot remember the face of the man who hit him.

"Who knows," he always says. "It could have been you."

At home, on the computer. In a chat room. I am typing real-time thoughts to Blux583. We are talking about the world's greatest public places. The garden of one-thousand roses in Madrid. Bethesda fountain in New York. The Embarcadero in San Francisco.

"What are you drinking?" he types.

"A somewhat disappointing Côtes du Rhône," I answer. Then I get to the point.

"I am sitting by an old statue on a wedding cake of stone steps. A car or van backfires and all the pedestrians stop. Over the roof of a nearby building, a flock of pigeons, already curving back to their roost . . ."

I wait for Blux583's answer, but there is nothing after my sentence. Just white space about which I can infer anything. He is having a cigarette. He is having a coughing fit. He is angrily inspecting the shard of cork in his wineglass.

"Are you out there?" I type, ashamed of my slight panic.

"Yes," comes the answer, seconds later.

"The spires of the catheter in Barcelona," he writes. His voice recognition software is screwing up again. I imagine Blux583 in his five thousand-dollar wheelchair. The Charlie McCarthy remains of his legs. He'll be fuming at the latest technical glitch. He tries again.

"The spires of the cathedral in Barcelona. Urine reek. Black mold on the walls. Echo of voices of other tourists. I climb higher and higher. Catch my breadth. Above me, someone has thrown a paper airplane from one of the slits. It sales out and goes into a helpless, tight spin. Out there, the hazy see. Islands I can't name. Great stretches of history I have no clue about. This is all I know. What the person before me sees and the person after. They scratch their names in the window . . ."

"I've never been," I type back.

"Shame," he types back.

I am standing near the dusty rectangle where the Lanford building once stood. Now it's just smoothed-over dirt. A chain-link fence. A strip of plastic paper running across the ground. A billboard illustration of the future skyscraper. Each window glazed and reflecting. Passersby become out-of-focus sticks. Unrealistic shrubbery. A sameness of trees. All saplings. No one smokes and everyone walks alone.

I am standing near the community garden. Taking notes. The fists of withered sunflowers. The tufts of dusty grass. The glass and wood coffins that hold this summer's seedlings. Cracked panes of glass. Windows buried in the earth.

She Remembers

Edgar Degas
The Bath, c. 1895

Honor Moore

From a distance, he makes something of me.
Even in the scant light of that darkness

my flesh burns as if his colors were true.
When he finishes, I step into the bath

naked, and he watches me as he has
the others, unspeaking, almost dead-eyed.

What are those behind me? Flowers.
He'd say it doesn't matter what they are,

only what he makes of them. And I break
the water with my left foot, underside

of my right knee slipping down the porcelain
incline, right hand steadied by a towel

slung across the tub's lip. I remember
how dark came, and the radiance of sheets.

My friend accompanied me to Vollard—I hoped
she could keep her face impassive. I wore

a stylish hat like that American woman
he painted once in the Louvre, her arm

long and slender as a closed umbrella.
Should commerce have kept me aloof?

I never was, from the first afternoon
he guided my leg to that angle, and bent

my nakedness until I looked like a jockey
mounting. Afterward, I unbuttoned him

and slid my hand in, pulling with my teeth
at the burnished hair near his shoulder.

We took each other between sheets
he later charcoaled. To the plain wooden bed

and its roil of orange hanging he gave half
the canvas, leaving the shadows for me

to step from air to water, from him
back into myself. I won't say what we did

that I wanted again and again, only
what grief I felt in his wanting, which I see

now in others he painted, women
who come to him, undress for money

and step in and out of water. My face,
praise God, is barely visible in the sedge

of paint. But I was not ashamed, even when
I lay on the floor and he touched me

with his foot. It was as if we were animals.
Look at the bath. What fills it isn't water

but a wild smudged black, as in the countryside
when night rises, beginning at the ground.

The Heron

Honor Moore

1.

White city sky, pull of blood down the body,
sleep in which I don't lose consciousness:

a dark-haired woman with a stump for a hand
wades soiled water, stone to stone; whirr

of heat, wallpaper, a hired room; past
doubled glass, white loops of wrought iron,

uptown skyscrapers breaking the clouds.
What replaces loss? A pay telephone, rain,

night, the separate bed, too much salt.
Shift your eyes from the empty chair. Horizon,

path through the woods, a river that flows
upstream, then at the bridge a bright rush of gray.

2.

She was fifty, I suppose, or even younger.
I was five, falling toward her wide soft flank—

though she was not my mother, not that
complicated darkness or thin sallow arm.

Again I dial the number, again busy.
It was afternoon, gray light, her English jarred

by the language of a place where snow
comes early, that the Germans conquered, blonde hair

burning to her scalp at an open oven
comes back brown, something about a red dress, how

she met her husband, who was German, uptown.
Take me back to that long afternoon.

3.

My mother and father's bed: outside, a paved
courtyard, broken privet, gate to the street,

the old man with one short leg and high black shoe
muttering Polish; and out of sight, families

whose houses burn in the night, a rat scuffing
tissue near a hole cut to pee through.

She speaks my name as one long vowel, she
teaches me the words for *cheese, thank you*

as upstairs I lie with her, refusing
love because she works for us and

because her face offers tenderness—simple
as a hand, as ironing a dress.

4.

I walk stubble, water through it like silver
filigree. It is here I have seen

the heron, at a turn in the brook.
This is the hill I climb, this the bridge

I cross, sky I look at. Each time
I wear these clothes: dirt road, then left

into the field, farm equipment rust
in the pasture. This is where I measure

what I've lost: her voice with its northern
accent speaking my name, my mother

close to death, or how my father looks
now, his white hair and crooked teeth.

5.

A black figure on the street passes
a white city wall. Light hangs behind

a silk shade, and a woman tries to comfort
the life I live out long past her death.

A bottle of water on dark polished glass.
I was in my twenties, she was in tears

on the telephone and old. She wanted me
happy, she said. Or was it green silk

that day she met her husband in Yorkville
where you could dance in the afternoon?

The brook turns here, and the great bird rises,
wings like the shoulders of a lover.

For Aagot Weickert, 1903–1985

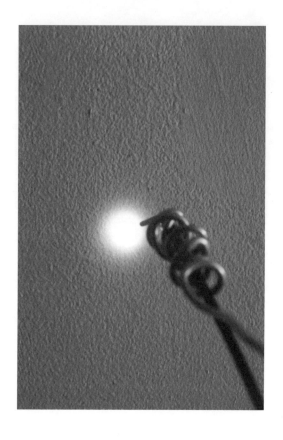

Helen Keller described her remaining senses as a "vibrascope."
(Francis, page 149)

The Short Story of My Family

Will Eno

BY WAY OF INTRODUCTION, WE WERE ALL BORN IN EASTERN
Standard Time. To the Northeast we came, crying or not, tangled or
facing the wrong direction, introduced in breech presentation or like
Caesar. We were given the test the hospital gave for newborns and
scored highly in the category of self-quieting activity. We weighed less
than the phone book of an average city. We were a family with our
own gravity, a rural quality, a name, address, and area code. Papers to
certify our birth were put in a scrapbook with a newspaper clipping
from the day we were born that began, "If you were born on this day,"
and went on to spell out our destiny and the tendencies of our sign.
You could swaddle us in one page of the sports pages.

We needed shelter.

"Here should do," our father said, before a piece of empty land.
Papers were offered. He took out his glasses, read to the bottom, nodded, and put his glasses away. The landowner made an X and pointed
to it and our father signed his fatherly signature.

From nails and two-by-fours, our house arose. From seeds and
roots, trees arose, grass, our yard. We painted our name on the mailbox. We stained the house. We all moved in. We survived the ways
you can die when you're a child—playing, sleeping wrong, swallow-
ing funny, or touching something electrical. Our dexterity grew,
our grasp of things tightening as time slipped through us and our
personalities hardened. We pointed at life. More trees grew. Their
leaves fell. We got a dog. Our dog barked. A car drove by, the driver

screamed, the car skidded. We got another dog. We dug a hole. There would be yard work in our future. We had a book to identify poison ivy. There was going to be a love of reading with us. Everywhere were the signs, the symbols, the letters, an alphabet. Our blondness faded and our blue eyes browned and words organized themselves around us.

"Berkeley Springs, Berkeley Springs," our mother said, rocking us on every syllable, instilling in us the mystery of Berkeley Springs, about which, later, we would learn nothing.

We recognized faces. We pointed more. We read our lips with our hands and touched whatever we could reach, going over all the Braille stamped into the world. We wet ourselves, got hungry, fought, cried and drooled, and dealt only in appearances, in accordance with modern philosophy. This is perfectly normal. We made early noises, allusions to contentment or distress, sounds that sounded like things, pre-words, babble, bubbles of saliva, dad, da, ma, mom, mother, or some other regional variant. We achieved immense personal growth, in terms of height and weight. By the age of walking, we learned to crawl, to put anything in our mouths, feel shame, be different, and then walk. Perfecting this, getting nowhere, becoming the same, we learned to sit.

Our father read. We sat across from him, in love with him, within earshot of him being so quiet. Once, he pointed to the words "Santiago, Chile," in the newspaper and said, "This is very sad and faraway." The picture was of a dead-looking cow caught in a tree branch floating down a river. What was a cow in a tree for, we wondered. What was a family doing on the roof? Serene photography of natural catastrophes. We didn't understand and didn't ask and our pretending we knew became our knowing.

If we had to ask our father something, we would go and ask our mother. Where is Santiago, Chile? Or, where was the rake, for instance, or shoes, or a blanket. "Did you look?" was the question she rightly answered the question with, for we asked these last questions rhetorically, lazily having made no effort to locate anything in reality. When the lost noun was found, or a South American capital, or the nonfarming implements of our North American youth, we, our then-photogenic family, got on with life. We, though snow was coming anyway to muzzle our state with snow, would take the rake and a blanket into the yard and rake. Our father sat down with whatever he was always leafing through, books or papers made of trees, possibly bound in the leather of a drowned Chilean cow. He would look out at us and his view of Massachusetts, one of the thirteen original states. We saw him cry at times in parts, reading certain writing, obituaries of past teachers and speeches of the late Abraham Lincoln. He had a reading sweater, a reading chair, a reading light of which much could be written. Whatever dog we had seemed to know it was a reading dog and would sit next to the chair and light, head on paw, breathing, studious, dog-eared.

He, our good father, would look at us over his glasses when we came in and say, "*Et tu*, Brutus?" We smiled and didn't know how to speak Latin. We looked at the floor and said, "Yes, Dad, *et tu*."

Our family had a family room. In this, we are not alone. There, by the dog, by the light of the reading light, we talked about literature and writing: Did you read this, Did you read that, Do you know how to read, Why don't you know how to read, Can you use the word "such" by itself, Why don't you ever say anything, How are you supposed to pronounce French?

Other than raking and how to be born, how to lose things and stare and be stung by bees, we didn't know anything. We were never a family before we were a family. There was no way for us to know anything about what to say or do. "There is no textbook," my mother would say, at night, as we stood around smiling in our yard, while our property got dark around us. We lived in a book-lined house on a tree-lined street, beset by sunlight lining our faces, beset by electric light, by the Encyclopædia Britannica, and leaves.

We were serious readers before we learned to read, furrowing our brows at simple things, squinting suspiciously at widely known facts, dazed by nightfall as if it were an essay question. When we would learn to write, we would write our names half-backward in our father's best books. We were adding some humanity, some crayon, and entering the only word that we could read, destroying his library from a collector's viewpoint. We were expressing an ancient desire, what cave painters knew, what Adam was after in the Garden, even though we didn't know anything. So began the scribbles, the graffiti, the reams of signatures that we would sign, in hopes of composing our Signature. So began the beginning of words cropping up all over.

Ex Libris, our father's books said on the inside cover. We looked through them to see what was not our yard or Massachusetts. Speaking for myself, and for everyone else, there was something in them to be preferred. Maybe it was order, a seeming order, an apparent neatness and meaning on the pages that we could never muster in ourselves or anywhere in our house. Gradually, through our studies, we grew to learn that we did not know how to read.

Nighttimes, in the meantime, we were read to by our mother. Did she want or not want the day or night to come when we could read ourselves, could read ourselves to sleep, when the family would become a book club and the whole house a reading room? Probably, as with all mothers and all questions, yes and no. Probably some nights she was tired, and tired of the story, and she had her own book to read, her own sleep to go read herself to, and was not interested in the destiny of a bunny or a talking steam shovel. Other times, she probably loved to read to us and see our then-unending surprise at the endless repetition. She must have loved how we loved her and looked at the pictures and up at her, mouthing whatever word she said, widening our eyes when the story we had heard the night before took a turn we didn't see coming. We asked for help with things that we didn't understand in the book, despite the completely understandable drawings. She believed our hearing stories about animals facing difficulties and making friends despite them was good for our personalities. Surely, it was. We all went on to become people who were deeply concerned about the animals in children's books and things that can't really talk that could talk. After the story, in bed with an indoor blanket and founded and unfounded fears, kisses were given, childish questions asked, sweet everythings whispered, and she turned out our lights.

Mornings and Saturdays would come.

"Saturday morning is here," our father would explain.

There was our yard for us to tend to and stand apart in. There were little plants and tender trees that were not meant for the climate our house was set in and so would die in the coming winter if they didn't get wrapped in burlap. We wore sweaters with simple wintry narratives knitted into them. We used twine. Afterward, during breakfast, we would use the word "twine," dropping it casually, if children can drop things casually, using the word in a sentence. We did this for our father's sake, to fill him with pride for his little children, for moving so easily between signifier and signified.

"Burlap," we thought, and made plans that would fall through or that we would forget.

One Saturday, our father pointed out the word "mulch" in a flyer we had been sent, altering our future, changing us as people.

One Saturday, he pointed out in the church bulletin that the apse was being repainted. We said the word "apse" to ourselves all day. Nobody liked cats, but we wanted to buy a cat and name him Apse, or Apsey.

During this time, the days of the week were written inside our underwear.

After breakfast, the word Saturday pressing in against us, our mother made us lunch. We were growing more intelligent. There was no evidence of this. We sat down to dinner.

Things continued, and we did, too.

Life flew, changed, fell, rose. We didn't notice life doing anything.

We were distracted from our yard work and the beauty of our home life by our homework. We were learning to read so that one day we could stay inside and read. We would let the leaves fall where they may. Someday, our noses and the rest of our bodies in a book, we would disregard the season, the early dark and dying flowers, our father reading and our beautiful mother motherly, and all of the other things that we, as children, so highly and deeply did not disregard.

Our brother learned to read completely one Halloween. It was quieter in our quiet house. Greenery and weeds lined the walk, ready to die for the year. A pumpkin with the shape of a pumpkin carved into it sat by the door. Our brother always stared at his hands, but now he had a book in them to stare at. We more or less disappeared for him, as each of us would for each of us. He dressed up as Robert Browning. He made a sign that said, "Trick or treat. I am supposed to be Robert Browning. Important poet of a gone age." Our sister said into the kitchen, "John, is there any more corn?" He said back, "Dust and ashes, dead and done with, Venice spent what Venice earned." Our sister asked again. He said, "Dear dead women, with such hair, too—what's become of all the gold." He came back and sat down. Our father said to my sister and me, "We'll make a sign for you two, too."

Our mother was adamant that someone say something during dinner, though nobody usually did. Someone asked somebody to pass something. Somebody said, "What does 'adamant' mean?" Our dining room was like a library. The ones who could read thought about reading. The rest of us waited for the dog to come in and do something funny. For the illiterates in the family, we had a long line of dogs who had scholarly names and came into rooms doing something funny, later to die in some unfunny way. Poor Baron Melchior Grimm, German shorthaired pointer, run over one night by a furniture truck. We dragged Grimmy off the road in a toy sled and buried him in a shower curtain that had the alphabet on it. This nighttime act brought us closer.

Not that we ever fought, ever. When we were little, the word "internecine" was not in our vocabulary. We were quiet. Quiet family, quiet town, Massachusetts, original state. We felt people were to be seen—seen going up stairs, patting the dog, touching their faces, seen staring at books and the trunks of trees—and nothing else. We watched and listened, in the hope of someday understanding, someday correctly reading something into anything.

Someone left a rake in the yard. Our father said, "Doesn't anyone in this house know where anything belongs?" We stood in the yard with the rake. "No," one of us said. "No," one of us said.

Life went on more. Man went to the moon. Woman did. Presidents were laid into the earth. There were headlines. Years of seasons went by. Snow, the ocean, crocuses, and pails on maple trees. Time was not standing still, but we were, and our faces reflected this. More and more lines appeared, little marks that were not birthmarks, our lips and eyes drying as we stared at our lives.

We readied ourselves for serious things, impossible futures, compelling narratives and prescription glasses. We imagined differences. We craved absolutes. We looked without pointing. Relatives died. We pictured cities. We looked for typos in the Bible, went through the Koran with a Hi-Liter pen, and then gave up on all gods and tried reading new writing from Europe. We studied Latin, to no avail, except to learn where the word "avail" comes from and that the word "dexterity" is more of a mystery than people usually think. Word spread of our speechlessness. We tried changing, made résumés, bought telephones, huge notebooks, typewriters, and tried to grow in ways other than weight. We involved ourselves in marriages and book clubs. We took note of things advertised in language, nonsense, sense, jingles, and slang. We wrote our names forward in our books. We subscribed to anything printed. We proofread our diaries, revised our high-school yearbooks. We devised names for dogs and then went to pet stores and animal-rescue leagues in search of the actual dogs who would fit them. We missed our quiet silent dinners together. We missed each other and ate alone, studying cereal boxes and reading milk cartons to see who was missing and what we could send away for. We missed listening to our mother read aloud and to our father to himself. Our underwear made no sense, nor did the days whose names were not written in it. Reduced again to our hands, we read our bodies, our breasts and testicles, for lumps and knots, any sign of some final growth. Things were more behind us than ahead. We longed for things, sappily. We pined and oaked and birched. Every word we traced back to our mother and father, we traced back through their mouths down their throats to their hearts, which were old and beat only half-heartedly. The Autumn Years became all our years, and we did not move gracefully into them. The children got gray and did not have children.

Leaves turned.

We did.

We would have made such a good book, our family. Or such a good cover of a book. We were practically a photograph anyway. Picture us looking at you. Everything is in our yard. Our arms are by our sides. The leaves are red and gold, they are brilliant. We are not. Hold us by the edges. See the tail of our good dog leaving the frame to get food or go into some room and be funny or tragically die. Our yard looks American, the way it is cared for, the dented mailbox, the red flag down, the species of trees, the bicycle, the tricycle. The house behind us is cropped so as to be only one story. One of the children is cropped in half. The father is beautiful, is out-of-focus. The mother, beautiful, is out-of-focus, is holding a rake, is protective, is mindful of her hair, and she is almost smiling. We are open books in our family photo, waiting for the future and the rest of the writing to come. The winter storm-watch advisories, the wills, the diagnoses, prognoses, and obituaries.

Picture the newspaper. A thin column about a local family. It reads, "They are survived by their bookshelves and yard and final dog, Miss Emily Bingo Dickinson, who will be given to the state of Massachusetts and has arthritis." There are other columns about other people. A few pages away: upcoming events, the weather, things that we will never read, a coupon for a haircut, the schedule of a parade.

The Following Information

Erica Baum

MONSTERS.

MONSTERS

MONSTERS.

MONSTERS.

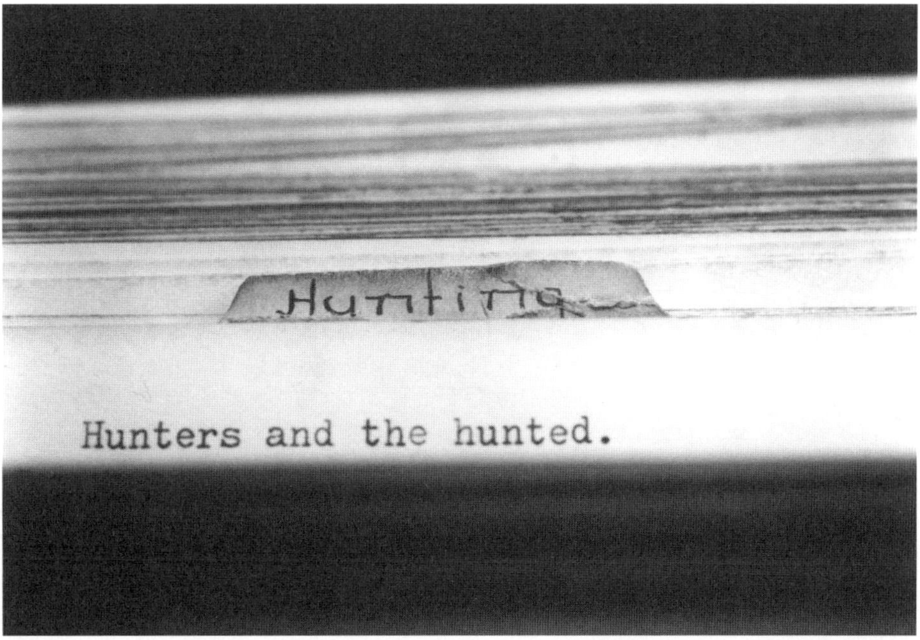
Hunting
Hunters and the hunted.

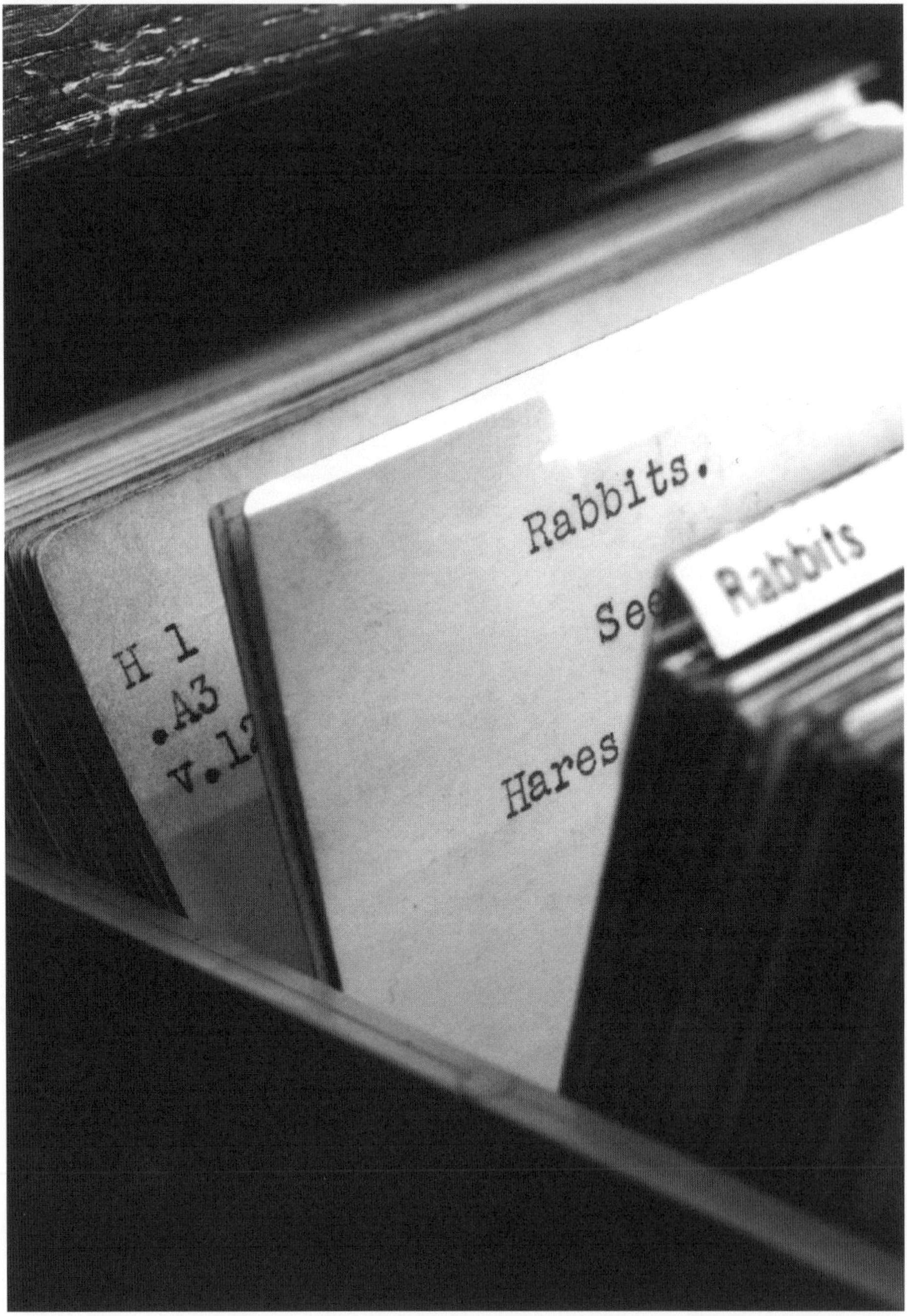
H 1
.A3
Rabbits.
Hares
Rabbits

Subversive activities
Suburban homes

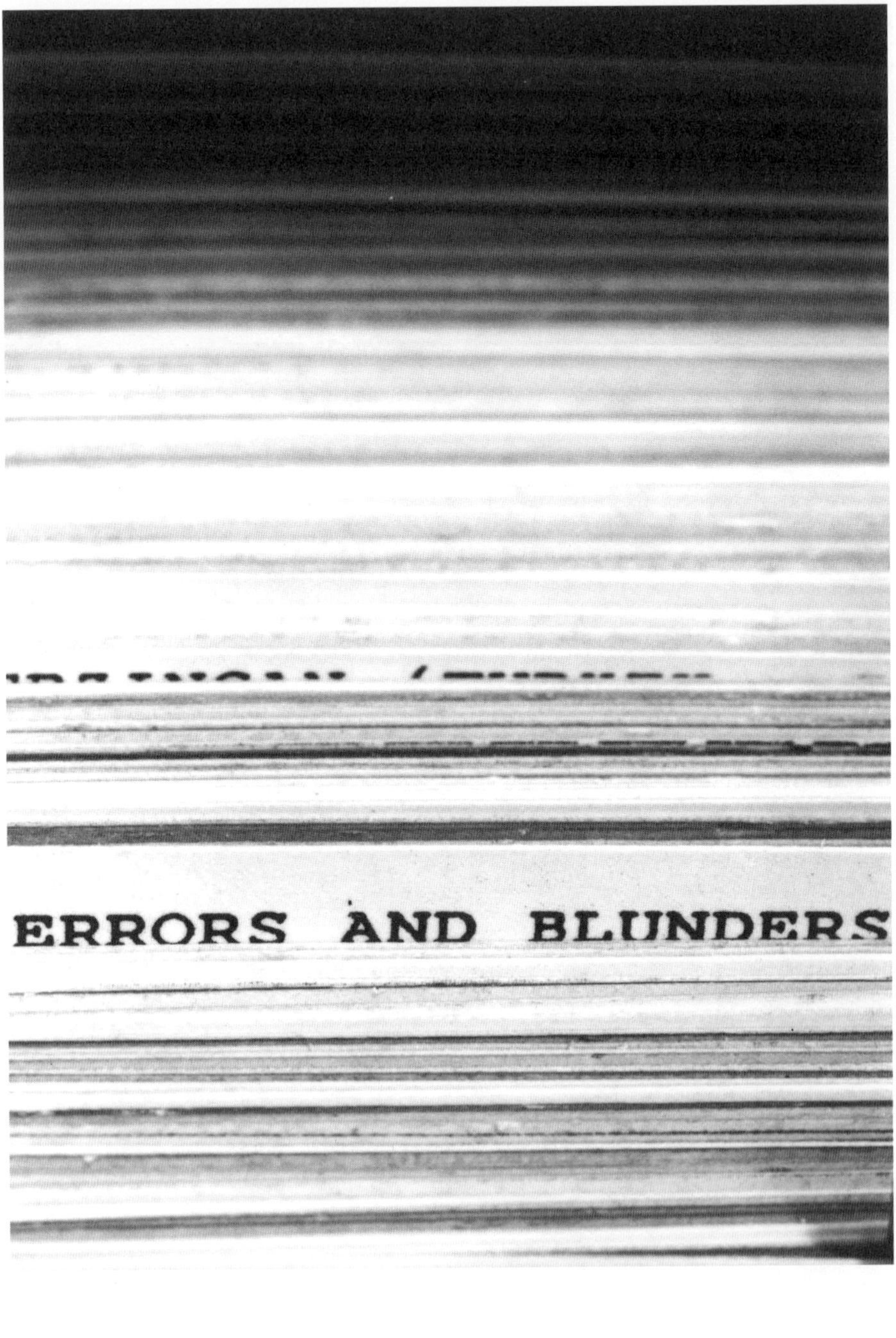
ERRORS AND BLUNDERS

God

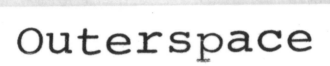

Outerspace

Gone

Toby Talbot

Anna: December

BARCELONA WAS A GHOST TOWN. EMPTY STREETS, SHOPS CLOSED, shutters lowered for the midday break. It was 1:35 P.M. when Anna checked into El Duque Hotel on the Passeig de Gracia. She remembered the hour, for the receptionist, glancing at the clock through steel-rimmed glasses, said she was early and that her room wasn't quite ready, but it wouldn't be long. She was startled at being addressed by her maiden name, having forgotten it was the one under which she'd made the reservation. When asked for her passport, she said it was in her luggage. The clerk, noting her reluctance to be served a refreshment in the lobby, suggested the bar.

Settled grudgingly on a stool, she sipped juice from fresh Valencian blood oranges. The barman was alone. He set a dish of almonds before her, and remarked on this unseasonably hot November weather: a loyal native, apologetic to tourists for unseemly spells of heat, cold, or rain. To show appreciation for his civic concern she nodded, whereupon another small dish, green olives stuffed with anchovies, appeared.

In Madrid it was twenty-nine degrees, he told her, and so dry that people had been hospitalized for dehydration. "*Tiempo feo*"; he screwed his brow at foul weather. As Anna set to calculating the Fahrenheit equivalent of twenty-nine degrees centigrade—in the eighties probably—she heard his voice in the background: "But that's

Madrid for you." The eternal rivalry of two cities: Barcelona berating Madrid's provincialism, snobbism, and indolence; Madrid spurning the other's materialism.

Here she was, in the same mirrored lounge as on that first visit—nine, ten years ago? The same blue carpet, the same tufted maroon leather chairs. Arturo, invited by his Spanish publisher, had insisted that she come. It was shortly after their marriage; she was his mooring, he insisted, and not just the translator of *We the Disappeared*, his book about being kidnapped and tortured in Argentina. Hard to believe that Arturo, given up for drowned last July, was in Barcelona now.

Mentally, she replayed the scene of the dance in Selores, the village where she'd been visiting Wendy and Gregorio: *"What the hell are you talking about!"* she shouted when Wendy drunkenly blurted out the news that Arturo was alive. Grabbing Wendy by the shoulders, she shook her and kept shaking her: It was like shaking a rag doll. Suddenly the music, with a discordant scraping of the fiddle, stopped. Dancers came to a halt, glued to their spots, holding each other like figures trapped in Pompei. Firecrackers exploded in Anna's head; Wendy remained mute. Anna dug her fingers into the doll's arms and imagined clawing her till all the sawdust fell out. "Talk! Say something!" she commanded. Wendy, sweating, eyes bulging, jaw limp, put up no struggle.

Their neighbor, Cuca, came over and separated them. *"No, hija, no!"*

For days, immobilized by shock, Anna sat in front of her translation of Arturo's book, scheduled to be published posthumously. How could it be? How could the person she trusted most engage in such deception . . . after all she'd done for him. These last months of loss, hope, and then mourning were sheer delusion—the double bereavement. At one point she came close to tearing up the manuscript: *Get the hell out of my life!*

When Wendy was asked for details, she only shook her head. Her husband, Gregorio, loyal to Arturo, had bound her to secrecy. Did Wendy know more than she revealed, but was loathe to be a messenger of bad tidings?

Why was Arturo in hiding? Had he committed a crime—though knowing him so well (or did she?), criminal behavior seemed unlikely. Had he received threats from the Argentine secret police and vanished in order to protect her? The words of *We the Disappeared* rang in her ears: *I live in fear of being alive. I'm the memory of a life, and memory fills me with fear.*

Yet, fury aside, what a relief knowing he was alive. An incredible, goddamn relief. And by the end of the week, she set out to find him. To confront him, accuse him, abandon him.

Gregorio had insisted on driving her to the airport in Santiago de Compostela, almost an hour away, though she wanted to take the train. She glared at his banalities: "It's a process . . . It's in God's hands . . . Time will tell." More than once, he assured her that Arturo was well: "I spoke to him just last week." But he could not, or would not, predict the precise date of his return. What to believe? Somehow, she believed Gregorio when he gave her Arturo's most recent phone number, and believed when he vowed that Angel had left no forwarding address.

At the gate, he waved goodbye, Wendy did not, her face a chalky mask. "Be sure and phone us," were her last words.

"*La señora Pereda, por favor.*" A bellhop entered the lounge: Room 317 was ready.

Anna paced up and down before the phone, preparing what to say if Arturo answered—a voice from the grave. Spinning zero for an outgoing line, she dialed the number in her notebook. The phone rang four times before a machine with a woman's voice answered in Catalan. All Anna could decipher was *vacaciones*.

Güell Park had been one of Arturo's favorite spots in Barcelona. Set on a mountain overlooking the city, it was close to the cemetery where his parents were buried. Antonio Gaudí, its visionary creator, and a virtual recluse, had been run over by a tram in 1926 on his way to church. A pale, bearded man, God knows how old or young, gospel book in hand, rusty black jacket fastened by safety pins, empty pockets. No ID.

The four spires of his renowned church, the Sagrada Capilla, dominated the city. "It's the best place to worship," Arturo had remarked, standing in its hollow center exposed to the sky, towers soaring above like candles of molten wax. "No sermon, open air, not one straight line." Unfinished, like Gaudí's life.

Now, wending her way through the spiraled arcade of the park, asymmetrical pillars leaning in, it felt like treading beneath waves of curling rock. Each bend yielded echoes of children playing hide-and-seek, and glints of Arturo's image. She headed for the Crocodile Plaza with its serpentine ceramic bench. A riot of greens, reds, yellows, and purples, embedded with shards of crockery—tiles, plates, bottles collected by Gaudí's workers. Leaning back against the shimmering mosaic, arms outstretched, she felt herself becoming part of that constellation of curlicues, icons, and cryptographs.

Children, deaf to maternal admonition, clambered gleefully on the ceramic paws and flanks of the Crocodile, poking their fingers into its harmless maw—little Pinocchios flirting with the whale. A wedding party was gathering for photographs around a newlywed couple, bride in ivory satin, groom in dove-gray morning coat. Young couples strolled by, arms linked, dutiful daughters guided elderly mothers, pensioners with canes and berets conversed in Catalan. Anna felt her solitude keenly.

Wife shadowing husband. How original! A Dashiell Hammett yarn: shadow-shade-spirit-ghost. *I have a little shadow that goes in and out with me, and what can be the use . . .* The verities of children's chants; shadows indeed left no footsteps. Anna Santos Pereda, a dangling marionette, movements decreed by a phantom puppeteer. Damn this tired script, damn Arturo! What in the world had prompted this vanishing act? Something *she* had done? Or had he simply flipped? Guess again. Another woman? Supposing she found them, in some nice little roost? In Spain, under Franco, a crime of passion bore small penalty. Her thoughts rambled on, disjointed as the bits and pieces of Gaudí's bench. She shut her eyes to blot them out. But a child's laughter and a mother's outcry penetrated: *"Juanito, ven aca!"*

"Se puede?" She looked up. Silhouetted against the sun, with camera and tripod, was the wedding photographer. Yes, she *did* mind. With hundreds of yards of bench, why must he plant himself here? But she merely shrugged, since he was already seated and arranging his gear. Locking a pouch, closing straps, folding the tripod into his black canvas bag.

Busywork done, he turned to survey the panorama. Treetop foliage, terra-cotta roofs, church spires, and yonder the sea. Linking thumb and index finger, he encircled his eye as to frame a shot, then swung around to observe the children perched on the crocodile. Finally, with background and foreground exhausted, he turned to her.

"Do you mind if I smoke?" Hmmm, she'd obviously been spotted as an American, no such permission requested of Europeans with their black tobacco. His native tongue was Spanish, she could tell, though not peninsular Castilian or Catalan. *La lengua del pecho*, one's nursing tongue, reigned on one's lips forever. With a motion of her head she granted permission, silently determined to remain seated a few minutes before casually moving away.

"Do you live in Barcelona?" With a photographer's eye, he scrutinized her. Discomfiting, that close up. Unnerving his dark, opaque glasses, those maddening shades favored by Spaniards indoors and out. She shook her head. "Are you on holiday?"

"Not really." Far from it, she thought.

He reached into his pocket for a blue pack of Bisontes, lit one, and took a long puff. Black trousers, black turtleneck, black sunglasses, even black tobacco—*artiste.* He leaned back, inhaling smoke and releasing its fumes as he watched the children at play. How irritating, the frank voluptuousness of each puff—*jouissance, douceur de la vie,* as the French put it. Sensing her imminent departure, he turned to her: "May I invite you for some ices?"

Miguel Pintero. Eyes, dark glasses removed (no need for blinders on the shaded terrace), an astral green. He ordered *la especialidad de la casa* for them both, three scoops of sherbet, coffee, hazelnut, and chocolate. This time, it was she who asked the questions.

"Do you work here?"

"I'm a freelance photojournalist and go wherever sent."

She raised an eyebrow. "Was the wedding one of your assignments?"

He gave a little laugh and spooned some ices into his mouth. "The bride is the daughter of my concierge and I've known her since she was born, even shot her baby photos." A fleck of chocolate, like a comma, rested at the corner of his mouth. He licked it off.

"A busman's holiday," Anna remarked in English, and in response to his puzzled look: "Impossible to translate."

"Where did you learn your Spanish?"

"The best place to learn a foreign tongue is in bed," Arturo had said the first time they made love. She smiled. "At the university." And when complimented on her fluency, offered her stock reply: *Me defiendo,* I manage. In fact, a core vocabulary of about a thousand words made for seventy-five percent of conversation. In turn, she asked the origin of his. His parents, Chilean exiles, had arrived in Barcelona in 1979 after Allende's overthrow (similar to Arturo's parents who had fled the Argentine Junta). It was uprooting for a teenager, and his parents, unable to return as long as Pinochet ruled, remained homesick to the end.

"Nowadays I travel everywhere on assignment, including Chile." His voice dropped: "I'm a recorder of catastrophes: coups, earthquakes, slaughter. Destruction is news."

"Why so bleak?"

"I like to think I'm pessimistic on a large scale but optimistic on the small. But what brings you to Barcelona?"

She surprised herself by telling him.

Miguel parked his car by the statue of Columbus, and they wandered through the narrow alleyways of the *barrio chino*. It was that time of day when wooden shutters re-opened and tourists roamed the quay, the city catching its second wind.

Anna pointed to a small bar: "Here's where we used to have tapas," Far from having faded like an old, overexposed photo of memory, the place was bustling, and two Gustav Klimt ladies of the night posted at the door cast inviting nods to unaccompanied gents. At a puddle, when Miguel took her elbow, contact with his arm suggested more.

His studio at the far end of the old quarter was in a nineteenth-century stone building. The glass-enclosed grilled-iron elevator ascended slowly, offering cinematic views of a curved stairway, rococo urns on the balustrade, painted murals at each landing. It made you want to linger. The apartment was spare: One large room spanned the breadth of the building, with tatami-covered floors, tripods, cameras, rolls of film, black boxes, a corner area partitioned off as a darkroom, and a platform bed surrounded by stacks of books. The surface of the floor, an extended bookcase, freed the walls for photographs.

She scanned it all, searching for wife and children, but caught only images of devastation: a Haitian soldier in a city morgue with metal shelves of what resembled dolls but were in fact unclaimed bodies of children; Pakistani refugees, skeletal arms outstretched to the Red Cross worker doling out loaves of bread from a truck.

"Who was it that defined photography as light writing?" she mused aloud.

"I see the camera more as a gun." He handed her a book of photos: "Ever hear of Sebastião Salgado? I was his assistant."

Slowly she turned the pages. Gold miners swarming down a mountain like ants, caravans of starved pilgrims wandering the African desert, a father holding a wizened child, face indistinct, barely alive. She read the introduction as Miguel poured some rioja. "Out of every ten children who die, seven are killed by hunger . . . A dying child manages to move its hand in a final gesture, the gesture of a caress, and caressing, dies."

Miguel unfolded a map of the city and spread it on a table. "Let's approach this systematically. We can cover a different district each day." He paused and gazed at Anna. "Finding your husband in a city as large as Barcelona is slim."

She said nothing. Barcelona was one of those cities harder to exit than to enter, and she remembered Arturo's frustration, looking for its *Salida* sign. Miguel promised to use his press connections to inquire discreetly at police headquarters for possible clues. "Spanish police are known to be thorough," he remarked laconically. He would also check the guest lists of various hotels and question concierges, that secret network of vigilantes who supplied reporters and police with tips. Meanwhile, she was to continue covering places where he was likely to appear—the Sagrada Capilla, the Picasso Museum, his parents' cemetary.

"I'm scheduled for Istanbul at the end of the month, and then to Eastern Turkey where there's a Kurdish uprising, but until then *soy su seguro servidor.*" She smiled as he bowed in mock ceremony, offering his trusty services." If you wish, you can spend the night here and get an early start tomorrow."

She was ashamed at how much she wanted to. "Well . . ."

"As you see the bed is large."

They slept on opposite sides, energy from the two separate bodies radiating into the space in between. On the brink of sleep, she pictured Arturo in that empty space, arm outstretched after making love.

The next day in her hotel, she ran a bath and unwrapped the complimentary green cake of Maja olive-oil soap with its black cover and a señorita with mantilla and fan. She washed her hair using the miniature bottle of shampoo, and turned on more hot water with her toe. *How can you take your bath so hot?* Arturo used to say, entering the steamy bathroom to shave. She rubbed her scalp hard, then submerged completely, leaving nothing visible but a swath of lather.

At the window, she dried her hair. Across the courtyard, the panes vibrated like a glittering silver harmonica, each sounding a different note: a man shaving with an electric razor; a girl with red hair talking to the television set; an old woman, elbows propped on the sill, peering out, unseeing. Glancing toward the far end of the Passei de Gracia, she pictured herself, seen from a distance, a cartoon figure without its bubble of script. Cars wheeled down the avenue like a mirage in the glaring sun. Clusters of figurines united at intersections like choreographed dancers, then parted and drifted off. One lone particle on a bench remained stock-still, heedless of and unheeded by the swarming atoms. A particle that might even be Arturo. She dressed, transferred wallet, sunglasses, and notebook from her bulging leather handbag into a lighter canvas one, then dropped her key into the slat at the front desk.

"Going for a *paseo*?" the concierge asked solicitously, and suggested the Gothic Quarter. "There's dancing between twelve and two," he said cheerily. "Just follow the street names: Sant Pau del Camp, Sant Josep, Bertrand i Serra, Passeig Isabel." She nodded, unlistening.

In a café on the Paseo de Gracia, she ordered a coffee and, shaking the sugar to the bottom of its packet, listened to two men conversing at the table alongside.

"Now, take *Wild Strawberries*. They don't make movies like that anymore. What a cast, what cinematography."

"Well Bergman keeps using the same actors, and writes from his own life. Amazing output for someone suffering from depression, retreating periodically to his bleak island . . ."

"Could be he suffers from manic depression, and writes in his manic phase. Temperament and creativity, you know, often go hand in hand. The list is long: Byron, Poe, Blake, Coleridge, William James, van Gogh, Robert Lowell, Graham Greene, Leonardo da Vinci . . ."

"How come you know so much about this?"

Sensing that Anna was eavesdropping, the expert lowered his voice. She wrote in her notebook: Is Arturo manic-depressive? Can that explain his behavior? Idly scanning the page, she noticed that lately she'd been pruning her upward stroke of cursive script, and that entries were squeezed into the space between lines rather than on them. She read like a translator reading someone else's text. Things Lost: miniature pepper mill for travel, mother's gold link bracelet, *Elective Affinities,* and at the very bottom of the list: Arturo. Alongside his name, like an asterisk, she placed a question mark.

The men at the next table observed her with interest. A foreign woman alone. Anna turned her chair and shielded her notebook like a schoolchild concealing her writing, whereupon they signalled the waiter for their check.

Another overheard conversation:

"Really, you must try the *zarzuela* at Casa Juanita." It was the red-haired woman seen by Anna from her hotel room, talking to the man from the floor below, he of the electric razor, who at closer quarters displayed a set of gleaming white capped teeth. *Small world,* thought Anna, savoring the platitudinous measure of the universe.

"I have a passion for *zarzuela,* fish of any kind," said the capped teeth. "Flesh is the most corrupt thing for our bodies. *Yo soy una persona . . .*"

Not waiting to hear what kind of person he was, she reached again for her notebook to record his carnal remark. How pertinent it seemed to her translation of Arturo's book, as was often the case when random phrases echoed others in the manuscript. She hadn't even brought the translation in her luggage. Travel light! To hell with deadlines. To hell with . . .

"Do you know why I like you?" Capped Teeth was asking Redhead.

"Why?"

"Because you like me . . ." His voice dropped to an intimate register. "Tell me, what do you dream about."

"About the mistakes in my life."

"Really? Me, I try to solve problems in my dreams. *Yo soy una persona . . .*"

Anna ordered a second coffee. At her feet, bosomy pigeons lunged at stray crumbs; one impudently alighted on the polka-dot shawl of a wizened *churro* vendor. Two baby-faced soldiers went by, awkward under stiff tricornered caps, pathetically displaced from some remote little village. A mother and child passed, the little girl running ahead, mother lagging behind, her tear-stained contorted face unheeded by the young one. Anna signalled to the waiter, paid the check, and left.

She stopped a man and asked for directions to the zoo. Scratching his head, he pulled at his moustache and blurted out: "I wouldn't start from here!" then vanished into a pastry shop. Stacked neatly in its window were almond tartlets and butterflies—Arturo invariably chose the latter. A wedding cake sat in the center—four tiers, pink roses, green petals, *Felicitaciones, María y Pedro* . . . Watch your step, María and Pedro!

At the corner, a deranged man in a woolen cap kept gazing up at a thermometer that registered city temperature. The mercury had risen to an unprecedented forty-three centigrade. "It's not the way it used to be," he howled. "It's not a joke. I'm not a joke!"

Finally, the zoo. In their travels, they would always visit the local zoo. She remembered that bright-green parrot in Chapultapec Park, tied to a perch and shouting: "Down with government!" And in London, that mother orangutan, baby clutched to her chest, gazing warily at the human oglers across the bars. And in Central Park, a polar bear inside a glass cage, swimming back and forth from one end to the other, banging its regal body each time against the glass. Arturo, turning white, had fled. Now, at the grilled gateway of the Barcelona Zoological Park, she paused under an umbrella pine, but decided not to enter. Arturo, she realized, would not be there: He'd gone to those caged parks simply to please her.

On the steps of the cathedral, an eleven-piece band costumed in taupe trousers and bright-red vests was tuning up. Little girls in their Sunday best, husky men in berets, women in white rubber-soled espadrilles readying for the dance. Anna took a vacant spot on the ledge bordering the plaza, next to a buxom woman in black holding a solid baby. The child held out a key ring to Anna; Anna took it, returned it, and changed her seat. A white-haired man with one lone tooth patted the space alongside and made room. At the first chords of the *sardana,* parcels and handbags fell to the ground, hands joined, heads rose, toes pointed, and the dance commenced. The old man clapped gayly, bobbing in place, working his feet, even getting short of breath. Only when he turned to address a friend at his side, did Anna notice that the small furry sounds emanated from an artificial voice box. His lips moved strenuously, as if addressing a deaf-mute, while his interlocutor, eyes glued on the speaker's mouth, replied with lips barely stirring. Anna felt like an alternate player on a side-line bench, yet when beckoned by two women in the circle, she shook her head. But at her neighbor's prodding, she hesitantly joined the circle of linked bodies, and, swept along, she recalled that last dance in Selores with Wendy . . . *Arturo is in Barcelona, and has been there since he disappeared!*

The dance over, panting dancers retrieved their possessions, collected children, and wished each other a fine Sunday meal. Anna, setting out on the emptied streets of the old quarter, entered a dim tapas bar. Inside, the air breathed red wine, olive oil, and fried sardines. Regulars, crowding around the counter, called out their orders. Hams and sausages hung from timbered rafters; underfoot, shrimp carcasses and napkins strewed the sawdust—the measure of a good tapas bar was how many napkins littered the ground. Taking off her sunglasses and putting on her reading ones, she glanced at the menu on the blackboard, but ordered just a sherry, gulped it down, and left double its price on the counter.

The sun-drenched streets were not totally depopulated in that no-nonsense Mediterranean way, midday and after dark, responding as it were to volcanic or earthquake warning. Replacing her sunglasses, she turned onto a side street, one that might lead to the waterfront. But suddenly, just a few steps down, she felt her handbag yanked from her shoulder by a speeding motorcycle. Racing after the two helmeted drivers, she cried out: "*Mi bolsa, mi bolsa!* Stop, stop, my purse got caught on your machine!" By the time she reached the intersection, the roaring vehicle had vanished around a curve. Stunned and helpless, she listened to its fading stridence. Her reading glasses, miraculously, were still in her hand, with one lens missing. Retracing her steps, she stooped to hunt for the lens on the sun-drenched cobblestone. Silverfoil candy wrapper, cigarette butts . . .

"May I help you?"

Startled, she looked up. It was Miguel. Towering overhead in the glare. How on Earth had he arrived on the scene? Incoherently, she tried to explain what had happened. He knelt beside her to search for the missing lens. Nowhere to be found. She stood up. "What are you doing here? Are you tagging me?" Confused however by the speed of the event, and upset by the loss of lens, handbag, and most of all the notebook, she merely registered incredulity at the quirky accident.

Miguel scowled. "It was no accident, it was robbery. What a bad impression this gives of Barcelona! We must report the incident." He hailed a cab to take them to police headquarters. There were two uniformed officers at *Denuncias,* one at the counter, the other behind a computer. They handed her a four-page form to fill out: Permanent Address, Local Address, Telephone, Description of Lost Object or Objects. Uniform Number One questioned her forensically: Could she describe the assailants? Color of vehicle? Number on license plate? Description of purse? Any passport or credit cards inside? Noiselessly, the computor entered her responses. Missing: Wallet with about eight-thousand pesetas, pen, tube of lip gloss, three-by-five-inch spiral notebook with mottled blue cover. As if anyone cared about her moveable compendium of book titles, restaurants, physicians, movie images, gardening plans, and ideas. Who needed to know that Nu Wah's Tea Parlor was at 13 Dover Street? Or that Burpee wasn't stocking fraise des bois seedlings this spring. Or that Simone Weil had lived at 549 Riverside Drive, Apt. 6G, and Hannah Arendt just a few blocks down, less than a mile away from Anna's apartment. Or that indelible image in *Aguirre, Wrath of God* of a raft on the Amazon, conquistador and haggard sailors encircled by floating corpses and swarming monkeys. Or that last week, December 18, was Arturo's birthday.

"Lucky you weren't carrying your passport," said the Uniform. "Fragile individuals are, unfortunately, most vulnerable." He cleared his throat, scanning Anna's scant five-feet-three inches. "Lucky you weren't thrown and dragged on the ground. Some *débiles* wind up in the hospital with fractured elbows and shoulders. But rest assured, Señora, if your purse turns up in a trash bin, empty of course, a *guardia civil* will deliver it personally to your hotel."

Outside in the vestibule, Miguel reiterated that purse-snatching of this sort, original perhaps to a New Yorker, was not so uncommon here, drug addicts and junior delinquents the principal perpetrators, particularly at the end of the month when salaries were paid. Muttering something about gold chains in Manhattan and fur hats in Russia, Anna scanned the photographs of Dangerous Wanted Criminals posted on the wall. Grainy mug shots of rapists, killers, and terrorists, "Wanted Dead or Alive." One, blond in last year's photograph, with black hair now. Another, clean-shaven once, currently sporting moustache and scar over his lip—good God, supposing Arturo had changed the color of his hair, grown a beard, and assumed an alias. X last seen in a tobacco shop. Y last seen in a train station. Arturo last seen turning off their bedroom light the night before his last swim.

Exhausted and drained, she felt like weeping like a child, or phoning her nearest and dearest as one might for consolation or congratulations . . . Let me tell you the good news. Or, Guess what happened to me. But self-pity swiftly turned to rage. Her nearest, and once dearest, was not picking up.

"Cities aren't safe for anyone nowadays," said Miguel, just to say something. Addressing her for the first time in the familiar "you," he put his arm around her.

In the hotel lobby, no one. The concierge handed her the key and asked if she wanted a wake-up call. They went upstairs, through the corridor with its night light, and entered Room 14.

Miguel leaned over and kissed her on the lips and took her hands.

"I loved my husband," she said.

"But supposing he wasn't faithful? Would you love him then?"

"You're questioning one of the frail," she said wryly.

"Who at some point or other isn't frail?"

"But Arturo *was* faithful."

"There's a difference between fidelity and faith," he replied. It sounded like a translating maxim.

"Why doesn't he kiss me again?" said Anna to herself, blood rushing to her face. Forgetting that she was a wife, forgetting that she was a translator, she went to the door and hung out the Do Not Disturb.

Anna and Arturo: January

Driver and passenger, safety belts fastened, embarked on their journey to Long Island. They knew its roundabouts and detours, which had been covered and recovered countless times in countless seasons. Driving close to the wheel, Anna kept an eye out for signposts not to miss their turnoff.

Jericho Turnpike, Sunrise Highway. They crossed into Suffolk County, and as urban gave way to rural, traffic snares were unlikely. On the Long Island Expressway she inserted a cassette into the deck, an aria from *Rigoletto,* Pavarotti singing. As he pleaded with Violetta not to leave him, Anna skirted numerous potholes: the road further on would be smooth. At the Manorville Mobile station, red stallion in flight, she pressed on the accelerator. Level countryside unfurled in stark wintry beauty.

Arturo gazed out in silence, confirming landmarks and memories: deciduous forest, circles on a map; triangles, conifers. The roadwork begun in June seemed near completion, with an extra lane added, and yellow-helmeted workers busily removing debris. As Anna swerved to avoid a stancion, he noted the speedometer at seventy-nine. He turned to her, voice tentative: "How about cruise control?"

Suddenly a de Chirico landscape sprang into view. Blackened forest, skeletal branches—the charred vestiges of the Shinnicock Pine Barrens. A faint scent of smoke hovered in the air.

"What happened here?"

"A wildfire sparked by a cigarette raced through the forest. Whipped by the wind, it devoured trees and vegetation like tinder. August was without rain . . ." It was like reporting a disaster to a tourist, or returning relative, certain details omitted. "You could see the blaze from far off. It took five days and nearly two thousand volunteer firemen to extinguish it. Birds took flight, deer raced away. Moles, chipmunks, and mice dug into their burrows. Most survived I think though ants may still be clearing ash and sand from their tunnels."

It seemed the exfoliated forest, with its scorched ranks, had been decimated by a slash-and-burn scepter. Yet at closer range you could see green shoots sprouting from the stubble.

Under the intensity of the flames the resin had melted, whereupon the cones unfurled like petals on a flower. Blackened on the outside, they'd remained rosy within. Combustion destroyed, but granted revival. Stump, stick, even fence post might regenerate. Summer wounds might mend, without visible scarring perhaps, yet required tending.

Exit 41.

They swung onto the turnoff of the last lap. The smell of brine drifted off the ocean. With a deep breath, Anna pressed on the accelerator: cruise control cancelled. Picking up speed, they sailed through the underpass. Momentary darkness, then light. And on the signpost above, like a quivering buoy:

Normal Conditions Ahead.

Like

if

you

had

a

hole

in

your

sock,

he'd

start

singing

about

that.

(Walls, page 237)

Bacchus at the Water Tower, Continuing Ed

Sarah Gorham

We gather this was homework: *Mix the godly*
with the mundane. Paint some place
you know. The tower is 1890s,
Greek Revival, and Bacchus looms in front
with purple lips and wandering
bloodshot eyes. There's plenty of drapery,
including a cement-colored toga
sheathing the left half of his body.
The artist didn't have to paint another arm,
and good thing, for the naked one's yellow
and lumpy like coffee cake. Our God of Libation
is showing repercussions of excess,
a hepatic glow spreading up his chest and neck
though the warning we guess is unintentional—
Our artist "Spike" proclaims in all caps
on onion skin that he himself
"loves the application of paint to canvas…"
it is a *"sensual* process" for him.
How charming in late life
this second look at profit-sharing
and I-beam manufacturing
which we gather from his
shaky signature has damaged more
than our good friend's spirit.
He's following the whiff of long-ago pleasure

and, amazingly, hasn't hurt anyone.
Except Bacchus perhaps, who looks distressed.
Some afterlife, he thinks, and would bolt
right off the canvas, if only his creator
had left him a proper skeleton.
It's as if the boy survived the lightning blast
only to miss the reconstruction,
nestled inside his father's shapely thigh.
Spike has an inkling of this lack
but unlike his subject he's no lush—
a practical man who enrolled in "studio classes,"
and hopes to "pursue his masters at U. of L."
In closing, the slightest flicker from his past:
"I truly enjoy the process,
and I hope you enjoy the product."
Sealed with a fire-engine red, nickle-sized price tag.
Eighty bucks. A real bargain.

Middle Age

Sarah Gorham

Way too early, a call
from the East. Sun poised on the sill
like a match before striking.
I muster a soft *Hello.*

Get your work done, now! my caller
advises. *Trust me, I'm dying in this heat,
it's hours till I'm out of here. Broke*

*a heel on the train, clean off—can't you
just see me limping
all the way through pre-sales?*

Where am I, where are my pants,
why did the phone
hook me from dream
and toss me here

a trout in the grass? Sun
rounds the corner and my skin
overreacts, temperature soaring. Is this natural?
I feel the heat, but not my age.

I meant to thank you, caller says.
*When the book arrived, I mean.
Forgot . . .* Outside, sparrows at the birdbath

seek yesterday's blessing.
Another dozen hackberry leaves
descend out of season. *Are you there?*

Why I Miss Junkies

Peter Nolan Smith

LIKE MILLIONS OF OTHER NEW YORKERS, I HAD DRIVEN BY, OVER, and under, yet most certainly never touched, the East River. While in recent years I had sighted people fishing off FDR Drive I had never seen a single kid gleefully leaping off a decrepit pier, an around-the-island swimmer, or even a bobbing floater. All that water seemed a shame, especially as July of 1999 stretched into an unbroken chain of 95°F-plus days.

Most people think you can't survive in Manhattan without an air conditioner. Unfortunately, AC has always made me feel as if some dirty old man from the Arctic who isn't Santa Claus is breathing down my neck. So I braced myself to tough out another New York heat wave. Maybe I was getting old but after ten days of body-sapping humidity, I had reached the point of surrender. I either had to buy an AC or get someplace cool.

The Hamptons were a good three-hour trip on the LIRR and the Rockaways took an hour and a half on the subway. Both seemed far away. Then I recalled Crazy John from the Russian Baths saying he had gone swimming at East Twentieth Street, and found myself asking, How bad could the water be? There was only one way to find out, so I put on my reef-walkers and headed over to the East River.

The streets of the East Village were gooey and the sidewalks radiated a wilting heat. No one dared play on the frying-pan asphalt of the Tompkins Square Park basketball courts. Old men in tank tops played dominoes on East Thirteenth Street, while on Avenue C a pack of children ran through the spray of an open fire hydrant. I could have joined them, except I had it in my mind to go swimming no matter what, and continued east to the river.

Underneath an elevated section of the FDR I passed a cluster of improvised cardboard shelters, whose inhabitants lay before them like dead men waiting for the hearse to haul them to an icy slab in the morgue. I heard each passing car gun its engine to the red line, as their drivers decided that I must be a member of this ramshackle commune. My feelings weren't hurt—I was much closer to the losers than the winners of this life. Plus, I was already feeling the cool of the East River on my skin as I ran across the road to the chain-link fence guarding the river from the city.

The water was a very cold green. I breathed in air heavily scented by sea salt. If the water looked clean, smelled clean, then it might well *be* clean. I continued to Twentieth Street, where a peninsula of rubble extended into the river.

People on lawn chairs were sunbathing on this no-man's-land while two jet skis noisily skated across a boat's wake. They weren't scared of the water, but then they were wearing wet suits. As I wondered whether I should risk going in, a man's head popped up from the river and he wasn't dead. I smiled and said to myself, "Damn! They weren't lying. People really are swimming."

I worked my way down to the water's edge, though my eagerness for a plunge was somewhat dampened by the slimy green algae covering a stack of railroad ties. Sensing my hesitation, the swimmer called out, "Don't worry about that. It's fine out here."

Recognizing the voice, my head snapped, for as far as I knew the swimmer had OD'ed for good in the early nineties. "Jamie Parker, that you?"

"What? You never seen someone come back from the dead?" the swimmer shouted out. "Hell, I heard you'd died in Asia. Some kind of motorcycle accident in Burma, right?"

"Yeah, but it was more a near-death experience than the real thing," I replied, stripping off my shirt.

"Hey, those are the worst kind! What are you waiting for? C'mon in, the water's great."

Having always been the type of person who said one thing to lull you into thinking he was all right before ripping you off, Jamie stood up and announced, "Nothing to worry about. I don't have nothing up my sleeves or pants either."

His being naked meant little. However, he didn't appear to have contracted any skin ailments, so I dropped my clothing and waded into the river up to my chest, goosebumps from the cold popping on every inch of skin.

"So what you think?" Jamie asked, as he swam over to me.

"Not bad." He looked better than the last time I had seen him, so I asked, "Where you been?"

"Well, I went a little crazy. At least that's what everyone told me and I wasn't in any condition to argue. Once upstate I discovered I wasn't half as crazy as they said I was, and also that the State was hiding hundreds of madmen and women in these abandoned state facilities."

"What do you mean?" I was suspicious of conspiracy theories from the mouths of avowed maniacs.

"What do I mean? You wonder where all those squeegee men went? No, 'cause you were too happy with them all off the streets."

Very few New Yorkers missed the beggars and mumbling madmen, yet their near-extinction was a sinister mystery. I said, "I figured the Mayor had hired a death squad from Colombia to kill them."

"I wouldn't put it past the bastard," Jamie commented, and took a couple of strokes farther from shore. Suddenly the current began to drag him away and I almost started for him. But he broke free of the tide's tug with a frantic flurry of flailing arms and kicking feet. When he reached the safety of shallow water, Jamie said, "Damn, it's kind of dangerous out there, but exciting too."

"I have to admit it is nice swimming in the city."

"Yeah, but 'they' don't like you doing it." His tone made no bones about who "they" were. "Last week, a friend of mine dove off the helicopter port. Everyone thought he was killing himself. The fire department and police came to rescue him, but he kept on doing the Australian crawl. Hah! Even the divers were scared to go in the river, but it's not bad. Not after you become used to it."

I dropped my nose to the ripples and inhaled deeply. "Smells better than Jones Beach in the 1980s."

"Hey, why shouldn't it? The river gets flushed twice a day by several billion gallons of Long Island Sound and the ocean," Jamie stated, then warned, "Only don't swallow any of it."

As we swam, joggers stopped at the edge of the highway and ran away shaking their heads.

A shout stopped our swimming and Jamie yelled to a grizzled old man on a bicycle, then turned to say, "That's Dynamite. I met him upstate. Used to be a fighter, but he took a couple of punches too many. He's all right most of the time, but he doesn't like strangers, so you'll have to forgive me if I go. I'm trying to ease him back into society, 'cause he can't go back to where he was. None of us can. They threw us all out of there, 'cause the Mayor's running for Senate and he doesn't want to piss off those upstate hicks anymore. You'll be seeing lots more of my friends in the next months."

"I'll keep my eyes out for them."

"You do that." Jamie carefully picked his way across the debris-strewn bottom toward the spit of rubble. I supposed I should have kept my eyes on my shirt, but I had heard too many people say the first commandment in New York is to never trust anyone, so I swam out into the river.

The current sucked at my body as if Poseidon had a claim on my soul. Kicking hard to keep pace with the undertow, I couldn't believe how good it felt when the wake of a passing tourist boat crashed over me, filling my mouth with water. A dozen passengers pointed at me and I could easily imagine their saying I was mad. At least I had given them a New York moment.

Someone called my name from the road. It was Jamie. He had both hands raised over his head. I saluted him with a clenched fist, then swam slowly back to the decrepit shoreline. My things were still there and I dried off thinking how good a day it was.

The exhilaration lasted even longer, for my friends were shocked by the news of my exploit, then said apologetically that had they known I was so desperate they would have invited me out to the Hamptons. I thanked them for the belated offer and fought off a grin. The last time I had seen such a bold-faced expression of distaste had been from the nuns at my grammar school the day I wore a leather jacket to Mass.

I went swimming a few more times in the East River without running into Jamie. As summer slowly rounded the homestretch into September, his prediction bore fruit; homeless people stood at the banks begging change and haranguing passersby with an arcane litany of dementia. But they were ignored, as if they were unpensioned veterans of a long-forgotten war. Times were different and people were happy, too happy to be bothered by anything but being happier.

One afternoon, I stood on a corner of Third Avenue, watching the passing parade of NYU students. There were so many of them. All wearing the same clothes, smoking cigarettes the same way, and walking with the same turtle-backed stoop.

Within minutes I came to the conclusion that I actually missed the gap-toothed smiles of the needle-tracked Twelfth Street whores, the gravity-defying acrobatics of Union Square's Valium addicts, the ravaged face of William Burroughs shambling through Grand Central, Johnny Thunders falling off his stool, the constant patter of drug dealers on my corner, even the thieving spic smiles of Alphabet City. My nostalgia for that era of errors scared me, for not everything about those years was worth remembering.

I probably wouldn't have thought another thing about it, except a gravelly voice blackjacked me by saying, "Nothing stays the same."

"No one ever said it would." I recognized the speaker not so much from Jamie's agitated voice, but by how fast the college kids' postures straightened up, as if they were trying to protect a possession that wasn't really theirs from someone who would really take it.

I knew living on the street was tough, but yellowing bruises discolored Jamie's face and he was missing a front tooth. His hand quickly covered his mouth and he must have slipped on a loose cap, for this sleight of hand filled the gap.

"How are you doing?"

"Who gives a shit!" He growled loudly, "C'mon, when you first moved down here, you never imagined it would end up like this. None of us did! Over there were a few parking lots, where the whores worked out of vans. Farther up the street there used to be some pawnshops, a gay peep-show theater, and a couple of porno parlors. Man, this neighborhood was fucked up! Junkies, whores, people down on their luck. Now look at it!"

He was attracting too much of the wrong attention so I crossed the avenue, hoping he might remain at his sidewalk pulpit. But he tagged along, speaking in a tone most people save for when they're about to get into a fight. "I hate these kids. Nothing bad happens to them. Not like me. They look at you like you don't belong here, but it's them that don't belong."

"Maybe we got too old to be here," I said, steering him up Stuyvesant Street, where the crowd thinned out. Jamie was on a roll and snarled at a pair of college punks in baggy clothes. "Look at 'em. They have their fancy hairdresser clothing thinking they're what we were, but they're not even close. Little stick-pussy bitches! They'd last about two seconds where I been. You know what I'd do. I'd get a gang of thieves, pickpockets, con men, and grifters and suck every penny out of these spoiled brats' pockets and send them back crying to their fat-ass parents. Like some kind of Fagin gang raping the rich!"

All good feeling from our swim was disappearing. I should have left him rather than toss gasoline onto his psycho-fire by asking, "Little angry this afternoon, Jamie?"

"Damn right! Just finished a weekend bid in jail and for what? Because some motherfucking film crew was tearing branches off a tree that blocked their fuckin' shot. I told them to stop and they wouldn't, so I fought them and was arrested for trying to save a tree. Shit, years ago I wouldn't have even cared a rat's ass about a tree, but I hate film people. Always trying to make believe. Then I get out and find out they put Dynamite away. Said he was causing a problem. Shit, he ain't killing people with tobacco or brainwashing people's minds with advertisements. And if talking to himself is a crime, then they'd throw all these assholes talking on cell phones in jail too. I wish I had a hockey stick, so I could slap-shot them off their ears. I mean who are they talking to anyway? It's madmen like Dynamite that make it safe for them to talk in the street! Fucking cunts! Why they have to bust him? He was getting drunk, but the cops, they don't care, 'cause they have orders to keep people like him or me in line, so these fucks get to have their pretty little world." Jamie spun around, as if a sudden spurt of vertigo might shift the time back twenty years, then he pleaded with tearful eyes, "You gotta remember why everything changed. Why this ain't how it was. Why nothing is."

I was baffled and watched, disconcerted, as he staggered to the newly erected fence around a weedy garden. After a few seconds of deep breathing, he asked again. "You have to remember."

"Remember what?"

"Remember the night they took Hakkim away for good?" Jamie asked desperately, as if his sanity depended on my saying "Yes."

"Yeah, we were standing outside the Horseshoe Bar on Avenue B," I admitted, proving my memory wasn't as badly damaged from my motorcycle accident in Burma as I feared.

"Well, after that day nothing was the same. Nothing." Jamie seized my arm, as if he had suddenly read my urge to leave.

"Jamie, but you have to settle down." I put my arm around him and led him down the street away from anyone who could hear what he had to say.

"Yeah, I get a little nuts if I don't get enough sugar. They still make egg creams at the Gem Spa?"

"Far as I know."

"Shit, I get me one of those and I'll be as good." The desperation in Jamie's eyes made his request hard to refuse. I still suspected this was some kind of scam, however, so I warned, "Listen, you try anything crazy and you're on your own."

"Hey, chill out, I'm just getting me an egg cream. Nothing else." The evaporation of his rage had left him a fragile shell. Outside the newsstand he said, "Do me a big favor. Stay here and I'll be right out. For once I'd like someone to stay, instead of running away. For old times' sake, do me that solid?"

"Hurry up." While I didn't owe him any favors I waited for him. I began to remember things I had forgotten over the years, mostly because the neighborhood had changed too much.

The Gem Spa was here twenty years ago, as was the bank across the street, the B&H Dairy Shop, and the Stage Deli, though most everything and everyone else had been packed up in the depository of history. The St. Mark's Cinema became a Gap, the Orchida serving pizza and big beer replaced by an Italian restaurant, Binibons gone, the Baths now Kim's Video. And people. Steven Pines OD'ed, Carol Smith OD'ed, Johnny Thunders OD'ed, Clover Nolan disappeared into East Berlin, Klaus Nomi and Steve Brown died of AIDS. Hundreds more moved out to regular lives somewhere nicer than here.

It was all so very different back then, but its being so very different was one of the main reasons I moved into the East Village. That, and it cost nothing to live here, especially if you were sharing a three-room flat on East Tenth Street with a young actress who had seen the

New York Dolls' album cover where they posed in front of the Gem Spa. To this ingénue's way of thinking that meant the East Village was where you had to be and she was right. Hundreds of punks, artists, runaways, B-grade models, dancers, and actors flocked to the tenements beyond First Avenue, even though the neighborhood looked like a suburb of ancient Rome a week after the Huns had sacked the city.

The landlords had torched some tenements for the insurance, and other buildings had been abandoned when the city presented their owners with a tax bill they couldn't pay. Anything left standing were rattraps overrun by cockroaches with buckling walls and no heat.

Still, there was something apocalyptically appealing about the syringe- and condom-strewn acres, the graffiti walls toasting dead dealers and the blacked-out shooting galleries with the long lines of junkies waiting for their morning fix.

Back then the neighborhood was packed with thieves, whores, chicken hawks, hustlers, rapists, scammers, junkies, and every other deviant known and unknown to modern man. None of them wanted anything to do with our kind, unless it was to rip us off. But the worst of them all was Hakkim.

All the politicians, the cops, the shop owners claim responsibility for the East Village being the place it is today, yet it wasn't their being here that wrought the change.

Not at all.

The change was determined by someone's *not* being here. That someone was Hakkim, and anyone who tells you different doesn't know what they are talking about.

The morning of July 1, 1977, was a scorcher and not any kind of day for moving. But my girlfriend from West Virginia was eager to start her new life, so we loaded all our possessions into five boxes, then took a taxi crosstown to the East Village. At First Avenue the driver stopped and turned uptown. I told him to go down the block but he emphatically refused to go any farther east.

After a brief and fruitless argument we got out of the cab and stood on the corner. A flurry of near-naked children played in the spray of an open hydrant, their parents lounged on the steps, and old men played dominoes on milk crates.

I struggled with the boxes for several feet, until one of them fell on the sidewalk. When two scrawny kids offered to help us my girlfriend whispered, "I don't think that's a good idea."

"Hey, I'm carrying four boxes and you're only carrying one," I hissed, and added, "We let them help us and everyone won't think we're some stuck-up white people trying to kick them out of their neighborhood."

She didn't argue as I handed each of the kids a dollar and told them to pick up a box, but I could see from her face that I would be hearing about it later. The four of us proceeded down the block to our new address, before whose door lay a pockmarked junkie. One of the kids immediately said, "That's George. He ain't dead, just fucked up."

Asking the comatose junkie to move was useless, so I climbed the steps and nudged him with my foot. He responded to the pressure by sliding over but before I could open the door an enraged voice shouted, "Who the fuck are you to kick George?"

The two kids dropped the boxes and hit the sidewalk running. For the yellowed eyes of the black man crossing the street were fixed on me like those of a cobra who finally found a clear shot to his snake charmer. "I said who the fuck are you to kick George?"

"I didn't kick him." I would have backed up, only there was nowhere to go.

"You callin' me a liar, you white piece of shit!" he snarled from the bottom of the steps, the veins on his neck pulsing like they were ready to spurt blood.

My girlfriend stepped away as if she didn't know me and I couldn't blame her. I raised my open palms and said, "I don't want any trouble."

"Too late for that shit, you already in trouble. And now I'm gonna show you how much," he threatened, putting his right foot on the first step.

Being brought up scrapping with Southie boys had taught me the value of not fighting fair, so I threw both boxes at him. They struck his chest squarely and knocked him off the stairs. His body hit the sidewalk and his head whiplashed on the pavement with a crack loud enough to echo off the opposite building. A trickle of blood seeped under his head and everything grew very quiet.

George rose to his feet with a groan and asked, "Hakkim, what you done to Hakkim?"

The little junkie scurried to his friend's side and glared at me, saying, "You fucked yourself real good! Hakkim gonna come get you and your little girlfriend! Take everything you got and fuck her . . ."

I had learned long ago that anyone stupid enough to threaten you without doing anything about it deserved a beating, and before he could say another word, I kicked him in the head. My girlfriend stopped me before I put him in the hospital and said, "We better go before the police come."

I gathered up our boxes and carried them to our third-floor flat, then sat up most of the night waiting for Hakkim to take his revenge. Sometime past 3 A.M. my girlfriend lulled me to sleep. We woke to birds singing in the alleyway and made love on the dusty futon the previous hippie tenant had left behind. Afterward we talked about how happy we would be here, and with the sun streaming into the apartment, it all seemed too good to be true.

When I went to get groceries, the domino players across the street waved to me as if I had been living in the neighborhood forever. I smiled to myself and thought everything was turning out okay. For a short time I was right.

Of course, that afternoon Hakkim reappeared sporting a stained head bandage, and George had a black eye and a swollen cheek. Their eyes ominously followed me but they did nothing. This unexpected leniency toward us didn't prevent them from conducting their reign of terror against everyone else in the neighborhood.

Typically Hakkim would break into any newcomer's apartment within the first three days. When my friends, Valda and Mary Beth, moved to an apartment across the street, they heeded my warnings about him by installing a steel door and a theft-proof grill on the windows. A week went by, then two, without their receiving the unwelcome wagon treatment. But Hakkim had only been busy elsewhere.

One night they returned home to discover Hakkim had bypassed their defense by chopping through the walls. Once in, he had stolen their money, defecated on their beds, and thrown all their clothes into the street. They moved out the next day and never came back.

Another friend, Kurt, chose the unusual strategy of signaling with an unlocked door that he possessed nothing worth stealing. Kurt upped this security measure by never cleaning the apartment. He would throw pizza rinds onto the growing pyramid of trash in the corner, then announce, "That's all I have and, if anyone wants it, they can have it."

A lack of cleanliness was meaningless to someone so far removed from godliness as Hakkim. One day I spotted him wearing a jacket Kurt had buried under a pile of Chinese take-out boxes several months ago. Upon seeing my horror Hakkim pointed at me and said maliciously, "You're next and I been waitin' to get you. Waitin' real patient for a piece of your girlfriend too."

He ran off before I could get to him, but tough as I was, there is only so much barbarism you can take. After explaining Hakkim's threat, my hillbilly girlfriend thrust *The Village Voice* in my chest. The weekly was opened to the Apartments for Rent section. She didn't mince words. "Find us someplace else and quick. I don't care where as long as it's not here."

There was an opening for a one-bedroom in Gramercy Park. I called the landlord, who said it was still available. My girlfriend said, firmly, "Go over there and sign the lease. I want to get out of here."

"Just as much as I do," I replied, then kissed her before heading outside.

No one being on Tenth Street was strange, yet I'd seen enough weird shit on this block to last me a lifetime. I walked to First Avenue to hail a taxi. Loud shouting greeted me at the corner, where Hakkim and another junkie were arguing about who had broken into more apartments. When I shook my head in defeat, Hakkim snarled, "What? You really think you tough? You a punk bitch like the rest of 'em. All of 'em. I own you all."

I snatched a two-by-four out of the trash and charged after Hakkim, who scrambled between two tightly parked cars. He was trapped and I swung at his head, thinking of nothing short of murder. I would have killed him too, if he hadn't stumbled into the street to be instantly struck by a *Daily News* truck.

Several tons of steel sent Hakkim flying fifty feet in the air. A woman screamed as he landed on the other side of the street. I heard a bone break, then another, as his body tumbled to rest in a broken heap.

The other junkie looked at me, then at the man sprawled on the pavement. I expected him to rightfully blame me for causing this terrible accident. Instead he ran over and rifled through Hakkim's pockets, then cried out with joy upon discovering several glassine packets of dope. After kicking Hakkim twice he ran east into Loisaida, spreading the news that Hakkim was dead.

People came out of their apartments and stood ominously over Hakkim. If a cop car from the Ninth Precinct hadn't rolled up to the scene, they surely would have finished him off. Both cops laughed upon seeing that the fallen man was Hakkim, but did their duty and protected him until the ambulance carted him away. As the crowd dispersed, no one was afraid to pray aloud that their tormentor would die. Later that evening people walked down the block carrying home the TVs, radios, and stereos they had been scared to buy while Hakkim controlled the street.

My girlfriend and I decided to wait out the change. The ornamental pear trees bloomed and the sun shone all day long. People even took brooms to the sidewalks and planted flowers in the beaten ground around the trees. My girlfriend called it the springtime of love, and I benefited from her prediction. I hoped every day and night would be the same.

Two weeks later I was sitting on the stoop talking with my upstairs neighbor, an actor later to be famous. Suddenly his face went white. I could tell he had seen a ghost and prayed that this phantom wasn't who I feared it was.

God wasn't listening, because Hakkim came hobbling down the street on crutches surrounded by a coterie of derelict fans toasting his return from the grave. He stopped at a recently planted flower garden and said, "What the fuck is this?"

No one had time to answer, for he awkwardly bent over and tore the flowers out of the ground. Waving a clump of roots over his head he shouted, "Hey, you motherfuckers! Wake up! I'm back and back for good, so get ready for a Christmas in the springtime, cuz from what I been hearin' you got a lot of shit for me."

Hakkim glared about the street. Everyone other than his friends shirked his gaze. I shook my head, thinking, "I have to move."

When I broke the bad news to my girlfriend she started crying; Hakkim had told her he would come in and get what should have been his all along. Hearing that, I went to my closet and took out my five-shot revolver. It wasn't the most accurate weapon in the world, but if I stuck the muzzle in Hakkim's ear a single bullet would do the job.

It was dark by the time I hit the street. Hakkim wasn't at Brownie's or the East Village Artist's Club on Ninth or at any of the shooting galleries on Fourth. No one had seen him but everyone had heard he was back on the street. I ran into Jamie Parker at the Horseshoe Bar on Avenue B, and he pointed to a group of passing Puerto Ricans. "See them, they gonna get to Hakkim way 'fore you get to him. Seems he ripped off their bruja and that fucked with their juju or some shit like that, so you might as well have a drink and let them do the walkin' for you."

Something about hunting to hurt someone can give a man a thirst, which I tried to quench with a few beers, but my mind kept turning to Hakkim on the ground before me.

The gun in my hand.

My finger on the trigger.

Jamie could sense the rising tide of vengeance and ordered me a shot of whiskey. I knew he was trying to get me drunk. I pushed away the shot glass and patted him on the shoulder, saying, "I need some air."

"Don't go far," he pleaded. Once outside I started walking back toward the shooting galleries on Fourth, only to stop when the sound of running feet slapping against the pavement was punctuated by a shout for help.

At first I couldn't make out the figure coming my way. Someone was after George, but no one on foot would ever catch the little junkie and he sped by me before I could even think about tackling him. Jamie came out and stared. "What's that all about?"

"Fucking George! Which means Hakkim can't be far behind." My hand slipped inside my jacket to grab the handle of the revolver.

"Help me, someone! Please help me!" Hakkim cried desperately as he wobbled up the street on his crutches. Glancing swiftly over his shoulder at the gang of Puerto Ricans gaining on him, Hakkim knew he wasn't getting away. He shouted, "Someone help me! Call the police! They gonna kill me! Help!"

There were plenty of people on the street and lots more watching from the windows, but he was on his own. When I started to cross the street to get in my licks, Jamie held me saying, "This doesn't concern you."

I snatched away my arm, but Jamie was right. And I watched while the terror of East Tenth Street dropped one crutch and swung the other at the four young barrio toughs. When six more kids carrying pipes joined them Hakkim screamed, "Someone help me for God's sake!"

The oldest of the Puerto Ricans, a long-limbed teenager wearing only satin shorts and sneakers, turned to the onlookers and asked without a single drop of mercy, "Anyone want to save Hakkim's ass?"

The people in the windows responded by shutting them. Those on the streets walked away. Some court might accuse us of being accessories to murder, for that night we were a jury who could give no other sentence than a thumbs-down. And none of us lost sleep over our verdict.

I never saw Hakkim again after that night.

After Jamie emerged from the Gem Spa, he finished the egg cream with one long suck then pronounced, "Damn, that was as good as it ever was. Just like 1976."

"Glad to hear it," I replied, stepping aside for a quartet of retro punks dressed in new leather. Jamie wasn't having any of my being polite and pushed the punks aside saying, "Don't you know who you bumped into!"

I had to pull him away before he really went off. Once they were across the street, one of the punks braved a shout. His friends joined in a single chorus of taunts, until Jamie turned around. He didn't say anything, only looked. All four ran off like rats with their tails on fire.

"See, I still got it," he declared, tossing the empty egg cream into the trash bin. "Good seeing you."

"Same here, Jamie. You take care."

"That might be asking too much." Seeing the expression on my face, he added, "Don't worry, you ain't seen the last of me yet."

As if to prove it, Jamie strolled across the avenue, daring the traffic to hit him. When a cement truck lurched to a screeching halt he yelled, "See, I'm invulnerable!"

I watched until he vanished into the crowd of college students, thinking that he had the kind of luck no one cares about anymore.

In the following weeks I expected Jamie to creep up on me unannounced, but he had rejoined the ghosts of the past. More likely he had lost his temper and the police had carted him away. If not, maybe he had been able to get out of town. Whenever I went to church on Fourteenth Street I would light a candle for Jamie, hoping he was living in Florida.

Maybe he'll come back, once he has rested up, or even when the neighborhood reverts to its old self. Until then, watch yourself on those dark streets and listen for those steps behind you, because they can't keep a ghost like Hakkim in hell forever. Especially in New York.

**the clouds appeared
naked and fragile without
corporate sponsorship**
(Talen, page 173)

Night Flight

Melissa Holbrook Pierson

Sometime one May night, I watched the late news, for the comfort of crime. But then they got a funny look. This just in—rushed to the station via a series of signals carried on cable through ocean sand, and sounding as odd—: A pilot flying over Soviet airspace has reported seeing a column of flame rising straight up from the Earth for a mile through the blackness. It appeared in a distant region of Siberia. We cannot say what it is.

And suddenly, you know, I was there, in a cockpit. No lights down below, stars just as far; each lighted dial on the screen trying green yellow red before claiming they are no match for the night. Air makes a thump on the fuselage in the dark, it too invisible. The engines buzz through the floor into my feet, their ground. I have been thinking. I have been flying. There is singing in my ears.

The black is unrelieved, as it should be. It seems so solid I could land. It has been hours that I have been thinking, Why, this is all there is.

When I saw that orange fire (How could I ever tell you what I saw? How can I ever be anything but alone henceforth?) the world tilted and I fell off the side. How lonely, strange, it made me feel; no longer held fast, I was instead the last human on Earth, above Earth, doomed to fly and never land. I could not hear the last cry of man behind the turbines' rush. In the distant flame was my fate: to live, to fly, to fly.

Later I forgot how the whole thing made me feel.

**people
stealing
shit just the tip
of the iceberg**
(Passaro, page 227)

A Peacock's Wings

Stuart David

I WAS GETTING READY TO DRIVE THE WIFE'S MOTHER HOME. I was fucking itching to be shot of her, to tell you the truth. I'd been sitting twirling the car keys round my finger for the past half hour, while the two of them discussed my merits as a husband, and a bread-winner.

"It's a constant worry to me, hen," the mother was saying. "I never know what he's doing, from one visit to the next."

"I don't always know myself," the wife told her.

"I mean, as far as your sister's concerned, I can put my mind at rest there. I know she's being looked after. I know what her man does. But with this one . . ."

The mother looked at me.

"We manage, Mammy," the wife told her. "Mary struggles a lot more than me sometimes."

"Aye, but she's got the security, hen. Donald's a good man. He's still getting started out, but he'll do well. He's got a good head on his shoulders."

It's hardly fucking surprising I was itching to get rid of her, is it?

I carried on twirling the keys.

"I mean, what's he doing here just now?" the mother asked.

"I'm waiting to drive you home," I told her. "Are you about ready?"

She turned to me.

"Why aren't you at work just now?" she asked. "This is my daughter you know. Why aren't you looking after her? You're a bloody disgrace. Sitting there in your Hawaiian shirt."

"We're still doing all right with the money he made when we were over in the States, Mammy. He doesn't need to work just now."

"But what was he doing over there? I still don't know. He had some *idea*; that's all I'm told. It's a constant worry to me, hen. I was telling your sister that the other day. Sometimes I can't sleep at night."

"We're fine, Mammy. We're fine. Don't worry about it. Will I get your coat?"

"Aye, hen, aye. Go and get me it."

The mother got up as the wife left the room, and I breathed a sigh of relief.

Finally, I thought.

She started walking around the room, looking at all the photographs we had about the place. Smiling at the ones of the wife, frowning at the ones of me. Totally confused by the ones of us both together.

"How's Jimmy?" I asked her. The wife's father. She carried on walking about the room, and then started looking at all the ornaments she'd seen a hundred times before. She gave us most of the fucking things herself, if the truth be told.

"Aye, he's fine, son," she said. "He's out at a wee do tonight, down at the bowling club. It's good for him to get out on his own sometimes. It gives us something to talk about when he gets back. You'll be doing fine if you manage to stay with Bev as long as I've been with Jimmy."

"How long's that now?" I asked her.

"Forty-two years. Forty-three in October. And I'll tell you what; I knew what he was doing for a living every day of his life until he retired. And I never had to worry about it either. Not like that daughter of mine has to worry. I know she worries. She might tell you she doesn't, but I know she does. And I'll tell you something else; Jimmy worries about her too. The times he's told me how he fears for her. It's not right for a man of his age to have to worry about things like that, son. It's not right. It puts a strain on his heart. If I end up widowed it'll be you to blame."

At last the wife came back into the room, just when I was starting to think I might end up making Jimmy a widower myself.

She held the mother's coat up for her and the mother pulled it on. Then she stood in the middle of the room, laboring over the buttons.

"There you go, Mammy," the wife said. "Peacock'll drive you home just as soon as you're ready."

"Has he passed his test now, hen?" she asked the wife.

I made an effort to catch the wife's eye, hoping she'd get the message and keep things simple, just so's I could get the mother out of there. But it wasn't happening. She wasn't looking at me.

"Well, he's *sat* it, Mammy," she said. "He's sat it, now."

"Oh, well then. Perhaps I'll feel safer with him, now he's got his license."

I tried to catch the wife's eye again, and I managed it this time. I shook my head, and she knew what I meant. She knew what I meant, but she didn't pay a blind fucking bit of attention.

"He didn't get his license, Mammy," she said, and I hung my head.

The mother sat back down again, and I stopped twirling the keys.

"Tell her what happened," the wife said, and I settled into the seat and made myself comfortable. I knew we weren't going anywhere soon now.

"Tell her yourself," I said.

I knew she was going to tell her own version of it anyway. There was no fucking stopping her. I put the keys away in my pocket and off she went.

"You know what he's like," she said to the mother. "Totally full of himself."

"He's always been the same, hen. I told you that the first time I met him."

"So he decides he can learn to drive in three lessons. Three. That's all he took. And then he decides he's ready for the test. So he books one, and off he goes to sit it convinced he's coming home with his license."

"'Get yourself dressed up for me coming back, Bev,' he says. 'We'll be going out to celebrate tonight, hen.'"

"'Aye, Peacock,' I says. 'Right you are.' Can you imagine it? Three lessons . . . He didn't have a bloody clue. So he pulls out of the test center, and he turns the corner, and who should be standing there on the pavement but wee Stott. So Peacock stops the bloody car. He pulls in and rolls the window down, and wee Stott comes running over.

"'All right, Stotty boy?' Peacock says. 'Aye, not bad, pal,' says Stott. 'What are you up to?' The next thing Stott's in the back of the car. The driving examiner's shouting at him to get out and Peacock's asking him where he's going. 'Just down to sign on, Peacock,' Stott says, so Peacock starts driving him there. The examiner's telling him to take a right here and a left there, and Peacock's going whichever way he fancies. 'Aye, Aye,' he's saying. 'We'll get back to that in a minute, pal. Just let me drop the wee man off first.'"

The mother turned round in her seat and gave me a look.

I shrugged.

"What? It's hardly a major offense, is it? Giving a mate a lift. The rain was torrential. I could hardly just pass the wee man by."

She shook her head and turned back to the wife.

"Aye," the wife said. "But the major offense is still to come, Peacock. We're still getting to that."

I sighed.

"He'd decided I'd failed as soon as wee Stott got into the car," I told them. "It didn't make a blind bit of difference what I did after that. The guy's head was up his arse."

"So they're driving along," the wife says "The examiner's trying to tell Peacock that the test's abandoned, and wee Stott starts saying that he's only got five minutes left to get to his appointment—and he asks Peacock if he can speed it up a bit. Christ alone knows how Stott thought he was going to get there in time when he was standing out on the pavement beforehand, but now Peacock's doing forty-five miles an hour in a thirty zone. And he didn't even realize. He didn't know that till he found out in *court*. And he wasn't in court for speeding. Oh, no. That was only a minor detail of the case. While he was doing this forty-five miles an hour there was a crash in front of him, so what does he do? Does he stop? Not Peacock. No way. He mounts the pavement, and *then* he slows down. To thirty. He just missed three pedestrians—and he only learned that in court too. And he disputed it. He didn't see any pedestrians."

"There weren't any pedestrians," I muttered.

"Then he bumps down off the pavement," she said, ignoring me. "And goes back to his forty-five miles an hour, all the way to the b'ru, where he slams on the brakes and tells wee Stott to wait for him— he'll come back for him when he's finished the test.

"By this time the examiner's just about having a heart attack. He's been screaming at Peacock to stop ever since he started speeding, and he's been sitting there shaking since he mounted the pavement.

"'Get out of the car,' he shouts at Peacock, as wee Stott's opening the back door. 'Get out *now*. The test is officially over.'"

"'What do you mean it's over?' Peacock asks him. 'We haven't even fucking started yet. I've just saved your *life*, pal.' I had to sit and listen to all this in court, Mammy. It was the most embarrassing day of my life. And you know how many embarrassing days I've had married to this eejit.

"So instead of coming home with his license he comes home banned for life."

"That was only because of the wee altercation," I told the mother.

"Alter*cation*, Peacock? Alter*cation*? You *assaulted* the examiner."

"So? That's the only reason they banned me. If I'd managed to keep my temper I'd have failed the test, that's all. And I'd have passed it the next time."

"Peacock, you were driving on the *pavement*."

"That wasn't why they banned me. It was 'cause I hit the guy."

"Then," she said to the mother. "Then, when he gets home from the test, he starts shouting at me 'cause I'm not dressed up to go out.

"'Did you pass?' I asked him. 'Did I fuck,' he says. 'So what are you shouting at *me* for?' And he says he's shouting 'cause I didn't believe. he'd pass. 'Peacock,' I said. 'You *didn't* pass.' And he starts going on about how maybe he'd have passed if I'd believed he was going to pass. Mr. thirty-miles-an-hour-on-the-pavement."

"Are you finished now?" I asked her.

She looked at me.

I asked her again.

"Aye," she said. "Aye, I'm finished." And she looked at the mother and shook her head.

"It was nothing like that," I told the mother. "That's how they told it in the court, but you know what they're like. They look after their own."

So I told her what had really happened, in the faint hope that I could still get her out of there.

It was true what Bev had said, I did pick up wee Stott, and there *was* a crash in front of me. Some fucking idiot pulled out from a junction without looking. So I swerved to the inside to miss it, clipped the pavement, carried on. Then the examiner starts screaming at me to pull over. Fucking screaming he was. Then when we get to the b'ru he tells me the test's over and I've failed. How the fuck could he have known if I'd failed or not? We hadn't even started the fucking test yet. I tried to tell him that, tried to reason with the guy, but he wouldn't fucking listen. So I lost the place and hit him—then he made up all the other shite.

Ungrateful bastard.

I *did* save his fucking life.

"Peacock," Bev said. "You're a bloody liar. You were on the pavement, and you know you were on the pavement. You're a maniac. Stop trying to convince anyone else otherwise."

"Ach . . ." I said.

And I knew what was coming next; the mother started unbuttoning the coat.

"Maybe I'll just stay here until your dad can come and pick me up," she said to the wife. "He'll be back from his do about seven or eight. Is it any wonder I worry about you, hen?"

I closed my eyes.

"I'm away for a pint," I told them, and I put the keys down on the table. "I'll see you both later."

Drawings

Luisa Kazanas

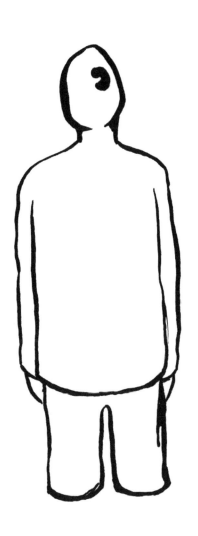

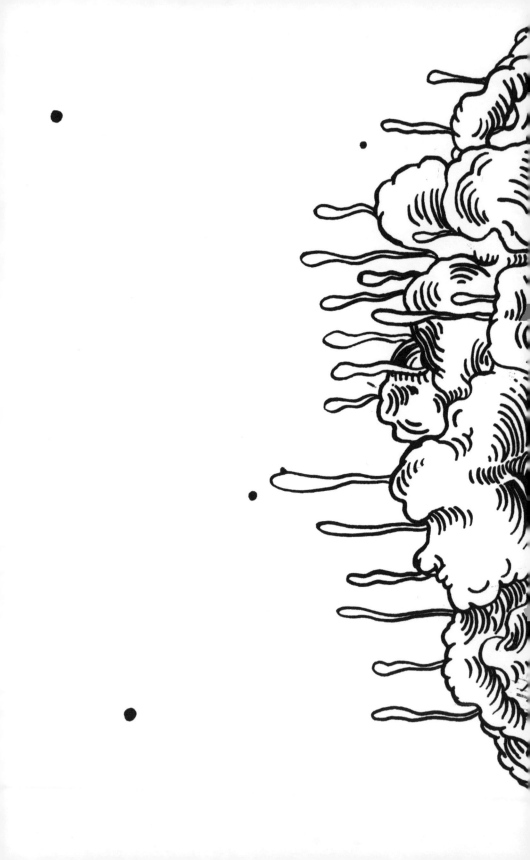

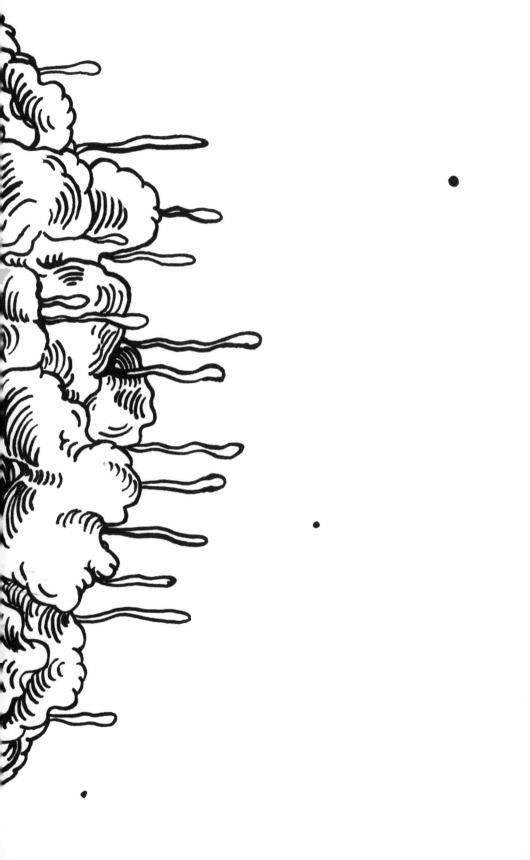

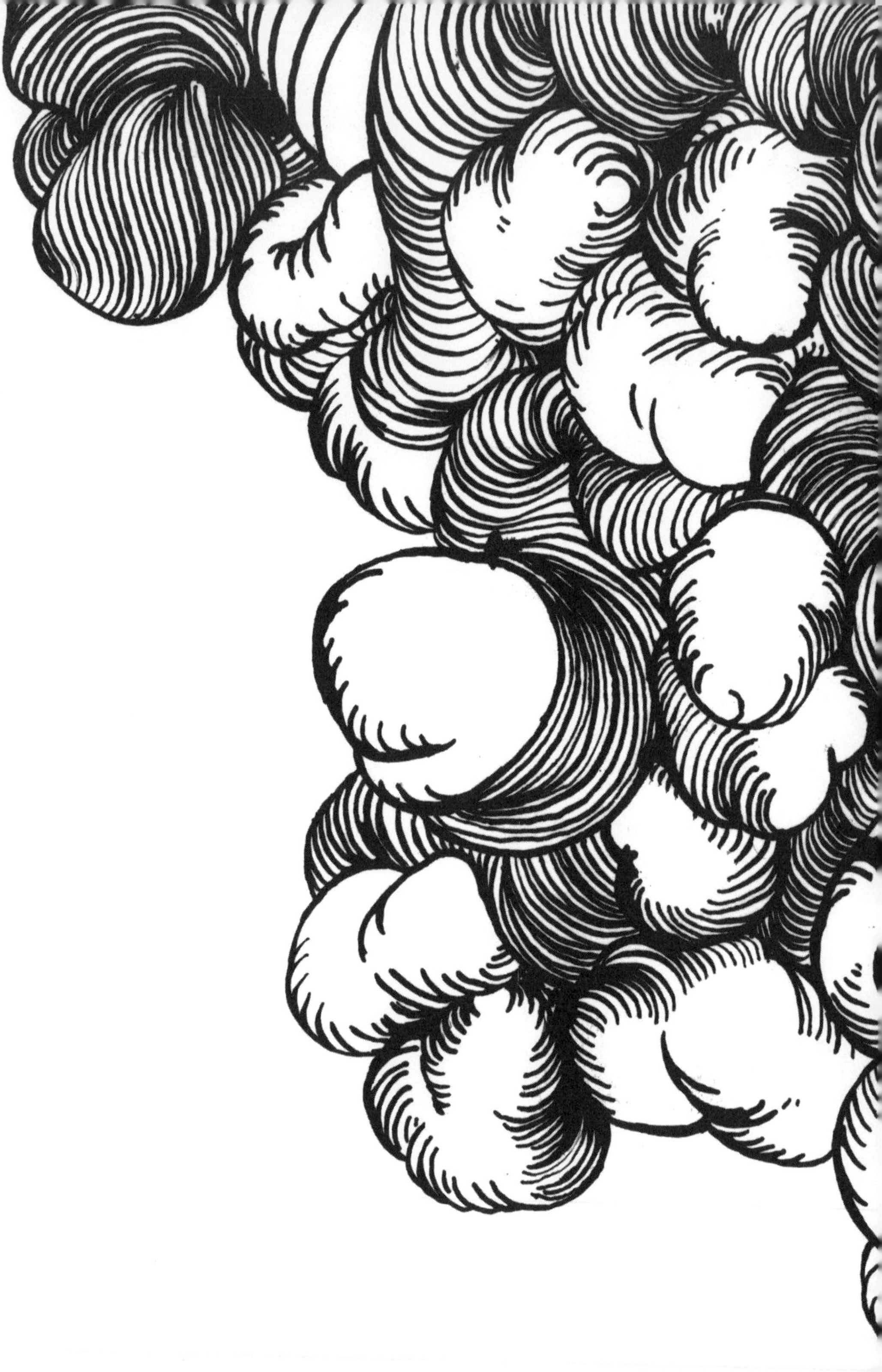

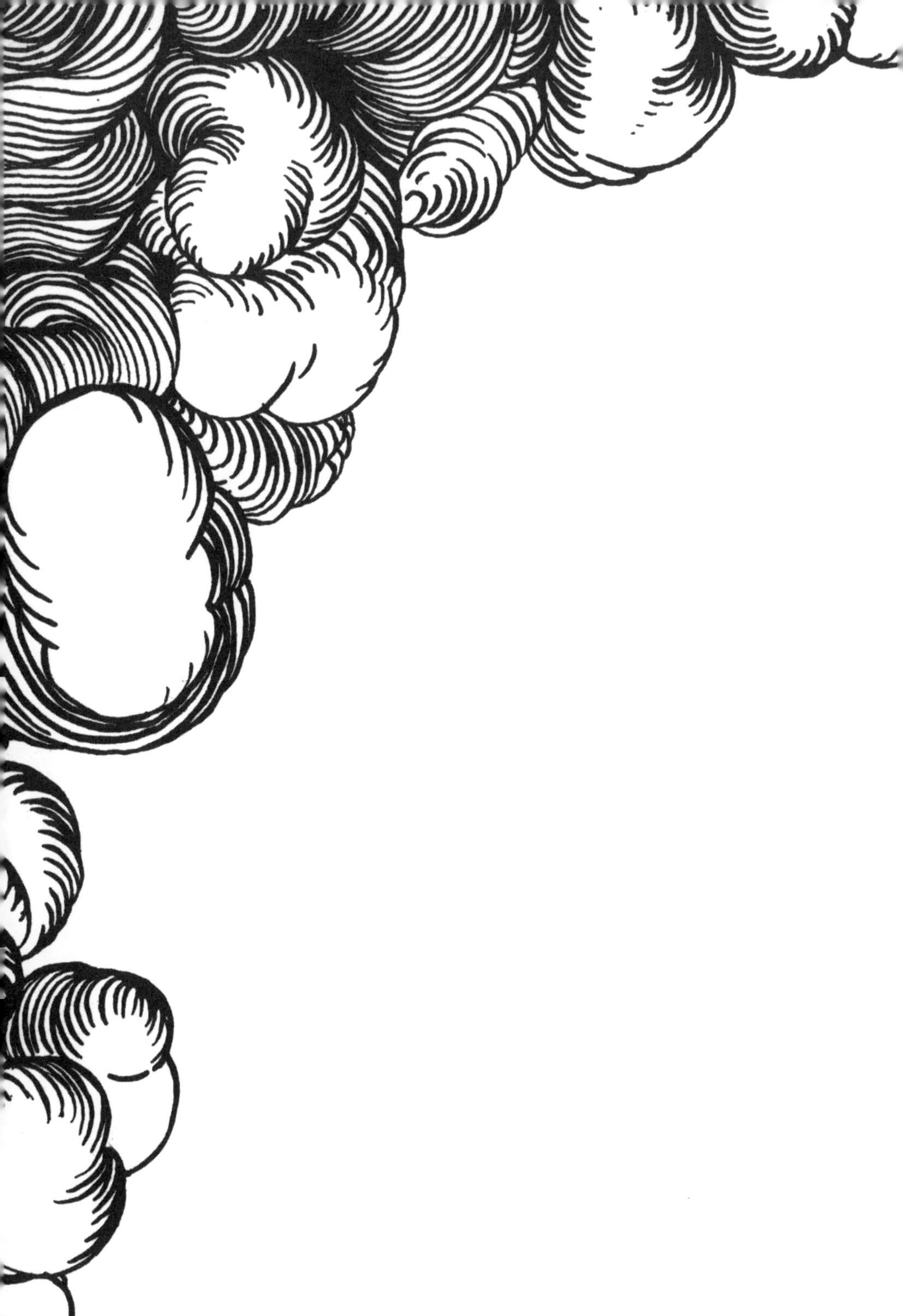

Four Plays

The following four dramatic works give diverse answers to the question: how does a dramatic text work on a page? They blow in wildly from all four corners of a theatrical compass . . . north wind, south wind, east wind, west wind.

Juliana Francis sends us tumbling headlong among boxing Victorian prostitutes, Ukrainian mail-order brides, a hallucinating ingenue from the Garden State, and a mysterious Artaud-reciting redhead. We find ourselves witnessing the theatrical equivalent of one of those Hindu icons, where the goddess's face is framed by an infinity of alternative manifestations.

Bill Talen offers a piece in a theatrical genre of his own invention: the Reverend Billy Sermon/Rant. As a postmodern anticonsumerist Paladin of the highest order, he is a hero to many for his intensely comic, politically charged message, and his peerless rabble-rousing ability. But the heart of his best "sermons" reveals a truly human personal struggle, that of an addict trying to live clean while being tempted on all sides by his drug of choice: pop culture.

Richard Maxwell gives us an everyday American vocabulary of language and behavior reduced to a blueprint of mathematical precision. This is a world where the typical (steak sauce, state fair) can feel otherworldly, and sudden absurdity (robotic humans, humane robots) can seem a welcome return to normality.

Finally, Carl Hancock Rux invites us into a heady garden of color, texture, and temperature, an echo in language and tonality to the abstract artwork at the play's core. Seduced, we walk happily into the trap of his hero's feverish headspace.

Having worked with all four of these authors in the New York theater world, I take great pleasure in seeing them published together in *Open City*. This is not to suggest these diverse voices form a school or movement of any kind . . . rather a cross section of a particularly fertile moment in playwriting.

—*Tony Torn*

The Baddest Natashas

Juliana Francis

If you bring forth what is within you, what is within you will save you. If you do not bring forth what is within you, what is within you will destroy you.

—*Jesus*, The Gnostic Gospels

This play premiered as part of the Blueprint Series at the Ontological-Hysteric Theater in New York City in the summer of 2000. It was directed by Tony Torn, with production design by the author and lighting design by Ben Kato. The original cast included Julie Atlas Muz, Funda Duyal, Juliana Francis, and Marie Losier.

CAST OF CHARACTERS:

MINNIE and QUINNIE, two Victorian prostitutes who are also NATASHA ALVALA and NATASHA ELVALHA, two contemporary Russian mail-order brides.

ACTRESS, in her twenties

REDHEAD, a girl who doesn't speak

VICTORIAN MADAM, MISTER UPSKIRTS, and THE TWO-YEAR-OLD KID, three performers on video

SCENE ONE:

MINNIE *and* QUINNIE, *asleep in a heap on the floor.*

Brief video flash of the VICTORIAN MADAM. *She looks like a cross between Catherine Deneuve and the Devil. She gestures furiously to* MINNIE *and* QUINNIE: *"Get over here."*

MINNIE *and* QUINNIE *don't budge.*

The video MADAM *disappears, then reappears with a cowbell. She clangs it, then disappears.*

MINNIE *and* QUINNIE *wake up groggily.*

MINNIE: Ooh ar. Here we go. Another funny one.

QUINNIE (*slightly alarmed*): Funny one what wants to stuff a bottle up me arse and break it?

MINNIE: No. That 'twere three bells. A little wild-girl show, knock this way and that, easy peasy pie.

(*Light changes like a door has opened.* MINNIE *and* QUINNIE *snap to it, address an invisible John.*)

MINNIE: Hello love. Hello cream pie. Aren't you a handsome devil.

QUINNIE: I wish you were my own sweet daddy.

MINNIE: Wouldn't you like me to be your own little wet spot of a girl?

QUINNIE: A smudge on your glasses that you look through, wipe on your handsome sleeve?

(*Pause.*)

MINNIE: Okey rokey.

QUINNIE: Doo hoo halla.

MINNIE: Let's get to it then.

(*They assume boxing positions.*)

MINNIE (*to* QUINNIE): Roll up yer sleeves you rancid big mess of a girl, I'm gonna flatten you flatter than you already flat.

(*They circle each other.*)

QUINNIE: Oh that's what you think you piece of meat sweating in clothes!

MINNIE: Ar. I'll knock the stuffing out of that blank head of yours.

QUINNIE: If it's blank, there's naught to knock. (*punches* MINNIE)

MINNIE: Ooh, you daft bitch. That was hard, but not as hard as this. (*punches* QUINNIE)

QUINNIE: Oh Daddy oh Daddy she knocked me on the head but she did not bite me on the wrist and not let go. (*bites* MINNIE *on the wrist, they whirl around*)

MINNIE: Oh, she's a wild one. A nasty unkempt wild one. WE don't let her sleep indoors. We keep her outside, behind the house, chained beneath the porch. She shouldn't be allowed indoors ever really, but Madam takes pity on her. Some girls just grow up wild, and some gentlemen just like 'em that way, Madam says. Madam is so beautiful and wise. She was born in a hole in the ground and now she's so fine, a fine lady, a businesswoman and compassionate too. But this one here, Quinnie, she'll never be fine. She don't like clothes and she don't like rules, but some fine gentlemen like to see things that they don't ordinarily see and that's little saber-toothed

Quinnie.

(QUINNIE *bites* MINNIE *extra hard.*)

MINNIE: OW! You're not supposed to really use your tooth you manky-mouthed God forsaken sag mattress! (*runs away*)

QUINNIE (*alone with "Daddy"*): Oh Daddy, stay Daddy, it's just you and me now! You can stay here with me now . . . (QUINNIE *alone*):

I got upset with her when she said I'd never be fine. Minnie knows naught about fine. She's just a stupid slag who used to be a scullery maid. Does that make her an expert on human affairs? Well, even so, nobody's story is finished, even if they do live underneath a porch. (*sobbing*) IT'S NOT SO BAD UNDERNEATH THE PORCH! YOU MAKE IT SOUND SO AWFUL AND IT'S NOT! (*recovering*) And besides . . . You're saying that cake is cake when it's still batter the baby will be president before it even knows how to hold its own spoon the cow being born is an old strip of jerky the mother cries out in the darkness but she's only eight years old there's a cave underground where there's only a watery crack my teeth are all broke when they're still sharp as razors the rain has ruined us before the dry season has ended the car hits the child before the ball even rolls out of the house . . . (*yowling, screeching, sobbing*) DON'T SAY THAT!!! DON'T SAY THAT!!! DON'T SAY THAT!!!

(*Blackout.*)

SCENE TWO:

Lights up on twenty-first century ACTRESS. *A heavily accented New Jersey striver. She might drink an entire can of Tab before she speaks.*

ACTRESS: Hi. My name is Natalie Ann Bovan and I'm an actress. I know, you're thinking: "Which restaurant?" or even more perniciously, "What's the point?" Well let me tell you. I'm not your garden-variety starlet. I'm trying to get in touch with something that might not be possible to get in touch with. For example: Let's say you're cast in the role of Helen Keller. You could wear a blindfold. You could plug up your ears. But all you are going to do is bump into the furniture. Helen Keller described her remaining senses as a "vibrascope." How many sighted and hearing people think to say something like that, eh?

But of course, Helen Keller could have a bad hair day too. I'm sure she had days where she wore mittens and sat in the corner. She edited herself. Or Annie Sullivan edited her or an editor edit-teded-her or some theater manager on the Helen Keller vaudeville tour said (*signed as well as spoken*): "Helen, why don't you smile and nod your head when you sing that song about smelling the flowers."

Helen Keller was a communist and she did sing songs.

So the truth, well it belongs to the bullies but they think it's diamonds when it's still just rotting leaves.

Me, I am trying to

find a way in where there isn't any. They say you can't rape a prostitute, you can only steal from her. Meow.

(*Blackout.*)

SCENE THREE:

A clip light switches on. MINNIE *is dressed as a Russian mail-order bride. She is being videotaped.*

MINNIE: Hullo. My name is Natasha Alvala. I am from Moscow. I am nineteen years old. I speak five languages. I am a dental hygenist. I won a modeling contest. I like traveling, disco dancing, and crochet. I am looking for a nice gentleman to love and go on walks with. I love vacuuming, children, and cooking gourmet meals from scratch.

(QUINNIE *enters dressed as a Russian mail-order bride.*)

QUINNIE: Hello, my name is Natasha Elvalha. I am from Moscow. I am eighteen years old. I speak fifteen languages. I studied medicine at school. I enjoy modeling . . . bathing suits, and other small things. I am a cheerful person who loves to go on picnics or to a car show. A simple girl . . .

MINNIE: Who loves simple things, like a sunset or a rainbow. I speak seventeen languages. I have a double PhD from university, ceramics engineering and child psychology. What I love best is . . .

QUINNIE: I have an eight-year-old daughter—

(MINNIE *smacks* QUINNIE *on the hip.*)

QUINNIE: But she is very quiet and works VERY HARD around the house.

MINNIE: Watch my video to see me walk up and down!

QUINNIE: Okay. Now!

(*They walk up and down.*)

MINNIE: Fuck this. There's nobody here. This is a fucking scam.

QUINNIE: Whatchoo mean?

MINNIE: I mean that bitch from the agency took all our money and now there ain't nobody here to put our film on the Internet for American gentlemen.

QUINNIE: Oh fuck. OH FUCK FUCK FUCK!

MINNIE: Calm down. Hyper!

QUINNIE: DO YOU HAVE ANY IDEA WHAT THE FUCK I DID TO GET THAT MONEY?!!! (*beat, glances at* MINNIE) OKAY, MAYBE

YOU DO!

MINNIE: Look, shut up now. WE have to be crafty, not loud. (*whispering*) There's a boat that leaves for Brighton Beach. We can go to restaurant school and wear lots of jewelry. I know a man named One-Eyed Sasha, he will get us tickets. Go to the dock in one hour, you will see a boat called *The List*. I'll meet you there. Don't be late. Okay baby sister?

(*Blackout.*)

SCENE FOUR:

Lights up on ACTRESS. *She looks pensive.*

ACTRESS: Hi! Yesterday I booked a commercial for the Japanese market. Strictly buyout. Shot on the weekend, so with the buyout, triple session fees. No residuals though. Starred a Japanese rap star who's huge in Japan but I never heard of him.

Everyone is so happy for me: messages on my answering machine: "Congratulations, Nat!"

The commercial was for sausage. Didn't Japan used to be a vegetarian country? The sausages were little, gray, and irregularly shaped, like little boiled arthritic fingers. They made a cracking sound when you bit into them; this was a selling point. The art director stuck the sausages on forks and had to keep mopping up the grease that kept flowing out of them onto our hands, our wrists, the table. Then we'd lift them up, bite, crack! and smile.

The commercial was designed to look like a Spike Lee film: Big American hip-hop kids terrorized the Japanese rap star who had just come from the grocery store, until they noticed he had a packet of these sausages, so they were glad and had a block party instead. Then the happy models came in from down the street. That was my part. Me and this other girl on roller skates.

I'll get paid in four weeks and by then I'll have amnesia and I'll go back to those offices and I'll . . . I'll . . .

(*Blackout.*)

Scene Five:

A cowbell rouses MINNIE *and* QUINNIE.

MINNIE: Ooh ar. Here we go.

QUINNIE: Oh. Another funny one. Easy peasy pie! (*leaps on* MINNIE)

MINNIE: Ooh! You daft squirrelly bitch, I'll knock you flatter than flat!

QUINNIE: Better flat than fat!

MINNIE: Fat, eh? Then how about me a-sitting on you then?

QUINNIE: Ow!

MINNIE: How about me giving a little jump a bump?

QUINNIE: Ow!

MINNIE: I've got you now, alligator! I could sit here for hours. Daddy, bring me a cuppa tea. Oh, okay, you're busy. Reminisce. The true story of Boxing Minnie, Prostitute Extraordinaire!

QUINNIE (*muffled*): Ha!

MINNIE: Shut it, slag mattress! (*raps* QUINNIE *on the head*)

QUINNIE (*muffled*): Awr!

MINNIE: I do pretty well for myself. Never been beaten into unconscious pulp. I've got syphilis, but I still walk pretty. I've got a sore on my thigh. I have a tooth.

Sometimes I have a dream. I dream I am in the shack I grew up in. The floor is dirt, covered with rotting reeds. The walls are black with greasy smoke from the fire in the center. The babies are whining. My mother is drunk in the corner, white track of saliva curlicued down her cheek. She is breathing and it rattles the fluid in her lungs. Suddenly I stand up, transfixed: There is a crack in the ceiling and a white knife of light is cutting through. It hurts my eyes but I look. And then I see inside the light there are a thousand tiny wings, a thousand tiny winged things swimming, darting, and then I hear them, because they are singing. They are wearing tiny crowns and holding tiny eggs and umbrellas and wearing dresses made out of gold and black spots and they move so quickly, and they are so happy, like little moths. I am the only one who can see them on this entire planet. Sometimes, if I am having a bad time at work, I can unfocus my eyes and there they are, singing (*she sings*): "Hello, favorite baby."

QUINNIE (*muffled*): Buggy bitch.

(MINNIE *beats the shit out of* QUINNIE.)

(*Blackout.*)

SCENE SIX:

The ACTRESS *applies lipstick to audition for a role. A man,* MISTER UPSKIRTS, *appears on video to explain it to her.*

ACTRESS: Hi!

MISTER UPSKIRTS: Okay, so your part in the video. Well, let me explain from the beginning. The magazine is having an auction of celebrity underwear—

ACTRESS: Celebrity underwear?

MISTER UPSKIRTS: Underwear celebrities, female celebrities and personalities have worn in movies, on location, you know. Not personal. And we've gotten ahold of this underwear and we're going to auction it off to our readers.

ACTRESS: For charity? A charity auction?

MISTER UPSKIRTS: More like for fun and profit. Now your part, what we've decided to cast you as is Geena Davis. Okay? Geena Davis.

ACTRESS: Just Geena Davis? Geena Davis?

MISTER UPSKIRTS: No, hold on. Geena Davis from *Thelma & Louise*.

(*The* ACTRESS *picks up a small Ziploc bag with a pink G-string in it.*)

ACTRESS: This is my whole costume?

MISTER UPSKIRTS: Well, no. You are also going to wear this vest and this bandanna, and we've got you this little gun here, and here's her face on a stick.

(ACTRESS *picks up vest, bandanna, little gun, and Geena Davis's face, cut from a poster and mounted on a stick.*)

ACTRESS: Oh. Okay. I hold this.

MISTER UPSKIRTS: Yeah.

ACTRESS: In front of my face.

MISTER UPSKIRTS: Yeah. So get changed . . . and we'll start.

ACTRESS: Okay. (*puts on the vest, takes off her skirt, tries to pull on the G-string but it gets caught on the heel of her boot*)

(MISTER UPSKIRTS *returns.*)

MISTER UPSKIRTS: Oh great.

(*The* ACTRESS *scrambles to finish dressing, holds Geena Davis's face in front of hers, and points the gun.*)

MISTER UPSKIRTS: You look great. Okay. Now, move around.

ACTRESS: Move around?

MISTER UPSKIRTS: Move around. Dance around. Pretend like you're Geena Davis. In *Thelma & Louise*. Oh terrific. That's good with the gun. Hold your face up a little more. A little more. A little less. That's good. Spin around. Spin around in a circle. Oh, don't shoot! Don't shoot! Oh-oh-oh—you got me. You got me. That's a wrap.

ACTRESS: That's it?

MISTER UPSKIRTS: That's it.

ACTRESS: Thank you.

MISTER UPSKIRTS: No, thank you.

(MISTER UPSKIRTS *disappears. The* ACTRESS *has a discreet panic attack.*

(*Blackout.*)

SCENE SEVEN:

MINNIE *and* QUINNIE, *dressed as the Natashas, are stowaways in a box on a boat.* MINNIE *is seasick, and has a plastic "I (HEART) NY" bag hooked onto her ears.* QUINNIE *is singing to herself.*

QUINNIE (*singing*):

Every night in my dreams
I see you I feel you
That is how I know you
Go on

(MINNIE *moans.*)

QUINNIE:
Far across the distance
and places
Between us
You have come to show you
Go on

(MINNIE *vomits into the plastic bag.* QUINNIE *holds it gingerly open for her. The* ACTRESS *enters. She looks distrait. She sees or thinks she sees* MINNIE *and* QUINNIE, *then realizes the audience is watching and crosses downstage.*)

ACTRESS: Hi! I think I am losing some sort of crucial identification with my surroundings. Everything is making me sad. Even my fingernails. I painted them orange last week. The magazine said orange is the new pink. I want to believe these things but . . . I had a dream about Marilyn Monroe. Did you know that she used to cut one of her heels down shorter than the other so she'd jiggle more when she walked? And that she sewed buttons into her bras so it looked like her nipples were always erect?

That was so thoughtful of her!

I dreamt Marilyn Monroe had gone mad, and that she had made a film about it. But the film was infected with the madness, and it looked like you were watching it through the eyes of a frog or a fly. It kept lurching from black and white to sallow yellow, and a horrible distorted electronic voice was screaming from underwater somewhere: IT'S TOO LATE. YOU'VE GONE CRAZY.

But she kept trying to make the film, even though the world kept spinning into fly-eye disks. What have I done for you lately? Walked down the street, wanting to feel things so nicely you'll go "clap clap clap clap clap clap clap . . ."

(MINNIE *and* QUINNIE, *dressed as Victorians intrude into the scene, dancing like two crack whores. They scare the* ACTRESS *away.*)

MINNIE: Ooh, Daddy, doncha like to see a girl dance!

QUINNIE: Dance dance dance dance dance.

(QUINNIE *makes a circle.* MINNIE *stops dancing.*)

MINNIE: Shit. You can stop yer twitching. We lost him.

QUINNIE: Shit.

MINNIE: Shit.

(*Silence.*)

QUINNIE: How much longer you gonna stay in this racket?

MINNIE: Huh?

QUINNIE: Well, yer getting a bit past it, aincha? Don't you ever want to pack it in?

MINNIE: Pack it in?

QUINNIE: Yeah.

MINNIE: I don't know.

QUINNIE: I heard Madam talking. She said yer getting too old and ugly, she's gonna turn you out.

MINNIE: Come right here and get slapped.

(*They fight.*)

QUINNIE: You could still work here. You could clean out the chamber pots. Ow!

MINNIE: I've got more skills than you'll ever have, you little maggot. Ow!

QUINNIE: Skills? All you got left is holes! (*grabs* MINNIE *by the throat*) And yer smart enough to use them in the dark! (*punches* MINNIE *hard between her legs then exits*)

(MINNIE, *in great pain, turns toward the audience.*)

MINNIE: Well, that's something, right? Everybody has one little thing that's theirs from God, and wot's God's is always good and won't get taken away! (*limps off*)

SCENE EIGHT:

The ACTRESS *appears, looking furtive. Her hair is very dirty.*

ACTRESS: Hi!

I haven't eaten or slept for a week.

Everywhere little black mice running in and out of little fires and centipedes falling.

(MINNIE *and* QUINNIE *appear in the audience. They are eating snacks.* MINNIE *is dressed as a Natasha and* QUINNIE *is Victorian. They stare at the* ACTRESS.)

ACTRESS: I am acting all the time now. I gave up on the offices. They sent me, they sent me to one of those things for maxi pads. You know, when they pour blue liquid in the ad to show how well it absorbs? Blue, huh? That's funny, right? The least human color, except for eyes. I was reading the part of the "young mother with two children," two children running around like bugs in the yard, and I was supposed to say "my flim-flam maxi pad always stays in place; which is a lot more than I can say for these two!"

I said it once, they said, great Natalie, do it again, more energy, like you're talking to your best friend.

Okay!

QUINNIE: Maxi? Who's Maxi? Is she a new girl? I'll cut her eyes out!

MINNIE (*Russian*): Oh, yes. They have those things in America. They are marvelous. Stick to your underwear like big thick Band-Aid. I am tired of using old newspapers.

(*The* ACTRESS *sees* MINNIE *and* QUINNIE *clearly.*)

ACTRESS:
Who am I
Where do I come from
My name
is Natalie Ann Bovan
And if I say my name
As I know how to say it
Immediately
You will see my present body
Fly into pieces
And under ten thousand notorious aspects
A new body will be assembled
In which you will never
Again
Be able to
Forget me.*

(*after "Post Scriptum" by Antonin Artaud)

(*Blackout. Wailing in the darkness.* MINNIE *and* QUINNIE *enter as the Natashas, carrying flashlights. They gasp when their flashlights reveal the* REDHEAD, *who is sitting in the corner with a bag of cheap crap like the stuff sold on the subway—plastic phones, key chains, deaf-education cards, and batteries. The* REDHEAD *is counting a Ziploc bag of change.*)

QUINNIE: Who's she, Natasha Alvala?

MINNIE: I don't know, Natasha Elvalha.

QUINNIE (*trailing her flashlight across the audience*): Is this the restaurant where we are going to learn to become cooker?

MINNIE: I don't know.

QUINNIE: It don't look like no restaurant.

(QUINNIE's *flashlight reveals the* ACTRESS.)

ACTRESS: Things dying and you're not helping. Personified dog-children. Cute baby animals. Marching in rows toward snuff films and drought. Wasted children and the seabirds that swallow plastic bags. Mother holding sick child in emergency room, tourist watching seabird spiral into the sea: What is it doing, that bird?

Is it—*eating* something?

Why did you choose that beach? 'Cause it was nice, pretty, free parking, not so crowded, you're allowed to have a barbeque, you can bring the dog, your favorite foster parents took you there, there aren't so many jelly fishes, no medical waste no dead dolphins, they say there's a nude section but you ain't found it yet?

Would someone fall in love with you at the beach? Your eyes, your toes, your burnt noses . . .

Nah.

What do I do for a living? I act in snuff films. I've done forty-six snuff films: *Dead Blonde, Dead Heat, Hannah and Her Dead Sisters* . . .

I want to look like Tinkerbell. Oh, okay!

I want to look like my cat. Oh, okay!

I want my lips pulled out of my mouth so they're all slippery!

Propped up on pillows in a silent room, fluids draining, face emerging from face.

Someone is sitting on a hard plastic chair, vomiting into a bucket.

Someone is bleeding into a fistful of napkins.

The mother filled out the forms nine hours ago.

Exit.

I am the last of the bad bad bad bad bad vagina girls.

I live in a cave with the rest of the last of the bad bad bad vagina girls.

It doesn't matter what you say.

You can turn the lights out five hundred thousand million times.

I spread my wings.

All good! All bad!

And so fucking unbelievably skinny you can see the blood tearing through me like a superhighway, like a magic flying zebra named . . .

Sometimes in the winter you wear a pair of leather gloves that you wish were longer because your wrists get cold. These weren't always your gloves. Someone left them at a party; you took them by mistake. At first they felt strange like holding someone else's hand. Now you're used to them.

I love you. I love you, gloves.

If someone loved you, you would buy a flower, put it in a jar on the windowsill.

Or ask the small, sad, cute little slave girl to do it. She's right over there and she does everything so—quietly.

They say, take a chance. The chance will pay off because of your shining faith. But if not, what happens then? Does it happen again, but smaller?

A voice in your head screams:

Noooooooooooooooooooooooooooooooooooooooooooooooooooooooooooo ooooooo!

This voice is always screaming but you don't always listen to it.

You just remember and there it is, moving like an underground river.

A suffragette falls through a time hole and marches down Fifth Avenue wearing a hat made out of paper, wondering, *Where's Lucy and Netty and the others?*

QUINNIE: *Don't worry, Alice, we're still here; it's funny!*

ACTRESS: Mother turns to daughter all serious, thinks things, says nothing.

Be the daughter that changes the world.

That smiles from all photographs

That's sporty and wholesome

That knows right from wrong

Don't

disappear into the darkness

Don't

smile in a way I never understand

Don't

dream of blood and fires.

Don't use antibacterial wipes

Don't be a stranger who hates me no more.

Hatred

(*scary gaspy hatred sound*)

having found a good body it could use, spiraled itself off the floor and swooshed toward the light switch.

Eleanora Duse died because she went to the theater in a snowstorm and she knocked and knocked on the door but there'd been a mix-up and no one was inside. She walked home, caught pneumonia, and died.

Allo?

(*knock knock knock*)

Allo?

(*knock knock knock*)

Dear a b c d efg hi j k l m n o p q rs t u v w x

I'm sorry but I quit.

I'm taking my stuffed elephant Bilbo and a Hershey bar.

You will never see or hear from me again.

Love,

(*The* ACTRESS *speaks in huge sign language, then exits. The Natashas watch her go.*)

MINNIE: Natashka Elvalha?

QUINNIE: Yes, Natushka Alvala?

MINNIE: I don't think this is the restaurant school.

QUINNIE: Shit, aren't you the damn genius.

(*The* REDHEAD*'s plastic toy phone plays a little electronic tune.*)

MINNIE (*eyeing the* REDHEAD): Hey. You. Red.

(*The* REDHEAD *looks up, smiling.*)

MINNIE: How long you been here?

(*The* REDHEAD *keeps looking and smiling.*)

MINNIE: How long you been in this place?

(*The* REDHEAD *smiles and shrugs, goes back to counting coins.*)

QUINNIE (*to* MINNIE): One-Eyed Sasha took our passport and papers.

Well, are you thinking what I'm thinking?

(*Beat.* MINNIE *begins wailing in Russian.* QUINNIE *grabs the* REDHEAD *by the wrist and they run the hell out into the street, which is filling up with fog.* MINNIE *and* QUINNIE *become Victorians.*)

QUINNIE: Ooh, I wish Madam 'tweren't making us work the street shift.

MINNIE: If wishes were horses.

QUINNIE (*Indicating the* REDHEAD): Why do we hafta work with this daft booby?

MINNIE: We're showing her the ropes.

QUINNIE: You can't show an imbecile the ropes.

MINNIE: Well, that's what we're doing. Ostensibly.

(QUINNIE *looks startled at the word "ostensibly." A whistle. They all turn and notice the* ACTRESS *facing upstage, disguised as a Victorian Gentleman.*)

QUINNIE: Oh, there's a bite.

MINNIE: Oh, a real gentleman. Look at his cloak and hat.

QUINNIE (*looks spooked*): Send blockhead. I don't wanna.

MINNIE (*to the* REDHEAD): Go on, Red. Be friendly.

(*The* REDHEAD *smiles at* MINNIE, *but does not move.* MINNIE *pushes her in the direction of the Gentleman. The* REDHEAD *crosses to the Gentleman.*)

REDHEAD and GENTLEMAN (*whispered*):
La vielle
a cheveux roux
est enterrée
dans le trou de la cheminée
il est ce trou sans cadre
*que la vie voulut encadrer**

(**after "Momo, 17" by Antonin Artaud*)

(*The* REDHEAD *walks back to* MINNIE *and* QUINNIE *and looks at them.*)

MINNIE: Oh he don't want her—

(QUINNIE *laughs.*)

MINNIE: He wants—

(*The* REDHEAD *points at* MINNIE.)

MINNIE: Me.

(QUINNIE *laughs harder. The* REDHEAD *points at* QUINNIE.)

MINNIE: And you.

QUINNIE: Whatever.

(MINNIE *and* QUINNIE *cross toward the Gentleman.* QUINNIE *turns to the* REDHEAD.)

QUINNIE (*with sign language, in a Helen Keller voice*): Wait here, we'll be right back.

(MINNIE *and* QUINNIE *approach the Gentleman. The Gentleman turns toward them, wielding a knife, Jack the Ripper style. He disembowels*

QUINNIE, *who squeals like a pig as the Gentleman pulls out fifteen feet of her intestines.* QUINNIE *tries to stuff her guts back inside herself; dies.* MINNIE *screams and runs out of the theater, dropping her hat. The* REDHEAD *sings a Russian folk song for the audience, places two chairs center, and exits. The* ACTRESS *removes the Gentleman costume, smiles at the audience, crosses downstage, and sits in one of the chairs.*)

ACTRESS: Hi.

I really appreciate you all listening to this.

Boy, that was (phew!)

But you know, I was reading RuPaul's autobiography in Barnes & Noble, and he said that everyone goes through a hard time in their twenties.

It's funny, the small things that make you feel better, and less alone.

I got two callbacks for a Hallmark Hall of Fame made-for-TV movie called *Hidden Choices*. It's a romantic drama about a mail-order bride from Uzbekistan. She comes to America to marry a farmer in Idaho. He turns out to be a cruel tyrant and much older than he said he was. He keeps her away from people, won't let her learn English. But then she falls in love with the young and handsome farmer next door and escapes to a new life. It's very moving. I mean sometimes the dialogue isn't—it's a little—but I like the story because it's moving.

(*The* REDHEAD *enters and sits next to the* ACTRESS. *They smile at each other.*)

ACTRESS: Hi.

(*They look out at the audience, smiling.*)

ACTRESS (*to the* REDHEAD): Did you know there was a period in history when they buried actors at the crossroads because they thought otherwise their spirits would wander the Earth, causing trouble? (*to the audience*) I mean, they sure wouldn't—well, it's just different. (*to the* REDHEAD) I'm not giving up. I know this because I had a dream—(*turning back out*) and in it was a little girl

(*Video image of* THE TWO-YEAR-OLD KID, *running and dancing*)

and she was running and smiling and talking to me, though generally not with words, sometimes she was speaking dolphin or bird or something transcribed by the Incas from the aliens who landed in Lima and taught them how to fly airplanes and do brain surgery on crystal skulls. This is a dream, remember. And she told me something that made my heart fall open like a flower. And then she vanished.

(THE TWO-YEAR-OLD KID *vanishes.*)

And I forgot it all.

(*sung, barely*)

Hello . . . Favorite . . . Baby . . .

End of play.

Free Us From This Freedom:
A Reverend Billy Sermon/Rant

Bill Talen

This "sermon" premiered at the final performance of The Church of Stop Shopping, *a comic church service, at the Salon Theater at 45 Bleecker Street in New York City in March 2000. It was directed by Tony Torn.*

A.
(Confidential, conversational, leaning over pulpit like sharing a secret)

How is it that we find ourselves in a time of apparent freedom and prosperity and yet we are as individuals we are quite sure that this is the most deeply conservative of times? The conservatism being of a psychological interior nature that we barely see.

This is a time when freedom is hard to develop, because we are not sure what it would look like or feel like. Why is that? Because freedom is so thoroughly mimicked, it is the delivery system for money. Products come to us down these colorful hallways of mimicked freedom. Freedom is surrounding us.

(Jerry Lewis on amphetamines)

Will I really individuate with my hand on that mouse?
Will I really kill my enemies if I drink this beer?
Will I really be free to dance with the tampon? With this Xanax?
Will I be able to smile unreservedly if I'm an actor with a product that

I lift into the sky flowing with cumulus clouds?
(Wailing rhetorical questions)

How did it come to pass that freedom would be
studied/replicated/manufactured and sold back to Americans? To the
world the word "America" means freedom. But how did it come to pass
that freedom would come back at us like a druggy storm?

Recent studies indicate that images of happy freedom are forced on
each of us nine thousand times a day.
Children we are gathered here tonight to seek protection against the
bombardment.
If we walked outside right now we would have to deal with a massive
Brad Pitt clone mixing fifty Skyy Vodka martinis at once. Smirking
that he has the freedom to tell such a shallow joke with such throw
weight. (The word "overkill." I'm thinking of the word "overkill"...
Overkill ...)

(Building to frenzy, far from pulpit)

CHILDREN WE WILL BE FREE OF THAT FREEDOM!
FREE FROM THAT FREEDOM!

(Audience now chanting with the Rev.)

FREE US FROM THAT FREEDOM!
FREE US FROM THAT FREEDOM!
FREE US FROM THAT FREEDOM!
FREE US FROM THAT FREEDOM!
FREE US FROM THAT FREEDOM!
FREE US FROM THAT FREEDOM!

(Ending in Alleluias and Praise Be's, get everyone onboard, walk up
the aisle, et cetera. Now commenting en route back to pulpit)

Oh where did they go with freedom of expression. Where did they
go with it?

B.

(Reading from the pulpit, scholarly)

And now I would like to read from an essay by Wally Cleaver Benjamin:

"What no one is noticing is that at the end of a day in Times Square people had returned from this mall grown silent—not richer, but poorer in communicable experience. For never has experience been contradicted more thoroughly than strategic experience by stealth technology, economic experience by sweatshops, work experience by the Wall Street casino, and moral experience by media moguls giving each other blow jobs on the top floor of the Condé Nast building.

"A generation that had gone to school and stopped the war and locked arms before doors, or became punks or beats or gays of conscience, now stood alone in Times Square—the Grand Canyon of retail—with logos going up the canyon walls, and nothing wasn't captured by a product except the clouds, and beneath the clouds which would move into sight above the buildings the human beings below half expected the clouds themselves to carry ads, for the clouds appeared naked and fragile without corporate sponsorship."

(Really boom, big-time preaching)

I was out on the sidewalk in Times Square.
Sometimes I have to go back out there and just preach, you know.
Just shout. Anyway, a few weeks ago I was out there preaching . . .
"CHILDREN, LET'S LIFT OUR HANDS FROM THE PRODUCTS
AND START A NEW WAY OF THINKING, A NEW WAY OF
IMAGINING! . . .
"PLEASE LOOK AT YOUR CREDIT CARD AND FEEL ITS
FORCE . . .
"SAVE YOUR SOULS CHILDREN. STOP SHOPPING! STOP
SHOPPING!! GO BACK TO LA JOLLA NOW!"

(A skit, the Rev. plays two people back and forth in conversation)

And then my girlfriend walked up to me. I was surprised—I didn't expect her.

She said "Oh Billy, you've been preaching all day, poor thing . . . I love you so much Billy, brought to you by Nike Sportswear."

"What? Honey . . . you've been taken over, they've got you!"

And she said "Billy, let's take a break, let's go get some coffee brought to you by Polo Deckwear . . ."

Christ!

"Yeah you look tired, brought to you by your local Coca-Cola bottler."

Honey!! Uh, what... oh God no....

(Billy in the skit has a change of heart)

Oh, I'm sorry . . . please honey . . . It's just that my emotions are just so . . . unendorsed . . . Can you be patient with me? Can you wait for me?

"Of course, my love. Someday you'll understand. I'll wait for you . . . I'll wait forever, brought to you by Toyota! Toyota! *We've Got What You Want!*"

(Shouting again)

HOW DO I TALK!
HOW DO I TALK!
MY TALK IS UNSPONSORED!
CAN YOU HEAR ME?
IS THERE WHITE NOISE POURING OUT OF MY FACE!!
I'VE GOT NO LOGO!
NO CONTEXT!

HOW DO I MOVE?
HOW DO I MOVE?
IT FEELS SOMETIMES LIKE I NEED VASELINE JUST TO CROSS
THE STREET!

CAN I BE FREE?
CAN I BE FREE?
WITHOUT ALL THE WORDS AND IMAGES
AND SMILING ACTORS THAT NOW GO WITH THAT WORD?
CAN I MAKE UP A NEW WORD?
IS THIS WHAT I MEAN BY "STOP SHOPPING"??
I WANT TO BE A CLOUD
I WANT TO BE A CLOUD
I WANT TO HAVE A SURFACE THAT RESISTS LOGOS . . .

(*Walking back to the pulpit and beginning to sing a blues*)

Let me turn my head
Let me lift my hand
From the sweatshop tchotchkes
That deadly discount deal . . .

C.
(*Conversation again, confiding with audience, letting them feel safe*)

How do I make words? How do I say to myself that I am free?

How do I recognize my own freedom and then report it back to
myself?

Yesterday I went to the local bodega to buy some coffee. I walked
there with my dog Jessica, who pulls me hard across Houston
Street. Her genetic memory is somewhere in the Northwest corner
of the Yukon Territory and she thinks I am a dogsled.

I see the Café Bustelo up there right away. It's stacked on this thin
sheet of Plexiglas that hangs from the ceiling on little chains and I
reach up for it.

So I reach up for it. I see my hand going up. I touch the can. The famous yellow and red Café Bustelo can; I'm grasping it. I'm at full extension now. But I am stuck in this pose. I am not taking the can from the shelf. I am standing there and my dog Jessica is too, because when I'm having a vision Jessica will stop and try to see it with me.

I'm having a moment of accidental entry into another world. I see coffee trees. My point of view lifts up and I see the villages around the plantation in Colombia. I see the money flowing from the hands and the people in the sheds and walking up the hills up the lines of coffee trees. I see the children of the owners flying away from resort towns in jets. I see the people watching each other from their stations on the ground, in the feudal-manorial arrangement of superiority and inferiority. I see the goon squads, the secrecy of the organizers.

(*Preaching but with a personal haunting to it, so that no request is made for call and response*)

Now I'm having a massive hemorrhage from a head wound. Somehow one of the goons hit me. I'm still reaching for the can in the bodega but I'm seeing the whole vision of coffee. I'm seeing the real cost of the bean. I'm seeing why it's so cheap and I'm feeling the ease of my life, this casual and habitual relationship to coffee, sustained by people living their lives.

I feel that for some reason the bubble of amnesia, the bubble of very supervised seeing, has burst for some reason. Where usually I'm ushered into the final acquisition, the final reach, touch, grab, and take to the register to pay and bag . . .
And always ushered into the purchase by a cloak of amnesia, a mental ride greased by the thousands of smiling actors and cartoon characters and forceful logos concentrated in the buying area.

But there is a vision hanging in the air, a major feature film of the production that made the product, the hours and hours, the lives of

people who brought these things here . . . Why?
Standing next to me is a man.
He's been standing there
Probably for a long time but now I see him.
He whispers his name but I can't hear it.
Something soft sounding . . . like Arian . . .

Later outside—I ask him how long his shift is and he whispers
"twelve hours"
—he's looking around for the owner—
I tell him to just nod when I say his salary and he finally
nods when I'm down at $2.80.

Let's stop in the middle of the shopping gesture children!
And let that vision rise in us,
I want to be like an artist—I have a vision and it changes me—
Let's see the whole picture
Let's get the information
Let's not let the packaging grab our hands
Let's slow down our shopping,
arrest shopping,
stop shopping . . .
LET'S STOP IN THE MIDDLE OF THE ACT . . . AND SEE . . .

JOIN ME NOW

(*Choir leads*)

STOP SHOPPING!!
STOP SHOPPING!!
STOP SHOPPING!!

(*During pause in music, invite audience to the post-show political*
action)

Join Jerry Dominguez and the folks at Unite 169. We're marching to
local bodegas that they are targeting and we'll support the green

grocers there. We leave from the front of the building directly after the show. Thank you, bless you, and good night.

(*Choir resumes the "No Starbucks No Disney" song and we march out.*)

A-1 Rolling Steak House

Richard Maxwell

This play premiered at the Ontological-Hysteric Theater in New York City in September 1998. It was directed by the author and featured the following cast: James Stanley, Alex Eiserloh, and Gary Wilmes.

CAST OF CHARACTERS:

STEVE
RAY
JUNIOR

STEVE enters and cooks at a Weber grill. Presently, RAY and JUNIOR enter.

RAY: . . . In a couple minutes, Steve's going to have sirloin for you all. Y'all ready? It's ten pounds of choice-cut, fressshhh-cooked sirloin to give away. Cut it up Steve!—Steve! How's it taste?! . . .

STEVE: (It's not ready yet.)

RAY: Is it done?! What's that? Rare? Rare!? Steve, you have to be better than that, baby. We don't want these folks to catch the ebola monster. Cook it up!

JUNIOR: Steve's a handy guy. I know you ladies be checkin' him out.

RAY: Yeah.

JUNIOR: Ha-ha. Ray, look at his sneaks . . .

RAY: Ha-ha.

STEVE: (Don't.)

RAY (*to someone offstage*): . . . What? . . . Okay. (*to the audience*) All right! We got hats, T-shirts, steak sauce. Tell-you-what!

ALL: Hey-oh!

RAY: I said, tell-you-what!

ALL: Hey-ah-oh!

RAY: Tell you what I'm gonna do! As I'm scanning with my X-ray specs, I'm lookin' at all these beautiful women out here . . . I'm looking at all these beautiful women out here. Ten pounds of sirloin goes to the first girl who can tell me . . . who can tell me . . . let's see . . . who can tell me how many pounds of sirloin we've given away so far on this trip? We've been out on the road for—what? Three months? Three months?! On this road trip, dude? Does it seem that long to me?

JUNIOR:

RAY: It's a lot of steak, but I like it . . . So I'm going to give it away— or wait. Junior. You're going—I want Junior to give this away. No, I want Junior to give this away. I see the girls eyeing that steak but I'm not sure, maybe it's Junior they be lookin' at.

JUNIOR: Ohh!

RAY: Huh? . . . Or maybe Stevie?

(*wrestling*)

ALL: Ha-ha!

JUNIOR: Seriously, I think this should go to the first girl who comes up here and tells us how much this piece of steak weighs. No, we said it.

RAY: This will go to the first person who has some literature on the—who can come up here with some literature from a . . . wildlife charity conservation program . . . Anyone who has some literature on the wildlife charity conservation program.

JUNIOR: How about free T-shirt to the first person who can come up here and tell us . . . how many cities we've been to. How many cities we've been to in the last three-and-a-half months . . . Anybody? . . . What he say?

RAY: Eleven.

JUNIOR: No, it's not eleven. Close. No. But not eleven. Any other answers? . . . What?

RAY: Fourteen.

JUNIOR: Yes! He got it. Correct. You are correct, Sir. Fourteen cities. We been to fourteen cities? Man.

RAY: Okay, I've got a free T-shirt. I'm going to go along with this! (*throws T-shirt*) Okay. Y'all. Watch the video monitor. We've got a little video demonstration up here for you to watch. I think you're going to like. Remember, we've giving away sixteen tons of beef over the last three-and-a-half months.

JUNIOR: Sixteen tons, G. Is like that song: "It's-six-teen tons—I-like-it-like-that . . . "

RAY: Ohh. Oh.

JUNIOR: "Some-people-don't-know-but-I-don't-knowwww . . . "

RAY: Ohh. Oh. Oh-oh. Stevie. Watch out. Junior's croonin'. (*to audience*) So don't go away. We've got a lot of steak here with the A-1 steak sauce.

(*Pause.*)

RAY: Steve, what are you marinating this with. That smells good.

STEVE: (Barbeque sauce.)

JUNIOR (*to* RAY): Call him Sandy. Look at that head.

RAY: . . . All right. Everybody. Who wants a Supreme A-1 hat? I got one steak hat to give to somebody. You could grill with this . . . No, guy. You had one, this guy got all the stuff. Check this guy out. Where you be puttin' all your stuff. You're like the—What? . . . No, I don't . . . You're like the Abraham Lincoln guy with a beer belly. Been drinkin' too much beer Abraham Lincoln? Black T-shirt. You know? Junior. I don't think I want to give to this guy. He ate all our steak I think. I don't think you need any more stuff, man.

JUNIOR: Okay, we got twenty more minutes until the next batch of steak comes out . . .

RAY: How we doin' Stevie?

JUNIOR: Steve, make sure how much we still got.

STEVE: (Don't.)

RAY: All right, we got twenty minutes. About twenty minutes and the steak will be done. We'll have more steak for you. Cool. Okay . . . It's time to play "What's at Steak?" You all know this. We played yesterday. I ask a question about A-1 and you come up and compete for the steak with another contestant and points are given to correct answers. Right?

JUNIOR: Ah-ight.

RAY: Okay, Junior. You know this, dude.

JUNIOR: Okay, here's the question. Ready? I want to ask a question. Here. There are five count 'em five flavors of A-1 sauce. I want to do something a little bit different this time. I want to have a couple come up here and answer the question, how many—What are the five flavors of steak sauce. A-1 has five. (*sung to "Anticipation"*): "Cou-ount-the-flavors. A-1 has-five-flavors." Can you come up here?

RAY: She don't want to come up, Junior. Ha-ha.

JUNIOR: What's a-matter?

RAY: She's scared of you, Junior! Ha-ha.

JUNIOR: No, I think she's scared of Sandy!

STEVE: (Junior . . .)

JUNIOR: You don't want to come up onstage?

RAY: No? Junior don't be biting. Yesterday, we had people coming up and singing songs. Now no one wants to come up here, dude.

JUNIOR: What'd she say?

RAY: She didn't say anything. Is there someone?

JUNIOR: "Lady, she's-my-lady . . . " (*He throws the hat.*) Okay, next question. What is the secret ingredient of A-1 sauce? A-1 has one secret ingredient. Do you know what it is? . . . What'd she say?

RAY: She said "tangy."

JUNIOR: Judges? . . . No, I'm sorry.

RAY: Next question. This is for the grand prize of, what else we got to give away? We still got steak to give away. And the question is, where. Who can tell me where A-1 is made.

JUNIOR: I'll give you a clue, it's a very famous state.

RAY: What state is A-1 developed in? There's only one . . . Who knows this? Junior, you know this, you decide if they're right.

JUNIOR: You know what? You know where it is, G? It's—Sandy—It's Sandy's home state. If that helps. What'd he say? Ohio?

RAY: Idaho.

JUNIOR: No . . . (*to* STEVE) Right?

RAY: Oregon? Is it Oregon?

JUNIOR: No . . .

RAY: How about? Washington?

JUNIOR: No. (*to* STEVE) Is it?

RAY: Let Sandy tell them . . .

JUNIOR: Sandy?

STEVE:

(STEVE *starts for* JUNIOR.)

JUNIOR: Ha-ha.

RAY: Horseplay! This is all horseplay! (*looks offstage*) . . . Okay. Come on. Steve. What is it?

STEVE: (North Carolina.)

RAY and JUNIOR: Ohhh!

RAY: We have a winner. Stevie is the winner. He knew that one, oh my goodness!

(*A* ROBOT *enters, he speaks to the audience.*)

ROBOT: Okay, please take a flyer and pass it back . . .

(*Pause.*)

ROBOT: Is Steve here?

RAY: Steve? . . .

ROBOT: Yeah.

STEVE: . . . Yeah.

ROBOT: Steven, will you come?

(STEVE *takes off his apron and follows the* ROBOT *out.*)

(*Pause.*)

Lights out. End of play.

**Oh that's what you think you piece of meat
sweating in clothes!**
(Francis, page 149)

Geneva Cottrell, Waiting for the Dog to Die

Carl Hancock Rux

This play was originally developed in 1992 at Mabou Mines/Resident Artist Suite in New York with dramaturgical assistance by Ruth Maleczech and Lee Breuer, directed by the author with choreography by Marlies Yearby. It was further developed at Playwright's Horizon's Forty-second Street Collective Project's One-Act Festival and The Nuyorican Poets Café, directed by Jude Domski, and produced in 1999 at the Penumbra Theater in St. Paul, Minnesota, directed by Laurie Carlos, with set design by Setu Jones.

CAST OF CHARACTERS:

RACINE

MUSE

GENEVA

The action of the play takes place in RACINE's *mind. There are two playing areas:* RACINE's *studio and* GENEVA's *South Bronx apartment circa 1977.* RACINE, *a visual artist who works in a variety of mixed media, is surrounded by paper, paints, brushes, tin cans, et cetera, as he sits in his underwear, drinking a glass of port, smoking a cigarette and observing his blank canvas. His legs, arms, and hair are splattered with many colors of paint. The* MUSE—RACINE's *conduit for memory, facilitating his confrontations and eventual reconciliation with*

GENEVA—*stands in a tuxedo, looking over* RACINE*'s shoulder and comparatively glancing back at* GENEVA, *who sits on her unmade bed, in a slip, staring out of her window, she is an image unfolding. At her feet are many albums, photographs, and several broken dolls scattered about. She lifts a cigarette to her mouth, and occasionally turns her head away from the window to listen to the voices behind her shoulder.*

GENEVA: Some haunting blues and violets weep, from corner to corner, wall to window . . . a call for soul's simplicity.

RACINE: This much I had: an urban space. A vacant lot near tenement dwellings, reaping abandoned Bibles and oversized chairs. Fire escapes leading to lovers or Jesus—one light box for laughter and a recipe for withstanding. A room with plastic flowers and broken plates, my gilded-cage imprisonment, tilted toward the plot beyond its window, listening to what bucked up from the bedlam of footsteps crossing language. The room's window hung on an opposing angle, dressed in shades against other eyes; a scrim for moving silhouettes on the other side. I stepped onto the ledge, leaped out of the frame, fell down . . . stood up—adjoining the canvas of negatives and exposures; a puppet show of city folks passing by with hats and grocery bags. On that plain of being I paint words and shapes on warehouse walls in strange configurations, waiting for a reply in chalk from anybody who has the answers. Anybody walking by. *This* is city living. *This* is how we withstand the wrecking ball of our lives . . . By walking . . . and remembering . . . I knew this much about the season of my deconstruction: It was the year of sanitation. Of erecting irrelevant statues and sweeping fetid bodies beneath the gratings. Old graves; apostatized and cemented over with neon animation. Forgotten murders shifted and then the litany began; a city was falling. My shoulders were tight. History belted itself around my neck and bent me down. An unrecorded history pressured into my spine, vertebrae by vertebrae—each disk twisting out of place. My head had been slumped toward my feet at all times, frail flat feet supporting a body of shame. The muscles becoming the consistency of granite, bracing themselves daily against my life. My whole body was a sculpture of trash heaped upon trash, until the sidewalk opened up into that chasm on the axis of the Earth, and the cinder fell from the cornerstone of a land-mark (crushing all composure beneath it), and fire began without provocation—consuming vanity . . . referencing what occurred before in rooms and corridors. This much I retrieved about myself on city sidewalks: a hint of gray and subtle blues present in a boy's eyes, eyes that required mourning when he laughed. Vanished mother trespasses the boy's memory, petitioning clear recollections of her Self, while he builds altars against retrospection—trying to *un*learn the language of the past. Scenes of forgotten gestures . . . But everything I am *is* that history. All that happened, the language shared, the music made, the songs sung, years before I walked this Earth . . . all of it . . . in my breathing. I know now it is possible to remember what you never knew. It is possible . . . Make . . . draw . . . some area outside myself . . .

GENEVA: Yesterway's soul simplicity.

MUSE (*coaching* RACINE *toward the canvas*): Make . . . draw . . . soft shadows, thin . . . light . . . white . . . not white.

RACINE: I want to remember her as she *was*, singing . . . scriptures . . . there were scriptures . . . *If thou* . . . *If thou* . . .

MUSE: *If thou criest after knowledge and liftest up thy voice for under-standing . . . if thou seekest her as silver and searchest for her as for hid treasure, then thou shalt understand the fear . . .* (*observing* GENEVA) Hers are the eyes fixed on the face, hiding in sketches of porcelain and lace—a lady who dies a very lovely death. Pungent bitter breath. Voice cracked like the mind.

RACINE: Would you tell me, this time? Just the facts. It's all I wanna know. Tell me one more time. Am I in the portrait too?

GENEVA (*calling out from her bed*): Faces? RACINE! Finished your painting Racine? All them colors in your clothes, in your hair, swear I can smell them colors in my dreams. You finished? You painting a landscape or shapes and things? A portrait of me or a river view?

MUSE: Hers are the eyes fixed on the face, hiding in sketches of porcelain and lace. A lady who dies a very lovely death, every day! Pungent bitter breath. Voice cracked like the mind. Great art! Fierce! Take off your clothes. Paint with your body, never use your hands again. Body against canvas!

GENEVA: You hear this Racine? You hear this music? Music suspending from cracked walls, open-pore walls . . .

RACINE: I try. They make me mess up.

MUSE: Who they?

RACINE: Dance with me.

GENEVA: Urine and shit and faces!

RACINE: If you dance with me it'll come out all right.

MUSE (*yawns*): Then I might as well do it myself. This is your process, not mine.

(RACINE *begins to put brush to canvas.*)

GENEVA: Does the night wind ever speak to you too, Racine? Call out your name and trade tales of celestial nocturnes? Rustle and rock you to a salsa soul, vibrate you to some foreign beat and speak your name, too?

MUSE: The eyes. Make the eyes beam. Do you see any light in those eyes? I don't see any light in those eyes. Light penetrates her window frame and falls gently onto her lids. Hides itself in the lashes, and the folds beneath her watery stare. The world as it was is just beyond glass and wood frame. Her window is her canvas, and she paints the scapes.

RACINE: But I'm tired, tired of the words.

MUSE: Stirring sighs and laughter fade. Towels and pain? Mmmmh. Interesting. Unlock the padlock to her door and breath like a holy virgin entered for the first time.

RACINE: There is no padlock to her door.

MUSE (*ushering* RACINE *toward* GENEVA'*s room*): Empty nightmares sleep on her breasts. First observation of subject.

GENEVA: Faces?

RACINE: None, just mine.

GENEVA: Smell shit and urine all day! Smell it in here? Open the god-damn window! Trapped! Breathin' shit and urine!

MUSE: God's light beams through and falls gently into her hair.

RACINE: Your flesh in my mouth . . . tastes like bitter leaves.

GENEVA: Don't know the air.

RACINE: Like dry and bitter leaves with poison veins.

GENEVA: Fair to say I don't know clean air, what circles like a carousel outside my room. Gloom and shit and dark—keep me locked in here—fear my imagination! It's a quick train ride, a glide to somewhere else! I'm a trip!

MUSE: Gently . . . gently. Scared virgin entered for the first time.

GENEVA: You got a couple of quarters, Racine? Buy me a loosey and a bag of Bon-Tons. Hair . . . comb my hair Racine. The lights are off at Yankee Stadium. They ain't never gonna come back on. I remember when I was . . . How old are you now Racine?

RACINE: Thirteen, without a clue.

MUSE: Spirits travel unaware. Come quiet. Come unannounced. Not loud. Not obvious. Ride in slowly.

RACINE: The words—tired of the lies!

GENEVA (*picking up her dolls*): Gifts of charm . . . my gifts of charm . . . Useta smell of my lover's peach wine and potpourri. Brought me pieces of colored glass and swatches of silk which I would mend and make and take home and clean. Make streaming gowns, gleaming gowns for my gifts of charm. Put them on top of blond wood vanities with shiny brass and crystal trays, stuffed with flowers. No sun or flowers in ditches.

MUSE: Not loud. Not obvious. Come quiet.

GENEVA and MUSE: Finished your painting Racine?

GENEVA: All them colors in your hair, in the air—swear I can smell them colors in my dreams—

GENEVA and MUSE: You finished?

RACINE: No.

GENEVA and MUSE: You painting a landscape or shapes and things?

GENEVA: A portrait of me or a river view?

RACINE: I don't know, not through . . .

GENEVA: Let me see it.

RACINE: No.

GENEVA: Let me see it.

RACINE: No.

GENEVA: Faces! Where's that damn dog, you know?

RACINE: Playing in traffic.

GENEVA: You keepin' him somewhere from me?

RACINE: No.

GENEVA: Sho'! You keep him locked behind some door like you do me! Ain't free to run—no sun, no flowers! Dogs got to run free, got to be where the light is! Can't keep a livin' thing in the dark!

RACINE: No!

GENEVA: Let it live . . . let it live . . . it wants to live.

RACINE: It wants to live.

MUSE: Close your eyes. Try to comb. See the tones?

GENEVA: Let it live.

MUSE: God's eyes!

GENEVA: I heard him, that dog . . . tappin' on the floor . . . scratching outside my door.

RACINE: Can I see the photographs again? I want to know the names of the faces. Am I in any of them? How come there are no baby pictures of me? The kids at school, they all have baby pictures. Where are mine? Is this you, holding the flowers?

GENEVA: Today I was drinking berry wine, fine drink . . . bathed in sandalwood. Should—should've let him in . . . He cried so awful that dog for me.

MUSE: The eyes—OOOOH!

GENEVA: You think I'm fat?

RACINE: No.

GENEVA: You think I'm ugly?

RACINE: No.

GENEVA (*engaging* RACINE *in a sexual pas de deux*): How old are you now, Racine? All them colors in your hair . . . today I danced to Brazilian love songs and my lover filled me with hisself. Today I ate Brie and goat cheese and melon cut in balls. He ran it down the small of my back, hisself sucked sugar squares from my tit, and licked peach nectar from clit and we—

RACINE: Spit at the moon? I know! Evening came too soon? I know! Was he made of your nightmares or your dreams? Was he flowing like drapes and dropping grapes in your open places, Mother? What lover was this?

GENEVA: The one with the Chinese marble eyes—and you were conceived by him. Today I conceived you. Shit! Goddamn! Can't be a mother to my own child! What, you don't wanna talk to me this evenin'? Shit! Goddamn! Can't be a mother to my own child! What you want from me, my left tit? Shit. Don't nobody hear this music but me? You finished your painting Racine?

MUSE: You gonna make it good this time?

GENEVA: All them colors in your hair, on your clothes—you finished?

MUSE: You gonna use other mediums besides pencil and paper this time?

GENEVA: What you painting? A landscape or a river view?

MUSE: Use your hand and body this time. Life and soul this time.

GENEVA: Lock the door! Feed the dog!

MUSE: You get it? It was all right there!

RACINE (*returning to his canvas*): There? Where there?

MUSE: All right there! Blood came streaming down from the womb of the wind—mighty breasts in hand, baring the pain of birth to bring forth hurt as metaphor. Stunning!

RACINE: Am I in it? Am I in the portrait too?

MUSE: As a fetus, left in somber solitude and starving for spirit. See it? It's right there. It's all there.

GENEVA: They stood applauding!

RACINE: I try but she make me mess up.

GENEVA: Hot tongue and berry wine! Chinese marble eyes! Hot tongue and berry wine!

RACINE: They're all lies. I try but all she tells is lies and I can't paint what's not true. I can't paint the questions . . . (*feeling himself*) I'm hard and I don't know why.

GENEVA: It was best he lay there.

MUSE: Use it. That's a lie too! Use it! Lies make fierce materials to work with. Go ahead—you gonna use me this time?

RACINE (*trying to paint*): Make . . . draw . . . some area outside myself, some stretch of area where the music is my own, the language is my own. Not tight. A space to be where soft light and shadows dance with me across the walls. Dance with me . . . are you hard too?

GENEVA: Too much. God made a mistake in me. Sick and dying. Dying. Dead.

MUSE: Burden-green and red.

GENEVA: It was best he lay there.

MUSE: You should use your hands. Put down the brush and use your hands. Never use a brush again. You need to connect to flesh and canvas. Violets and gold . . . red for the blood, the dog's blood . . . the grass, a burden-green . . . her skin . . . the shadows, make shadows . . . aaah. See that shape? Nice . . . nice . . . what more do you want? She's given you all the answers. Don't hate the lies! Lies are fabulous materials to work with—they're recreations. It's all there. It's all there. The confluence of powerful impressions coming from the natural world and corresponding with inner truths . . . now this can lead to a painting that is all at once an image of the artist's personality. An inspired interpretation of lies . . . or truth . . . or whatever you want to believe. (*suddenly annoyed*) Flat! That's a flat shape! No depth, no dimension! Look at what you're doing!

(*Leaving his canvas,* RACINE *exhibits a completed painting hanging on his wall.*)

RACINE: Aurelie Lanceau! Born in Lyon, 1906, to a poor merchant and his wife. Her mother used to sing songs to her down by the Saône but she died when Aurelie was very young. Aurelie worked for her father as a silk merchant, and was resting on the steps of the St. Jean when she was discovered by silent filmmaker Marco Marcevicci.

MUSE (*considering the painting*): What did the mother die of?

RACINE: What?

GENEVA: Faces?

MUSE: The mother. How did the mother die?

RACINE: I don't know. Who cares? This is a portrait of the child!

MUSE: Flat.

GENEVA: Racine!

RACINE: Marcevicci whisked her away to Hollywood and starred her in several silent films. She never went on to make talking films. She was depressed . . . and lost her mind . . . and drank herself to death and died in Lyon . . . overlooking the Saône . . . at age . . . thirty-five . . . it was . . . 1941.

MUSE: So she returned to France? First she was in Hollywood and she returned to France and died? It's stiff. No color. No form. Not real. Look at the eyes, there is no life in the eyes. It's all wrong! Look at the coloring in the cheeks.

GENEVA: Racine? You hear this music? You hear them chords and string? You hear the sweet crack in the falsetto?

RACINE: I don't know how.

MUSE: It's all wrong. No life. You make up stories, you make up the faces. Not real. They're all the same. All born poor, all beautiful. Translucent skin and Titian hair. They all have the same noses, and big breasts and full mouths. You don't shade in. You always use the tip of your pencil, you never turn it to the side to make shapes within shapes, darks and lights. Hues. They're all the same. They all die young.

GENEVA: Racine?

RACINE: I don't know how. Show me how.

GENEVA: You hear that? You hear the way the voice calls out and sounds just like a horn or something? Then it sounds like a whole string section!

RACINE: They make me mess up!

MUSE: They who? Who they? What they?

GENEVA: Can't nobody hear this music but me? Can't nobody understand this?

MUSE: You. Me. She. No they.

GENEVA: WHERE'S THE DOG? FIND THE DOG! It's poor and thin.
Don't eat, don't sleep. Hair lost its shine! Why you wanna kill the
dog?

MUSE: Try magenta and cobalt blue. The values contrast.

GENEVA: Shit! Don't nobody hear this but me?

MUSE: Contrasting values.

RACINE: I can't! Can't! Play with me.

GENEVA: Shit! Don't nobody hear this?

RACINE: Can't we just play?

MUSE (*pushing* RACINE *toward* GENEVA): Second observation of subject.

GENEVA: You goin' to church on Sunday?

RACINE: No.

GENEVA: Why not? Don't like alla that hoopin' and hollerin' I suppose? Jesus is a glass sky. Folk can't understand human nature, make
up another kind of nature. Another reality. King Pleasure is my reality! What they tell you when you go? What they have to say?

RACINE: Nuthin.

GENEVA: You tellin' lies. What? You don't wanna talk to me this evenin'? Shit. Goddamn. Can't be a mother to my own child. What you want from me? My right tit—Shit! Don't nobody hear this music but me. Who preach last Sunday?

RACINE: The prophet.

GENEVA: Where did he take his text from?

RACINE: Proverbs.

GENEVA: Yes?

RACINE (GENEVA *repeats under him*): "My son, if thou wilt receive my words and hide my commandments with thee, so that thou incline thine ear unto wisdom and apply thy heart to understand . . ."

GENEVA and MUSE: Yes?

MUSE: "If thou criest after knowledge and liftest up thy voice for understanding, if thou seekest her as silver and search for her as for hid treasure, then shalt thou understand the fear."

GENEVA: You know it was best he lay there. I put him to rest in the fields and forgot. Couldn't find him when I went lookin.'

RACINE (*to* MUSE): Can't we just play now?

(MUSE, RACINE, *and* GENEVA *pick up telephones and proceed to play a radio game.*)

MUSE: Helpful Harry here. You're on the air caller, go ahead.

GENEVA: Go ahead.

RACINE (*in a girl's voice*): Hello? Hello?

MUSE: Turn off your radio lady. You're on the air.

GENEVA: You're on the air.

RACINE: Oh, uh, hello? Hi.

MUSE: What's your name lady?

RACINE: I'm Nancy Drew.

MUSE: What's the story Nance?

RACINE: Well, there's an untold mystery kept away and she won't tell.

MUSE: That's her business, what's yours?

RACINE: I paint . . . but she makes me mess up. I can't paint unless I know how I come to be and why. I got names, hers and mine. I got one address, where we lived. I've seen old photographs of people, and one of her holding flowers, but that's all I know. There's no trace of me anywhere. I can't find clues to myself. Sometimes she tells me I was born here, in this room, sometimes she says it was a holy event. These are the only walls I know. I can tell there was paisley print paper in the bathroom before it was painted over a putrid green.

MUSE: To the point lady.

RACINE: She's crazy! Everybody knows she's crazy! The man who rents the room upstairs? He knows it. Sings and prays. Drinks and steals food from the refrigerator. He's crazy too. They're all crazy together. Miss Mamie, the woman who owns this house, she says Geneva is sick—but she won't call a doctor. If you know someone is sick, shouldn't you call a doctor? She just wants the check every month, because where we live—they give you money when you're crazy.

MUSE: Sounds like a plus!

GENEVA: A plus!

RACINE: Do you think I'm crazy too?

MUSE: I'm not paid to think kid, just listen.

RACINE: Well . . . Miss Mamie say I should go to school, it's right down the block—I go sometimes for arts and crafts. Get left back when you only go sometimes. I should be in the seventh grade by now.

MUSE: So what do you want from me?

GENEVA: What do you want from me?

RACINE (*his own voice*): I ain't got no soul in my pictures! My muse say—well he say—YOU SAY I should paint souls! I don't know how to paint souls. I don't know how they dance or what notes they hit. Last night I dreamed Snow White had red hair and I caught her in the kitchen of Noah's Ark. She let me touch her and when I woke up I was stuck to myself.

MUSE: Yeah? So?

RACINE: This is what I paint. Cartoon beauties. Make believe. I don't know how to paint souls!

MUSE: So go ahead and make your cute little pornographic cartoons. Long as it gets you off, what more do you want?

RACINE: I don't know if there was music the night part of myself escaped and made the whole of being. It ain't much to want to know.

MUSE: How do you see yourself, caller? I said, how do you see yourself? I said, how do you see yourself caller?

GENEVA: How do you see yourself, caller?

RACINE (*in a girl's voice*): In white organza and triple strand pearls.

Sometimes I borrow her shoes and wear them when I paint. When I wear them, I understand how her flowers wilted. They're not where they supposed to be. I understand when you try to grow where you don't belong—

MUSE: Well caller, we've run out of time. Sorry. Oh, what's your favorite radio station?

(*Game ends.*)

GENEVA: GODDAMN IT! GODDAMN IT!

RACINE: Hello? Uh—Hello—but I didn't tell you about the dog! Hello?

GENEVA: GODDAMN IT!

MUSE: You gonna make it good this time? Three dimensional maybe?

GENEVA: Racine! Tell Miss Mamie he did it again! Took some of my cheese! You took it old man, didn't you? Racine! Tell Miss Mamie we leavin'! I can't stay where people steal! I got to go!

MUSE: You hear the way the voice calls out and sounds just like a horn? You hear this music?

GENEVA: Limp dick old fool!

MUSE: Lovely! Lovely!

GENEVA: The rich man don't know God! Money is his God! GOOOD! God is on Lenox Avenue in an empty lot havin' breakfast and conversation. I got a postcard from Jesus!

MUSE: Make it real this time!

GENEVA: God is not dead! He's yet alive! I got a postcard from Jesus! Jesus is alive and well and livin' in sin!

MUSE: Gently. Gently.

GENEVA: There is an evil enemy operating the machinery of our minds! I can't hear the phone! Bessie? Billie? Aretha blues? I can't hear the phone!

MUSE: This is hotter than sex over an open flame!

RACINE: I DONT KNOW HOW!

MUSE: Let emotional disturbance and heightened creative function-ing coincide. (*pushes* RACINE *toward* GENEVA) Third observation of subject.

GENEVA: Where's the dog?

RACINE: Out having a drink.

GENEVA: You trying to kill the dog. Little Esther ugliest thing you ever wanna see . . . ugly voice too . . . You think I'm ugly?

RACINE: No.

GENEVA: You think I'm fat?

RACINE: No. (*runs back to another one of his paintings and exhibits it to the* MUSE) Dale Prichard, born in 1964! Died in a tragic fire!

MUSE: No.

RACINE (*holding up another painting*): Black-eyed Susan, born in 1970—Murdered her dog during a nervous breakdown!

MUSE: Obvious.

GENEVA: I give you the dog so you could have something you could hold. A dog that needed it a mother. Don't let it die. Make it fat. You got some quarters, Racine? Buy me a loosey and a bag of Bon-Tons . . . Little Esther ugliest thing you ever wanna see . . . What you painting, Racine? All them colors in your clothes, in your hair, swear I can smell them colors in my dreams. You finished? You painting a landscape or shapes and things? A portrait of me or a river view?

RACINE: Supposed to be you.

GENEVA: I knew. Yankee Stadium dark as my soul. They used to have—how old are you now Racine?

MUSE: Make the transition.

RACINE: Eighteen and I still don't know how. Will you tell me again?

MUSE: From fantasy to imagination. Make the transition!

GENEVA: All them colors in your hair.

MUSE: Make it fluid, subservient to wish fulfillment, oblivious to contradictions . . .

RACINE: Tell me one more time.

MUSE: . . . and other stringencies of reality. Make the transition. Gently. Gently.

GENEVA: The lines make sharp and jagged squares on Anderson Avenue asphalt. Interrupted shapes crossed by cracks in pernicious pavement channels. Square-root scribbles and fingernail scratches across gray cement.

MUSE: Gently.

GENEVA: This house was born when houses, not tenements, lined South Bronx streets. See? Small cylinder-shaped lumps on post and lintel, nailed there by praying Semites before the conquest.

MUSE: Parallels.

RACINE: What conquest?

MUSE: Don't interrupt the process.

GENEVA: Nailed there before the conquest of Caribbean tribes, in bright colored polyester—beating warrior rhythms on the hoods of the cars. Nailed there before the erection of bodegas and number spots. I remember the light from Yankee Stadium in the summertime shinin' through our windows, when I wore think-skinned rose and tulip-petal patterns and called my hair *my people,* but that was long ago. Once upon a time, before. Uncle James and I lived here, before the migration. He was an Apostolic Prophet, walked barefoot and wore olive oil on his head. But he played Coltrane and King Pleasure and took me to himself. The dog was all the family I had. The rest is vague.

MUSE: Capture the miracle.

RACINE: What part of yourself came from what part of someone else?

GENEVA: Where's the dog?

RACINE: He's dying fast!

MUSE: You're not listening!

RACINE: She's not telling!

GENEVA: Faces?

MUSE: Miracles seldom yield new facts.

RACINE: She's being vague!

GENEVA: Vague as the color of South Bronx skies.

MUSE: If we desire to conceive of another human being . . . of the imponderables, which transcend the circumstantial, it's the miracle that informs us—not the facts!

GENEVA (*singing*): The colors in my eyes are as vague as South Bronx skies now.

RACINE: Where am I from? Where are you from? When did you toss your mind to the wind?

GENEVA: I'm not from, I'm to! You? You were immaculately conceived. Blood came streaming down from the womb. I was a virgin rockin' myself to sleep. Thorazine. White walls. He took me in his arms, to the bathroom, had me on the toilet, quoting scriptures— you was born in water. I slept in the waiting room. I'm still healing. You my metaphor. My Messiah. Jesus is a glass sky. I'm trying to be a mother to my child.

RACINE: How do you see yourself?

GENEVA: In white organza and triple-strand pearls, holding wilting flowers. A holy virgin entered for the first time, before the conquest.

MUSE: Listen.

RACINE: She's lying!

MUSE: She's oscillating.

RACINE: No one is immaculately conceived! She FUCKED some-body—I'm here! The dog been dead for years! She's lying!

MUSE: She's oscillating between fluidity and rigidity. Miracles are rare, it's in their nature to be elusive. Don't interrupt the process!

GENEVA: You believe what people tell you about me, right? You believe it because I go walking at night, because I borrow quarters and dance to the percussion in my head? Who talks about me? The old man? Miss Mamie? Who tells you things? He drinks and prays and she never sees the light of day. I'm a blossom and they're weeds. WEEDS!

MUSE: And you believe what a weed has to say about a blossom?

GENEVA: They want to strangle me. Don't you see? They want me to shrivel up and die. My mind is a quick train ride to somewhere else. I'm a trip! And you believe what people who have never been any-where outside of themselves have to say about me?

RACINE: I just want the facts!

MUSE: Born, 1940.

RACINE: To whom?

GENEVA: I don't know.

MUSE: Capture the miracle in the hair!

GENEVA: Someone . . . a woman . . . once loved someone . . . a man . . . once . . . and pushed me through a plié. Then someone spiraled into the corridors of an urban maze and someone went to sleep on a coolin' board and rolled themselves into windin' sheets, and Uncle James—my mother's brother—took me to himself.

RACINE: When?

GENEVA and MUSE: Winter, 1944.

GENEVA: Took me to himself like the surviving litter of a dead bitch on a highway—let me keep the dog.

MUSE and RACINE: Summer, 1953.

GENEVA: He was whimpering and crying so awful that dog for me. In the rain, three legs, one gone. Looked so different from day to day I name him Faces. Uncle James told me it was all the family I was ever gonna have of my own. He grew me like an unwatered snake plant in a dry pot.

RACINE: Who—the dog?

GENEVA: The man! And I wore tulip-petal patterns and called my hair *my people* and stickball boys saluted me with the strength of their mojos. They said I was sick, need a doctor—made me take Thorazine and I held white flowers up to my white organza dress and smiled for my high-school graduation picture—but everyone knew something wasn't right. Something wasn't right. I wore the triple-strand pearls Uncle James gave me, and *my people* were tight and curly on my head.

RACINE: The talk . . . how did you talk?

MUSE: Lovely. Lovely.

GENEVA: To myself, in my own language. In tongues sometimes. You got to tarry for tongues, they don't come easy. You got to kneel and pray till you foam at the mouth and someone put olive oil on your head. They threw the medicine away and we danced to the beat of the drum till dawn. You could tell something was wrong. Never moved like they did. Moved with spirit. Talked to angels, conjured my own aura out of Morganna King's soprano prayers! And people moved away from me. Tried to run far. Limp dick old fool! People feared my mind. It's a quick train ride. Even Faces ran. On all three legs. Ran. 'Cause they told him to. Where's the dog? Help me find the dog. I'm gonna sit here and wait for the dog.

RACINE: And me? What about me? Am I in the portrait too?

MUSE: The fetus left in somber solitude.

GENEVA: You finished your painting, Racine? All them colors in your hair. In them clothes. You finished your goddamn painting? Urine and shit and faces? He's crying for me. You hear him? He's sick and wobbly and poor. I'm gonna wait until he comes back. I'm gonna help him. I am.

RACINE: You're crazy! Everybody know you crazy!

MUSE: No.

RACINE: She's not even here! She's a bad memory! Fuck all the psychobabble art therapy bullshit! I thought I understood something about it all—all the images—all the wasted paper—clean sheets scribbled on—trying to understand the images—trying to hear the music . . . I can't even find her face—her tone—her movement as it was—You don't get it! She was half of a distorted image in my mind and it's all bullshit! I grew like an unwatered snake plant in a dry pot—Not knowing. Grown and not knowing. She's composites, and images have to be whole—true—if you're gonna confront them—put them out there. Add color and tone! She's not even here! She's on Anderson Avenue circa 1977 with pale skin and wiry hair and I can't find the tone in her eyes—I'm not even sure if this is her face as it was—as it really was . . . I can't retrieve it. She's back where I used to be holy and gleaming, adolescent and scribbling on white paper—she's back where she was asking passersby for a cigarette or a quarter to cool the trouble of the day and the senseless rhythm of the night—she's looking for the dog . . . I'm looking for her . . . She was crazy! Everybody knew she was crazy.

(RACINE *laughs out loud, sits at his canvas and lights a cigarette.*)

GENEVA: I talk to myself because nobody else hears this shit but me . . . Who do you talk to, Racine? What do you want people to believe about you? How do you see yourself? How old are you now?

RACINE: Thirty and I—I want it to stop. You're a liar! A liar!

MUSE: Hers are the eyes fixed on the face, hiding in sketches of porcelain and lace. A lady who dies a very lovely death, every day. Pungent bitter breath. Voice cracked like the mind. Great art. Fierce. Take off your clothes. Paint with your body, never use a brush again. Body against canvas!

(RACINE *removes his clothes and rubs his body against the canvas— working his way into the painting.* GENEVA *moves from the painted dimensions of her room into another light.*)

GENEVA: I had a dream once, Racine. I dreamed I lived in a house as large as a foreign country. Dreamed it with my eyes open to peeling plaster dripping in small leafs from the ceiling of my room. Dreamed it when I walked barefoot through city streets, hiding behind demolished walls—a house as large as a foreign country. Seventeen garden rooms on sixteen acres of land filled with olive trees trimmed like Japanese lanterns. Redwoods, California native oaks. There is a rug hanging on the wall of my mansion, from India, with a thousand stories woven into its fabric. And over there, a lamp—fifteenth century from Indonesia. Mahogany tables layered in veneer decorated with hibiscus and tulips. A copper-top coffee table—from Morocco—holding silver and porcelain cigarette boxes. A marble fireplace, six feet high, with marble from the halls of Hercules at Versailles. I reside in a tower built of reinforced concrete with brick veneer—the steps are white Italian marble. I am standing beneath a chandelier that once hung in Versailles during the signing of the peace treaty. The crystals from the chandelier reflect little shapes on my shoulders. The floor is designed in a Venetian mosaic. French doors close you out, Racine. You are not allowed to climb in through the heroic-sized windows. There are so many people dancing in the ballroom of my mansion, Racine. So many people and so much music! Dancing in a ballroom—seventy five feet long and thirty-two feet wide. Twenty feet from marble floor to elaborately painted ceiling. So many people—and you are locked outside, so I have to escape into the garden. I am out here, Racine! I am in the garden, running through Irish yew trees, looking for you. You are hiding in seventeen garden rooms, running from upper terrace to lower terrace, running one-third of a mile down a path connecting sixteen acres of garden. Olive trees trimmed like Chinese lanterns, redwoods, California native oaks, two hundred and ten upright yews surrounding you. I am trying to find you, Racine. Are you trying to find me? Can you see me Racine? Can you?

MUSE: Contrast. Values. Tones.

Fade to black. End of play.

to step from air to water, from him
back into myself. I won't say what we did
(Moore, page 71)

A Project for *Open City*

Peter Pinchbeck

Peter Pinchbeck, the father of Open City *editor Daniel Pinchbeck, died last September at the age of sixty-eight. An utterly committed artist, Pinchbeck's work is a testament to a solitary, passionate, life-long dedication to the utopian ideals of abstract art. The paintings and drawings he left behind are probing and profound, abject and obstinate, luminous and eerie, eccentric yet true to their own inner logic.*

Pinchbeck was eloquent about his own work, believing that abstraction remained a viable way to explore the nature of consciousness, the history of art, and the latest ideas in physics and philosophy. The following note, found on his paint table at the time of his death, describes the concerns of his later work:

"Painterly volume is what interests me. What shapes have to have is presence, like a person, to have the reality of a figure in space, but still be abstract. I want to evoke this world, to some extent, in the rendering of form, but not in terms of the imagery, which is surreal and abstract. In style it mainly follows the tradition of the romantic abstractionists (Ryder, Redon, Pollock, deKooning, Kline, Cézanne). There are predecessors for this kind of extreme volumetrism. There is a group of drawings by Picasso in the thirties of these strange organic shapes, very three-dimensionally rendered. But I hope there are other echoes. I am influenced all the time by that Rembrandt self-portrait in the Frick where the figure sits against a dark background and the figure, face, and the amazing hands have an extraordinary volume and presence (the greater the volume, the stronger the form—the greater the presence). There are also those late blue Cézannes of the gardener. Painting goes its own way: It must always evade our understanding."

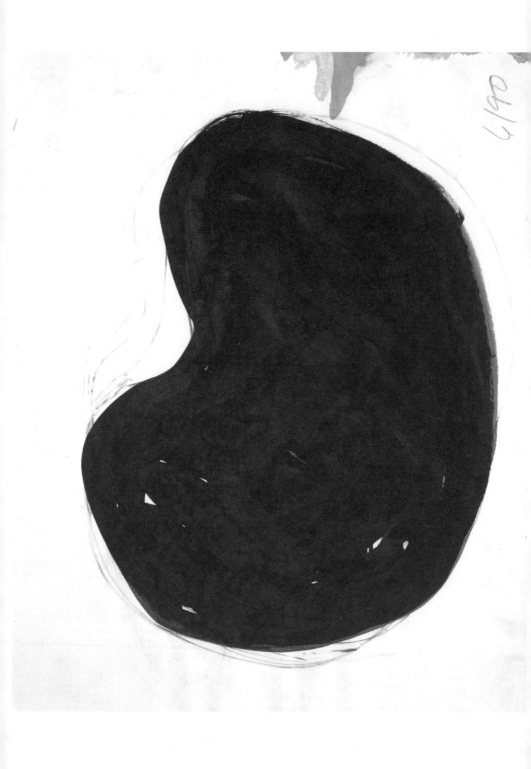

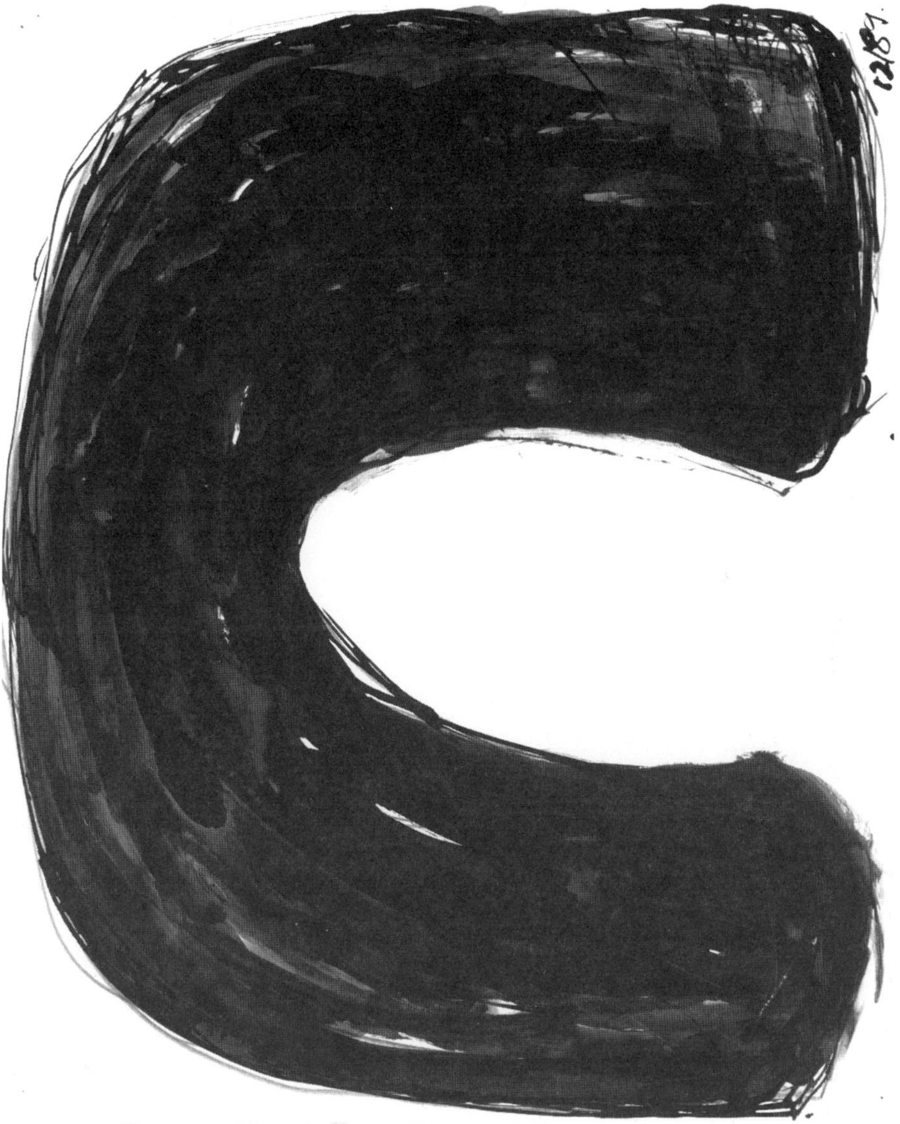

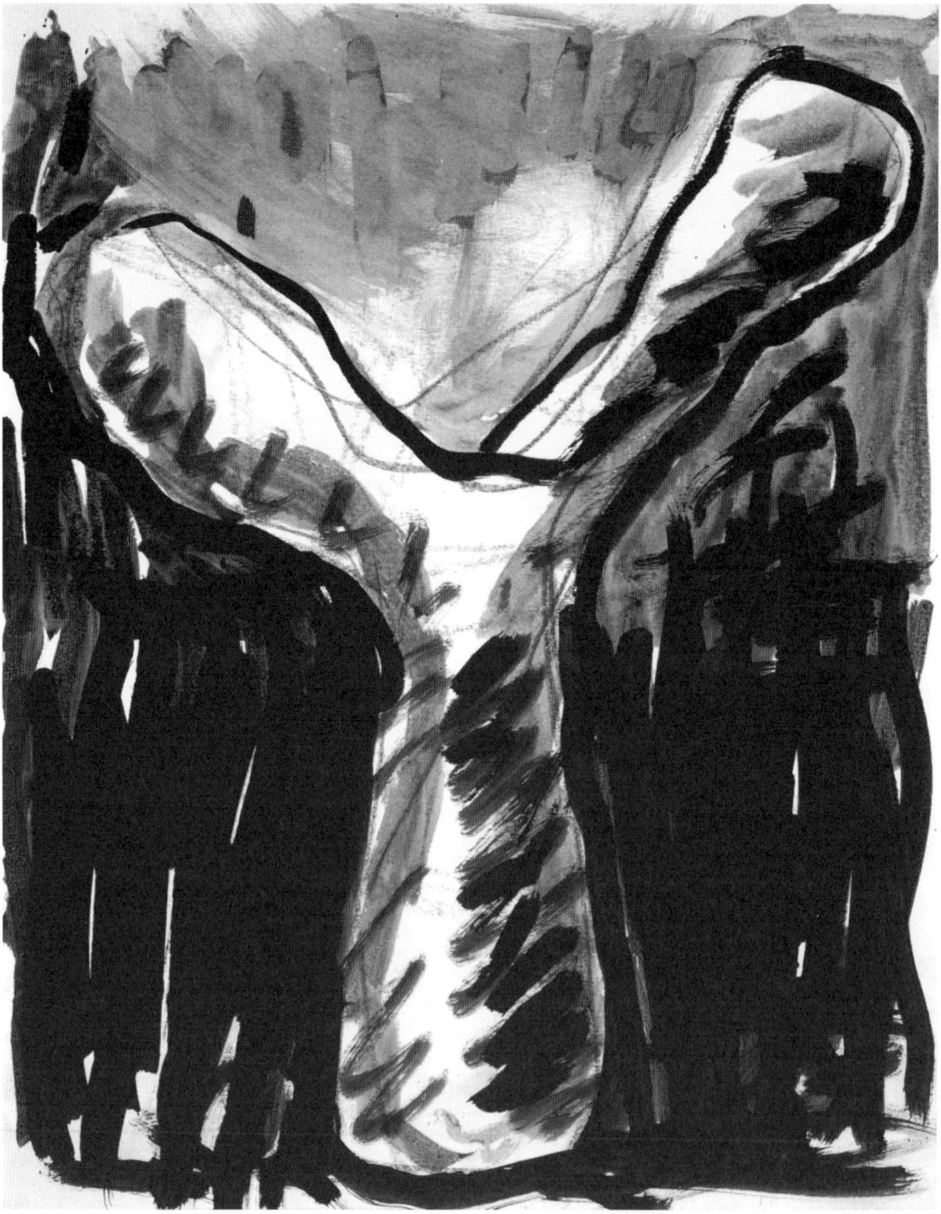

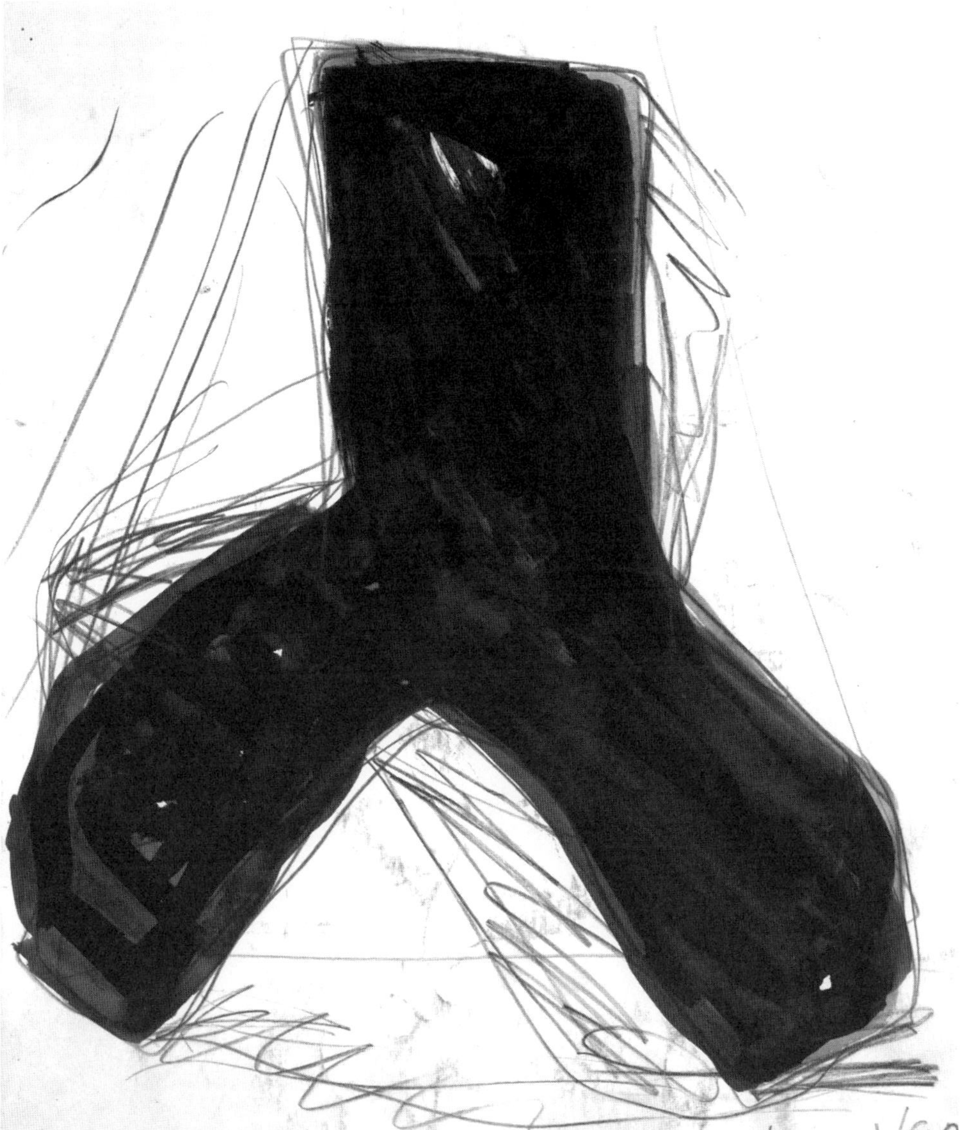
wishing bone 1/90

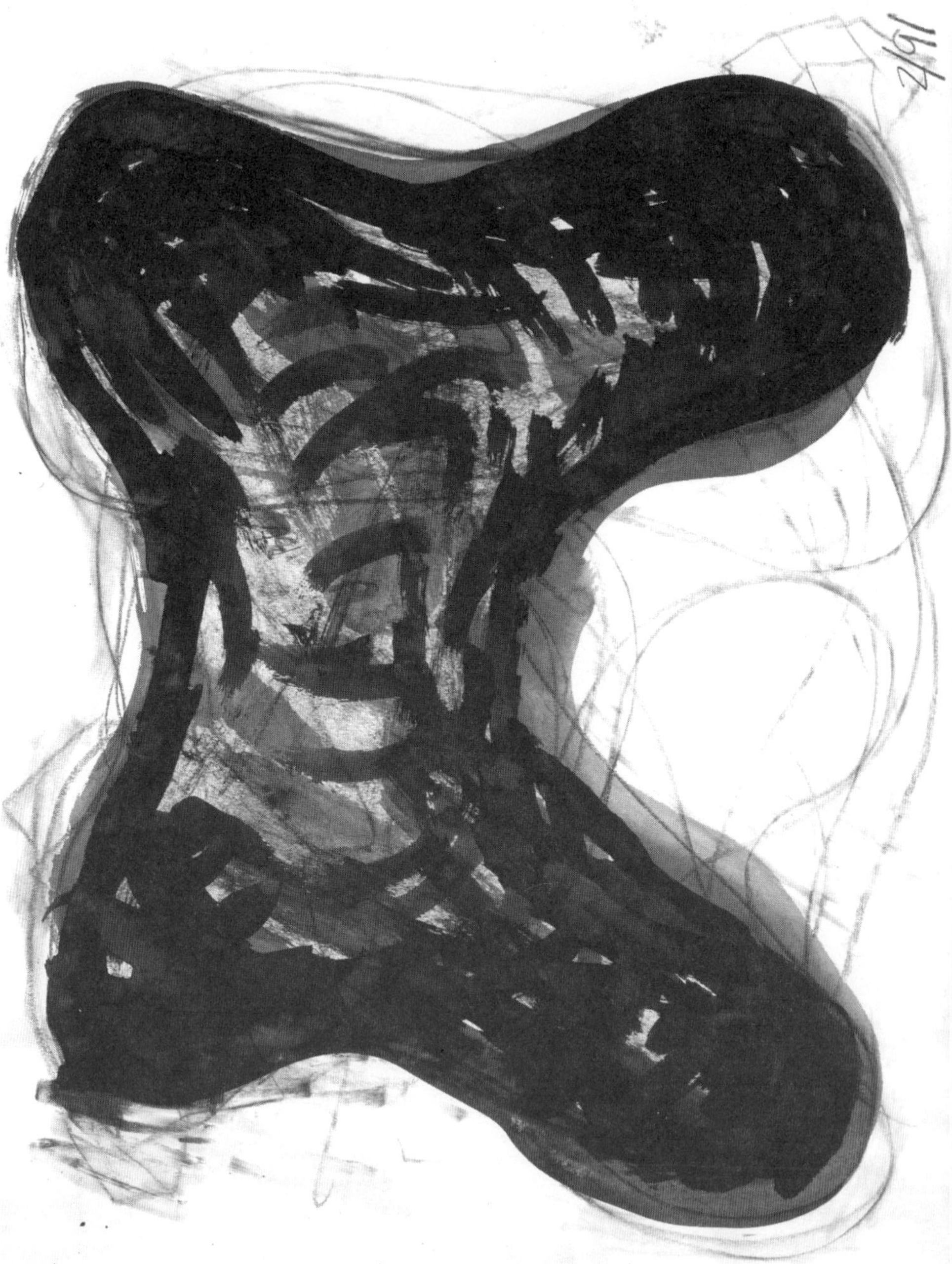
2/91

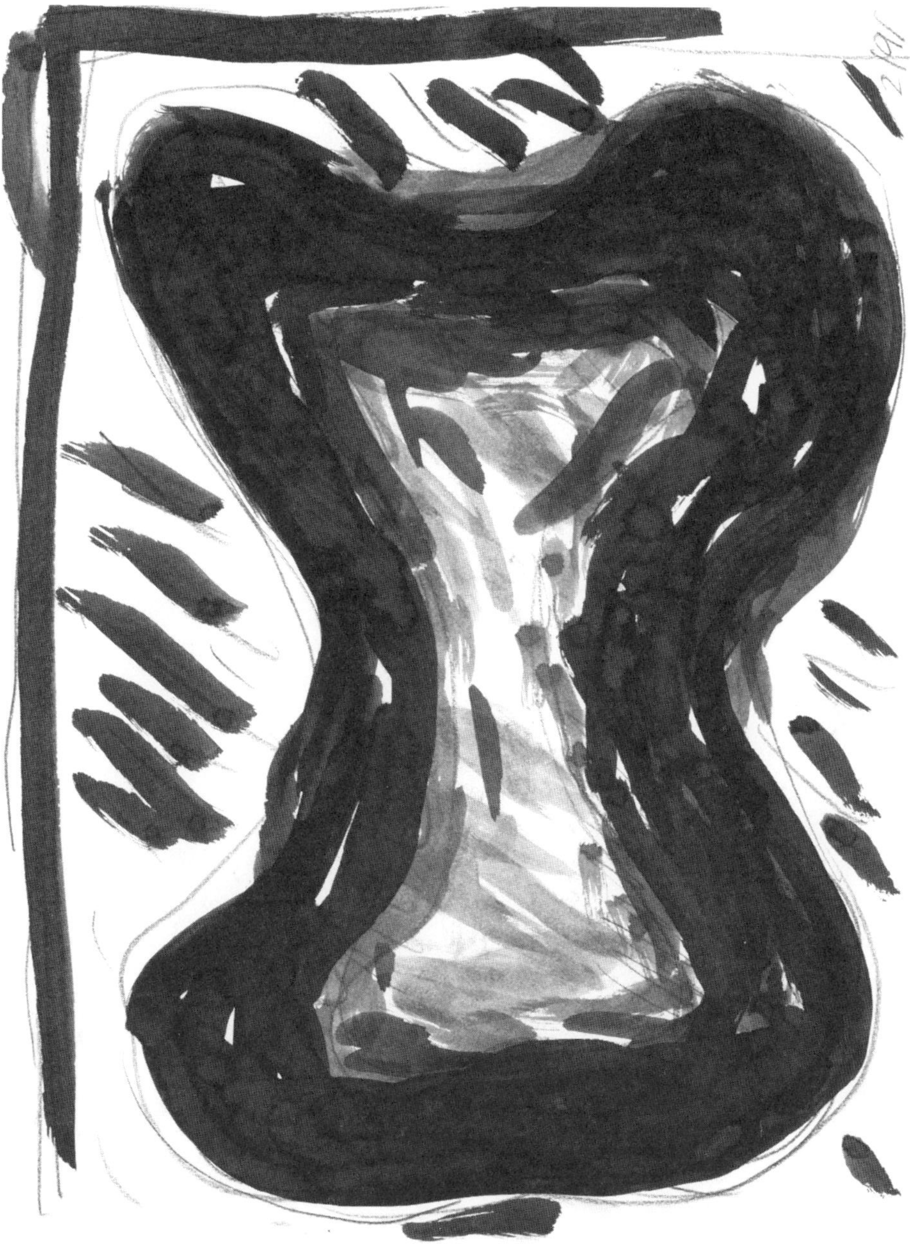

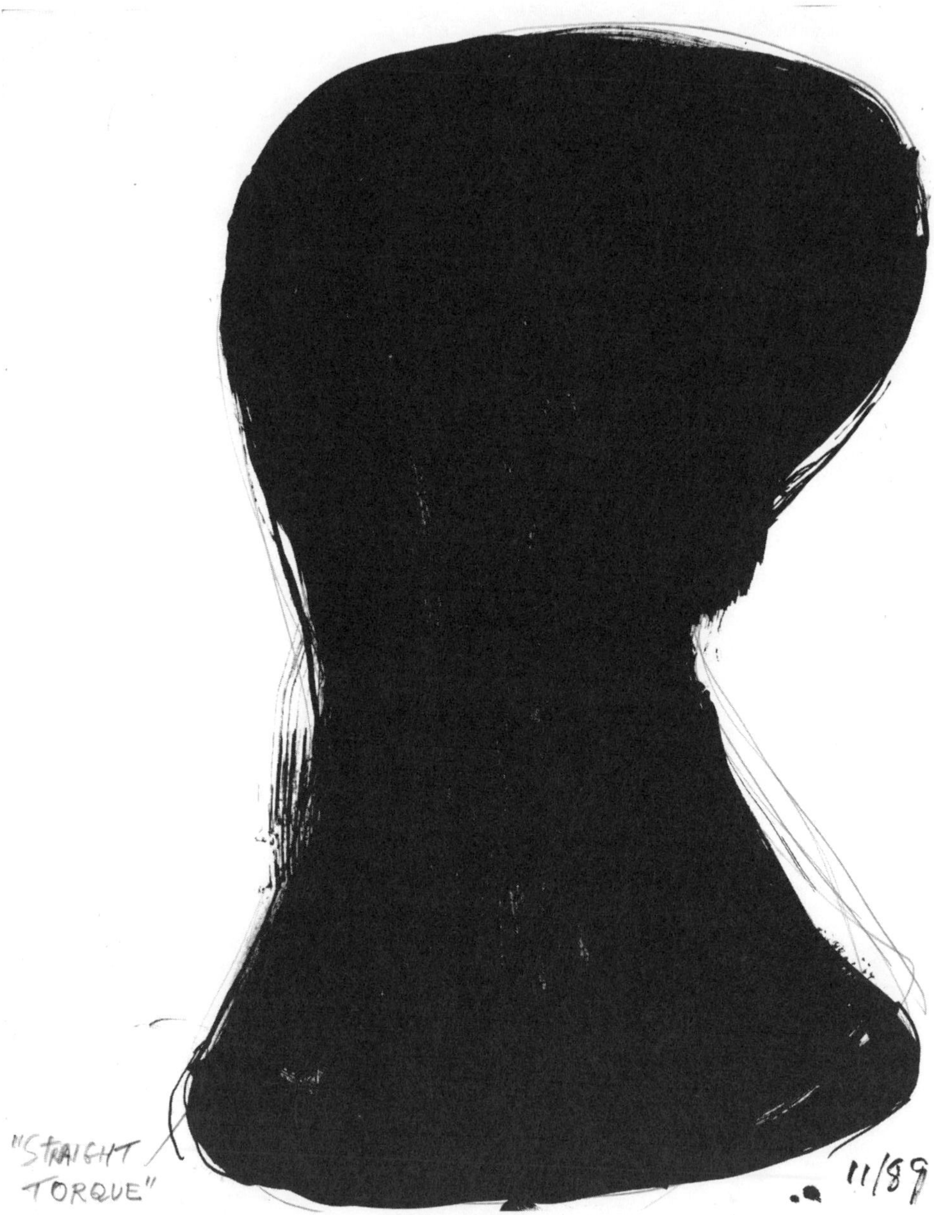
"STRAIGHT
TORQUE"
11/89

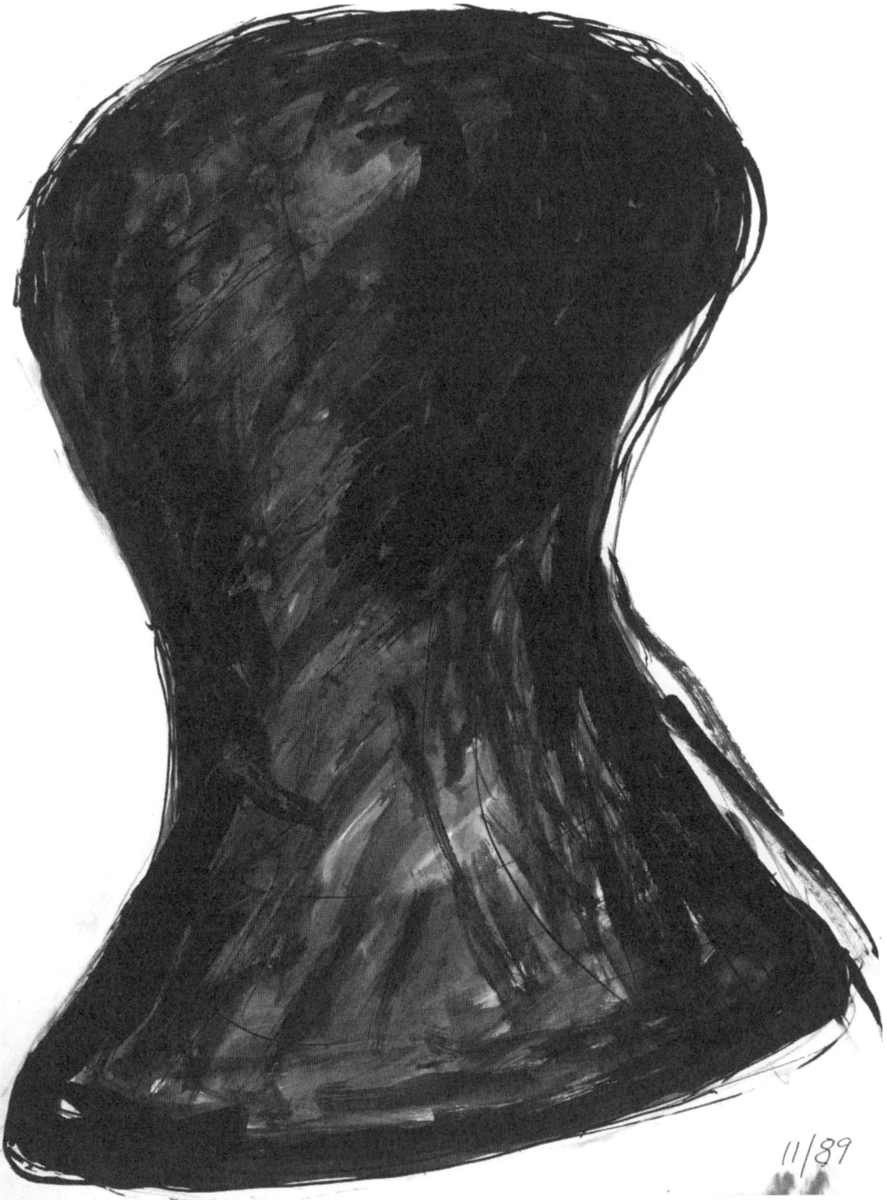
11/89

Adult Content

Vince Passaro

I AM TIRED BUT I CANNOT SLEEP.

Every time I think about the law firm and my upcoming partner-ship, I think: Hello, asshole. A little essay I might write, after I have been a partner for a time: "What I Do for a Living." I rely on the cash flow of six or seven normal American families. I put in a year, perhaps two, finding small cracks and handholds in the cliff face of the law, a minute process, while (if I am with the program, if my career has the same purpose as the careers of my colleagues) I plan my next big pur-chase and my next big vacation. These vacations are self-confirming narratives (as are most of the purchases; I'll have no other way to prove I exist), each is a tale of How-I-Can-Afford-This. Oh how proud I will be of my travels to well-advertised places. The high Sierras, a private sea, ravaged canyons with full-service hotels. A won-derful package offered by a creative travel agent promising some momentary electric contact with history; the travel agent's name is Terri and though she doesn't understand my longing to feel a part of the movement of time that is palpable in ancient cities, she does know that I wish to go there without missing the sensual pleasures of resort living. Weeks upon weeks pushing the dollies on which power and privilege rest, to and from the loading dock, grunt work, and then a holiday on credit: to Turkey, Crete, Athens, Rome; to New Zealand, Ceylon, Mozambique; to Cairo, Jerusalem, Damascus; *to Carthage then I came, burning, burning.* The vacation of a lifetime until a few years from now when I take another vacation of a life-time—this is what I have to look forward to, what partnership will bring.

In the meantime an unnecessarily large pleasant home that sur-prises no one, electronics galore, the refrigerator, set into the wall and full, Sub-Zero or Sub-Sub-Zero or Absolute-Zero, the temperature that stops even subatomic particles dead in their tracks, whatever is the best at the time because why not, that's what I'm working for after all; and if I am particularly enlightened, a couple of spots that indi-cate an effort toward beauty, an effort fully informed by online access to the *New York Times'* House & Home section . . . Something to be longed for and worth good money to maintain.

Your children—you are very concerned with reading scores, with growth charts. When they are small, how to explain their beauty? Secretly, one takes credit for it; then asks forgiveness for taking cred-it, and tries to grant the credit where it belongs. You pray first that they survive, second that they thrive, that they will be in every sense All Right. On selfish or worried days, you pray that they will not dis-appoint you, and in all likelihood they won't. You pray you will not disappoint them, but you will and you know it. They will probably, like the vast majority of their friends and peers, step graciously into their heritage of privilege, competence, and prosperity, even if (worst case) a few years late, because the alternatives in the world to come, in the new Middle Ages, will be unacceptable. They will be forced to hold on to every protection and hope of stability against what lies ahead, which you envision as a tectonic shift, an underlying *thunk*, after which the gatherings begin on street corners; isolated harangues will become political movements; in good time, only the priests and nobility will know how to read, the ultimate achievement of educa-tional reform. The money people will be the best barometer, this is something your children will know because you will teach them; the money huddles like cattle before a storm. The property types pull in their interests, safe-haven their capital, protect themselves—literally, too, in a real-estate realignment, out of the cities, they isolate their interests, the self-preservatory habits of a vulnerable genus; it's a pro-foundly reliable intuition they have. It hasn't happened in thirty years so it is due to happen again, like the early 1970s only worse, faster, more precipitous and terrifying. For a short time there will be a way to thrive in misery; play against the new inflation, the new unemployment, or both; you can bet on the burgeoning underclass, you can put money down on ever more restricted distributions of wealth, a gathering of all available net cash at the top of the economic ladder; you can bet on government cutbacks, deficits, deep imbalances; all of it means money is changing directions, moving from one place to another, like the salmon runs, and if you get up ahead of where the money is running you can expect to siphon off a nice piece of the action; but when the trouble really breaks out, watch the money hide; not a glimmer in the water. The word "overseas" will be important. Euro, Swiss franc, yen. The fortunes of five-hundred-thousand men and women will disappear in a couple of keystrokes. The big money moves away from the disturbance, like a retiree who spots some young men fighting on the street up ahead of him; literally like that. Crosses over. And the piddling mutual-fund investors and amateur traders will be left holding the bag; the pension funds will get totally fucked because some of the money always has to get fucked for the other money to survive and grow and if the system works as it should this means fucking the people who have actual needs; the dollar will sink, the markets will have no bottom; and the real people will have foreseen it all; they will have caused it, in the short term, so they're not surprised, and more important, they're not in it. They're long gone, baby. This is what you will protect your children from. Goodbye New York, hello Shanghai.

The point being that I cannot sleep. Since leaving Ellie and my two small children, my vulnerable children (but that is sentimentalizing, and I know it), I lie awake, passing the hours until three or four or even five, when exhausted, with work to come in just a few hours, I am finally able to fall away, to disappear into a dreamless rest.

The best thing to do is to leave my little box, to pass the time in the cinema of outside. It seems to be getting a little better in the neighborhood—one of the cops says, "It's like a self-cleaning oven," then he laughs.

I head up to 110th Street, to the all-night newsstand, the all-night groceries, the all-night bagel shop, the new café and bar on the corner which is open until four; I might go into any of these, depending on my mood, but I also like the walking, and usually keep on going, up to 116th and into the Columbia campus, a hazy white-lighted place at night, and my friend at work, David, is right, the sky is always purple over Harlem toward the east. I wander the campus's dark corners, watch the shadows, toy with a sweet nostalgia for my time here, all those drugs, the hope that rose in the presence of the many young women; I feel the quiet and the play of light on the big McKim Mead limestone buildings, glowing like sand in moonlight.

Then back downtown: when I'm walking down the street, a solid pace but slow enough to see things, to watch for the details, there it is again, a man behind me, I am faintly aware of the weight and darkness, a mumbling that keeps up and must therefore be directed at me. I turn and it is the cup: Aegean blue with the Parthenon on it, the take-out coffee cup, these cups being the last vivid icons of the West and its oft-lauded civilization. *Spare twenny cens? Spare twenny cens?* in a quiet chanting voice. The visionaries and shamans who have chanted through the ages: altered states of mind in which God speaks, and snakes rise from stones. All over the city, the quiet moan, the blue cup with its Doric columns and the rattle of coins. *How 'bout a little help tonight?*

I stop at the newsstand for cigarettes—what better company for the evening than these old friends. Ahead of me a tall, thick-shouldered, prosperous-looking man in gray slacks and a pink Lacoste shirt, maybe fifty years old, is buying dirty magazines, a goodly number of them too. I wait for my nicotine while the gentleman selects his pornography. With an air of expertise, he picks out several sets of four-for-$12.99s, the hardest-core stuff they've got, and negotiates the price down to thirty-two dollars for the whole thing. The Pakistani guy packs them in a bag. The gentleman strides off with an absurd air of confidence and pleasure.

"Pack of Marlboros," I say. My eyes drift overhead to the magazines, wander among the penises and open mouths. Ladies pose doggie style. Brown men with curlicues of black hair running down their middles in a thin lateral line. Invariably these men have mustaches.

On the other side of the newsstand a bedraggled man with fierce eyes sits on the edge of a trash can. To his chest he holds one of those little ironing boards, the size, roughly, of a child, a toddler, my son Henry. We exchange looks. "Yo, big man," he says, brandishing the little board, waving it in my direction, "No more ironing on the kitchen table man." He holds it out like an offering, an ancient sacrifice.

"No more ironing at all for me," I say. "It's all about the new casual."

He sets the board down and comes over. "Yo, big man, listen. Can you spare a hundred and thirty-nine dollars, you know, for a one-way ticket to Bermuda? I got a travel agent down on Forty-seventh Street she gonna give me the ticket for a hundred-thirty-nine dollars, man." His hand wraps around my upper arm, fingers strong as talons. "In fact, you know, you could just give me your credit card number, and she could charge that shit right up, give me the ticket. I just need to get away, you know? The warm air good for my lungs and whatnot. Charge it right to your American Express card man, Visa Gold, whatever. What you got, you got the Platinum Discover? Diner's Club? I can't take any more of this New York winter shit."

"My cards are all over the limit," I say. His hands, his face, the crusty unliving look of his hair and his beard, like bunches of old wool. Too much intimacy, too many people closing in and I'm just watching them like I'm a lizard, cold-blooded and slow, behind a glass.

"Just a hundred-thirty-nine and Bermuda is mine," he says. "Figure out where to go when I get there, you know, like the man says, definitely 'Better to Be Homeless in Bermuda.'"

"I don't know about that," I say. "New York is very understanding, a very tolerant place, we accept all kinds here."

"Fuck that shit, it's cold," he says. "You ever been cold? All night? No hope of getting warm?"

"No," I say.

"Makes *tolerance* look pale, man. Plus there's Rudy, he ain't so *tolerant* as the last few."

"You're probably right."

"Listen, my man," he says. "You know I'm just kiddin' around, right? No disrespect. No disrespect. Here's the real shit, man, I got a problem down at the welfare. They give me a ID card, you know, for my checks, but it got stolen in the shelter and now I can't get my check. They givin' me the runaround. Here look at this," he says, his grip loosening so he can pull from various pockets torn pieces of paper, gray and soft as chamois cloth.

"No documents," I say. "I don't look at any documents."

He folds the battered scraps back into his cracked palms.

I say, "This is a good story, by the way, a proto-narrative that comes up all the time, a major legend. I heard the same thing just a couple of weeks ago at the hospital, you know, the stolen ID at the shelter, et cetera, et cetera. It works."

"Yo man that shit happen all the time," he says. "All the time. There's all kind of shit going on out there, people stealing shit just the tip of the iceberg, you got no idea, man, no idea what-so-fucking-ever. And not just among the lower classes either."

"I know," I say.

"No you don't," he says. "Anyway, big man, it's like this see, I got to get down to Third Street to the shelter down there, they got a bed assigned to me down there. And in a few days I get my card back, you know, a new ID, and I get me a check and then hopefully I be off the streets. How 'bout a little help, man, you know, whatever. I gotta get downtown."

I give him a dollar. He moves on, I look down the block, three or four beat guys waiting with paper cups, a gauntlet I'll have to run to get, where, home? Can I even call it that? And beyond them Broadway stretches into the charcoal-lavender night, buildings loom black against the glowing sky, most of the windows dark, most of them always dark after nightfall although the apartments certainly aren't empty, who knows why, and down the gentle slant of the avenue hang the traffic lights, small red streaks, tongues of fire along the urban grid.

By this time of night the main thoroughfares can be a Fellini dream sequence: along the sidewalks, shifting like unquiet waters, a slow-motion flow of the lame and the halt—an Easter parade, or gaudy like it, but also unavoidably grim; in the middle of 110th Street, literally on the yellow lines, a crazed-looking woman in a wheelchair twirls toward the westbound traffic and then as quickly swerves back around like a mechanical drunk to face the eastbound, shaking her tin cup in midair like some kind of awful preacher of gloom and perdition—as if she believes the cars themselves are per-sonalities on the scene, listeners, inclined to come to Jesus and give her some change. She shakes the cup at moving cars that are going thirty-five or forty or even fifty miles an hour, cars that have shown her an uninterrupted streak of kindness only in that she hasn't been flattened by any of them. She is there for many nights, but a night will come when she will not be there, and no one will see her again. EMS will have taken her away, or the cops; she'll do time in a hospital bed, be sent to social services, be unable to follow the dotted lines that keep her in the system, and be dumped back out again in a new spot, among some different group of horrified citizens, to harrow them for a while.

There are others, always ready to take the spot, a steady supply of men and women of few means but strong public presences. Silhouetted, they have strange postures and forward-leaning, bony walks; one sees them either fleeing in a great and heaving rush to get to some probably imaginary appointment or else they are rooted to the spot. One man seems half twisted; turning and turning, one of Michaelangelo's prisoners. If a prayerful person were to pass by, he might phrase an address to the Almighty along these lines: *God, in your wisdom and mercy, what exactly do you have in mind for us out here on the street at night?* One believes that prayerful people are indeed passing by, at least a few; one believes this now because in the new medieval city there are essentially three groups—the powerful, the devout, and the bankrupt.

And here in the glowing white darkness of night in autumn in New York City, near the river, smoking a Marlboro and going slightly woozy with it, I think the only possibilities are devotion or nothing at all, devotion like the poet felt when he fell to the floor in front of the Pietà in St. Peter's, the hope of a moment when the idea of a thing and the thing itself are so perfectly joined that your knees fold and your legs collapse and your face lies flush on cool marble. In that moment, thick woolens wrapped him and deep gravity pulled him to the floor, an impossible union.

It has not happened for me. It almost happened for Ellie once, also in Rome, and might have happened, I like to believe, if there hadn't been a German; or perhaps it did happen and it was the German who caused it. This was the year after we were married, and we went for five weeks with not much money to France and Italy—we were in Rome the longest because we had friends there, although there were friends in Paris too but not as close a set, we had friends all over in those days. We went one day to see the *Moses*, which resides at another St. Peter's, San Pietro in Vincoli, which means Saint Peter in Chains. We went for the marble and art but ended up captured by the chains. Ellie gave herself to the scene; she had done it in Florence too, climbing the abandoned scaffolds in the Brancacci Chapel where they were doing a chemical peel on Masaccio—*chiuso, in restauro*—up she climbed and pulled back the canvas that draped Adam and Eve, banished and in agony. I thought somehow we would be arrested for such a thing. I don't really know how to live. She takes things on as they come, a deeply bred, intuitive fearlessness. In Rome, in an open crypt before the glass-doored reliquiarium holding St. Peter's chains, she stood utterly still, just watching. Her stillness seemed to me a kind of prayer, or a shawl used in prayer, something she wrapped around herself like a shell of less demanding and cluttered light, something more silver-gray than the brown-gold light of the air around her; it was grace perhaps; and then quietly up behind her came a tall German with a camera; he was studious, careful, and dull; you could see it in his shoes, those awful German shoes. He wanted a picture of this, as of everything else that caught his interest, the chains in this instance because that church was about the chains, though Michelangelo's *Moses* loomed off to the side and above, a carnival of unnecessary ideas by comparison. The German raised the camera and she did not hear him, and watching from above her on the main floor of the church, I knew what would happen but could not call out to her, it being a church, and then came the rude flash—white, sudden, air-shattering light. It made her leap—like an explosion. Time collided with the infinite and she was thrust back into the blinding world. White flash and black silence; it was Paul's fear and blindness reenacted, he'd been struck from his horse, all over again, and all over again he was hearing the irresistible voice, *Saul Saul why do you persecute me?* on the road to Damascus.

Fear on the road now—among the many disciples on Broadway, late at night, hearing voices. I know the feeling, a small portion of it, that chill and stillness, and if at this moment I do not have actual belief then I have the desire for belief. *He has risen, he is not here . . . Woman, why are you weeping? . . . Ich glaube mein Herr, hilfen mein unglauben.* The frightening moments are these, finding the stone moved back and the tomb empty, when you are forced to recognize that God is immune to history. *Before Moses was I am . . .* The problem of course is we don't get to see any of that, we live in the age of the invisible god, the age of flaming cities, mass human holocausts, gossamer surgery gently waylaying our avid search for death. *Why do you seek the living among the dead? . . . Go quickly, and tell the others.* He could be anyone, anywhere, anytime, and will be. He could be under the white and yellow streetlights, one of the women or men who live in this place, their figures moving slowly across the scene, shadows and memories of shadows. *Who is the third who walks beside you?* Shadows like the shadows that a child has seen, moving across graying walls, as sleep escapes him, as sleep teases him and frightens him. He lies still, watching, making out patterns and reflections, and taking comfort from these and from the sound of cars, the soft hiss of rubber on pavement and the low muscular sound of engines. All of it in time—real light, real walls, real tires—and out of time, the coded talk and semaphore of a supernatural side of creation. And distant in the house for that child—I remember this—is his mother at the sink; the pipes clink and shush when she turns the water on. Outside his window a little bit of rain. A sweet wind.

There are drops on my face now, and the soft bite of a northern wind on Riverside Drive, in the dark. *O dark dark dark, they all go into the dark . . .* The park below me is lush, black, a lattice of gray branches guarding a shadowed cathedral. I do not understand suicide. Suicide is too difficult. It is insufficient; it has never been enough. I want to be knocked down; I want to be flattened, atomized, crushed; I want to be annihilated, absorbed; I want to be assumed.

I want to go home.

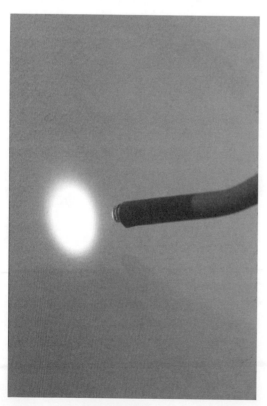

The black is unrelieved, as it should be.
It seems so solid I could land. It has
been hours that I have been thinking,
Why, this is all there is.
(Pierson, page 131)

Hi-fi

Jack Walls

THE DEATH OF JFK JR. MADE ME THINK ABOUT A FEW THINGS I hadn't thought about in many years. That little salute he gave his dad was one of my earliest memories. I was six years old, in the first grade. We had just returned from lunch hour. Several of the teachers were in the hallway crying. I didn't know why. I didn't even have time to take off my coat. They told us all to return home. Imagine as a child my glee, no school! Upon arriving home my happiness turned to sadness. My mom was weeping. I'll never forget that one silent tear running down her cheek. I've only seen my mother cry twice. That was the first time. She turned to me and said someone had shot and killed the president. Because my mother was crying I thought that I should cry too, so I did. And I cried again thirty-five years later when his son's plane went down. My tears came hard and fast. I was shocked at my reaction. What a sad but fitting end to this, our century, I thought.

That weekend in 1963 I sat cross-legged in front of the television watching the funeral procession. Every station was interrupted with the coverage. I was forced to watch it. I remember the horse pulling that simple wooden coffin down Pennsylvania Avenue in what seemed to me a very elaborate ceremony. I sat watching it as if in a trance. Thirty-five years later, I began to think of all the things that had happened to me since that day in late November, when little John-John stood there and gave that final salute.

Television was still in its infancy. Watching that funeral procession made me understand its power. I still remember the first time a black couple came dancing across the tube on *American Bandstand*. The telephone started ringing off the hook. Soon our living room was crammed with relatives and neighbors, all jockeying for position in front of the TV set to watch the "colored couple" dance across the screen. As a child at six I knew being black was being different. This I understood through the power of television.

I saw race riots, Vietnam, peace and love, LSD, The Beatles, the afro, The Stones. I saw them kill Lee Harvey Oswald, Martin Luther King, and Bobby Kennedy. I saw the Black Panthers, Gay Power, Black Power, and Charlie Manson. I saw the black man transcend the word "nigger." I saw them burn flags and bras and draft cards too. The Supremes, The Temptations, the whole Motown Review. And somehow during all that they managed to put a man on the moon.

My parents Willie Walls and Dorothy Mae Jones were born in Mississippi, Sunflower and Tunica respectively. These were the days of Jim Crow, a time when segregation was accepted by the majority of whites and begrudgingly by most blacks.

Most white southerners believed that all the people in the South, white and black, wanted segregation. This proved not to be true.

But still, the schools remained segregated, water fountains for "colored" only. Blacks sat on the designated seats at the rear of the public transportation systems. The major cities in the South had taxi cabs for "negroes," separate dining areas in restaurants, and some hotels didn't accept them at all. Black people usually had to travel out of the way to find lodging for the night, or slept in their cars along the road. Which at times could prove to be a fatal mistake.

The black population for the most part bowed and scraped to the "white folk." Yes Mammin' and Yes Sirin' all day long. The black southerners soon began to tire of this. Which led to civil unrest.

It was to be a hard-fought battle for all Americans, black and white. For white southerners, the scars that were just beginning to heal after the Civil War were about to be ripped open. By custom and by law, most blacks were servants, laborers, and tenant farmers. Went to separate, poorer schools, lived in separate poorer housing. It was like this throughout the country. But especially in the South, where they made no bones about keeping the "nigger" in his place. Blacks were held down socially and psychologically. Blacks were even denied the right to vote.

But there were always a few blacks and some whites who fought against segregation and racism. This was the South my parents were born into.

My mom had her first child out of wedlock on May 13, 1953, when she was twenty years old, with her first boyfriend. He had to leave town in a hurry before the child was born. It was either trouble with the law or the Ku Klux Klan, which in those days in the South was usually one and the same. My mom gave birth to my oldest brother who she named Charles Edward Jones, the middle name being his father's birth name.

Shortly thereafter my father entered the picture. When he came to court my mom, my grandmother used to greet him on the front porch with a double-barreled shotgun. He'd be standing there with some sorry bouquet looking down the barrel of a shotgun pointed at his chest. Somehow they got married. They weren't married too long before my dad had to do time for pistol-whipping some guy. Over what? Probably nothing. My dad had a temper.

He went to a work farm (which is a polite term for chain gang) for six months. Lucky for him, soon after he got there his appendix ruptured. So he spent the rest of his time in the hospital. My dad fancied himself a blues musician. He played guitar, called himself Little Willie Walls. When I was a child, the men who hung around the neighborhood tavern simply called him "Shorty."

He used to get drunk and play acoustic guitar. As children, we hated the blues. You always hate the music your parents like. We'd avoid going into the living room when he was playing. Because if he saw you he'd start making up a song about you. Like if you had a hole in your sock, he'd start singing about that. He used to run around with Howlin' Wolf and all those other blues cats. He idolized them. They had all gone to Chicago or "up North." So my folks decided that they too would go "up North." But before they did, on June 15, 1955, my mom gave birth to my brother Dennis, leaving my oldest brother Charles behind with my grandmother and her youngest sister. They took off with baby Dennis for Chicago. Now that they were starting to have children, they wanted them to have better opportunities than they'd had growing up in the South. After they got settled they sent for Charles.

I was born with a bad case of rickets, March 7, 1957, in Cook

County Hospital. My legs were so bowed, they say that when as a toddler, I walked like Tarzan's chimpanzee, Cheetah. I don't remember it being so bad though. They're still bowed, but they're not that bad. Years later, upon my arrival in New York City, Robert Mapplethorpe would photograph my legs and make them famous. Robert Mapplethorpe was also to become a key figure in my life. I spent the last eight years of his life with him as his friend and lover. It was he who thought I should write.

As a child I would often fantasize about the future. About what was out there, what lay ahead. For some reason, when I was very young I would hear that song "Green Onions" by Booker T. & the MG's and have really intense, for lack of a better word, premonitions about the distant future. I can hear that song today and get the same feeling I had as a little kid living in the projects on the south side of Chicago. The song is an instrumental. It was like a sound track to a movie, my movie. As a child I always thought that I was being filmed or watched.

In 1963 we moved from the projects to 2609 West Ogden Avenue, on the west side. We'd lived there before, I was to learn later. I'd also realize later that this was the apartment building where I'd had my first Christmas memory. The first time I saw Christmas tree lights all aglitter. And under the trees was a little plastic train set, for me.

Another fond memory for me is the snowstorm of January 1967. It was called the Blizzard of the Century. The snow began to fall as my brothers and I sat watching television. The snow continued to fall throughout the night. In the morning, upon waking, Mom told us that there wasn't any school due to the snowstorm. I ran to look out of the window of our third-floor apartment and all I saw was white. No cars were moving, no buses, nothing moved. Just all white. The city was paralyzed!

I couldn't wait to go outside and play in the snow. After a breakfast which consisted of grits, eggs scrambled soft, bacon fried crisp, and a bowl of Fruit Loops, we began to get dressed to go out and play, donning long underwear, three pairs of socks, overalls, and galoshes.

We set out through the kitchen and out the back door that led across the hall to a small vacant one-bedroom apartment, the door of which had no lock. By that time I'd been told that this was the apartment in which my first Christmas memory takes place. This had been one of the first apartments my parents had lived in upon moving to Chicago. I was the baby of the family, but since then they'd had three other children: my brother Carl, in April 1959, Gregory, in September 1961, then Michael, in February 1963. Through this apartment we accessed the third-floor back porch. From here we eyed the mountainous snowdrifts. The roof of the one-story factory across the alley from our building was laden with snow. We made our way down to the second floor and leapt from its porch into the snow below. We then proceeded to go to the apartments of all our friends in the neighborhood to see if they too could come out and partake in the aftermath of the blizzard, and we all set out together for our adventure in this wonderland called winter.

To most Chicagoans the storm wreaked havoc. Cars and buses were stranded all over the city, trains were frozen in and could not make their usual commuter runs.

O'Hare International Airport (then called O'Hare Field) was shut down! But to the children in my neighborhood it was Heaven come to Earth. Out we ran to make angels in the snow.

Mounds of snow covered everything. They were indeed mountainous. We started out playing King of the Hill. My brother Charlie found an old broomstick, made it to the top of the hill first, then took his red scarf, which had been a Christmas gift, from around his neck, tied it around the broom stick, and triumphantly jammed it in its peak proclaiming himself the king of the hill. Challenging any of us to remove it, he stood there defiantly, hands on his hips, and his young chest thrust forward. The older boys engaged themselves in a fierce battle to see who was to be the true king of the snowy peak. The younger children, we set out to build igloos. After putting much effort into building several igloos, under which we had dug rather intricate tunnels to connect them all, the older boys came and destroyed our little village. We retaliated by hurling snowballs, which led to an all-out battle *royale*.

Over the next ten days the snow continued to fall periodically. After it was all said and done, twenty million tons of snow had fallen across Chicagoland. The blizzard itself lasted over two days. There was no shortage of things to do in this winter paradise. Children erected armies of snowmen in the vacant lots all over the neighborhood. We built snow fortresses and challenged the kids from neighboring hoods to snowball battles. We did not lack ammunition.

One day, as winter turned to spring and the snow had all but melted away, my brother Dennis and I were walking home from school The snow mountain Charlie had once claimed with his makeshift flag was now no bigger than my foot. I kicked what was left of it away, turned to my brother Dennis, and said, "Remember when that piece of snow was a mountain?" He nodded yes. Then I said to him, "I'll race you home."

The following year, 1968, would prove memorable for other reasons. The war overseas in Vietnam was still raging. The American people were sick of it. As a leader, Dr. Martin Luther King, Jr. spoke out against the war in Vietnam in the national media, which pissed white America off. His most powerful ally, then President Lyndon B. Johnson, was bitterly disappointed in King. When King went public with his opposition to the war, J. Edgar Hoover, director of the FBI, tried to discredit him. The FBI monitored King's every move; though he had always been monitored, they turned up the heat.

Some saw Dr. Martin Luther King's outspoken opposition to the Vietnam War as his death knell. But King felt obligated to take a stand.

And we as black men were not only bearing the brunt of racism at home on the front line, but now on the front lines in Vietnam as well.

In April of 1967, Muhammad Ali was stripped of his World Champion title for refusing to go to Vietnam and fight a war he thought went against his religious beliefs. Born Cassius Marcellus Clay, he'd gone to the Olympics in 1960 and won the gold metal in the light heavyweight division. When he returned to his hometown of Louisville, Kentucky, Clay was refused service in a local restaurant. Stung by the rebuke, Clay threw the gold metal in the Ohio River. Nonetheless, he embarked on a boxing career. Advancing through the ranks of the heavyweight division, Clay quickly became a ranking contender, his boxing skills clearly evident.

Clay also gained increasing attention as a poet. Reciting sparse verse, he usually predicted the round in which his opponent would go down. In 1964 Clay, defeated the then heavyweight champion, Sonny Liston, and became the new heavyweight champion of the world.

Shortly after this victory, Clay announced that he was a member of the Nation of Islam, and changed his name to Muhammad Ali.

Ali's membership in the Nation of Islam and his friendship with Malcolm X made him unpopular among whites. Ali's straightforward declaration, "I ain't got nothing against those Vietcongs," rattled white America. He at once became a hero to black Americans.

Letters to Ali's draft board began to pour in. Initially he had been deferred from the draft on the basis of having failed the Selective Service qualifying exam. Numerous letters, often vicious, were sent to Ali's draft board in Louisville demanding his reclassification and induction. White America was still trying to keep the "nigger in his place." He was, in fact, stripped of his title and sentenced to five years in jail.

As the war raged on in Vietnam, the so-called War on Poverty in the United States suffered. One in seven Americans lived in poverty, many resorting to welfare just to have the basic needs: to pay the rent, for clothes, for food. So the poor organized. In the South, poverty was even more widespread. In the state of Mississippi, people were starving. The situation was so bad that Senator Robert Kennedy toured the Mississippi Delta to see for himself. Going from house to house he saw that the need for a solution was pressing.

In the summer of 1967, there were riots in one hundred American cities; eighty people had died. There was talk of a black revolution. Dr. Martin Luther King said, "A riot is a language of the unheard." Events were driving King to a more radical solution.

A poor people's march on Washington, D.C., was planned. They would recruit from all races, a nonviolent army of the poor. This, King said, was an alternative to riot, a last desperate demand for the nation to respond to nonviolence.

As King began to organize and recruit for the march, few were paying attention to a labor dispute in Memphis, Tennessee. It concerned the garbage collectors who were making $1.04 an hour. Three men had died in a freak accident while trying to seek shelter from the rain one day. They had climbed into the back of the garbage truck to seek shelter and were crushed. No one cared—the drivers of the trucks were white. Left the heavy work for the black sanitation workers. The workers accused the city of racial bias. Thirteen hundred workers decided to strike.

During the strike, a march was planned to protest the City Council's lack of action. During the march, a riot ensued between the cops and the protesters. Two months into the strike, Dr. King was asked to come to Memphis. He was to make a speech, and lead a second march.

The whites dreaded this. They'd already heard about Watts, Detroit, and Newark. And all the other big cities, and all the troubles in the big-city ghettos. They knew about the march in Selma, Alabama, and Rosa Parks' bus boycott, which had crippled Montgomery, Alabama.

Upon his arrival, King made the speech, which went well. But during the march a riot erupted once again. This was the first King-led demonstration that had led to violence. He braced himself for criticism; if he couldn't control a single march in Memphis, how then, would he control a poor people's mass movement to the nation's capital? The strike continued.

On April 3, 1968, King returned to Memphis, where on a rainy Wednesday evening, he delivered what was to be his last speech. He gave the now famous "I See the Promised Land" speech which closes with, "Mine eyes have seen the glory of the coming of the Lord."

The next day at the Lorraine Hotel, around six o'clock, as he and his associates were standing on the balcony about to leave the hotel, a shot rang out. It struck Dr. King. One hour after he was shot, Dr. Martin Luther King, Jr. died.

America's cities exploded. At around nine o'clock that night, in Chicago, my brothers, Charlie and Dennis, and several friends, and I were walking home from Marshall Square Boy's Club. That's where we went every Thursday from six to nine to shoot pool and play Ping-Pong. It was about one mile from where we lived.

As we turned the corner on Washtenaw Street off Cermack Road we could see the flames in the distance. Earlier that day, we had heard about Dr. King on the news. Even at that age I knew what was happening. We hurried home. I watched from our living-room windows; the flames went all along Roosevelt Road, the whole city seem to be a flame, everything was red. People were rioting. Directly across our block on Ogden Avenue were housing projects. Next door was a tavern where my dad would buy his cigarettes. Then, cigarettes cost only sixty cents; he smoked Pall Malls. He would oftentimes send me to purchase a pack of cigarettes, or "squares," as they called them in Chicago. This establishment was owned by an old white lady named Ann. Ann's Tavern. Her son, Wayne, would bartend in the evenings—he had a glass eye. Sometimes, when he would hand you your change, the glass eye would be amongst the change! Anyway, as my family and I watched the flames, we saw a band of rioters crossing the boulevard approaching the tavern. My dad, upon observing this, went into the bedroom that he shared with Mom and got his gun, a thirty-two snub-nosed revolver. He stuck it in the waist of his pants. He then went out the door and down the stairs to meet the rioters. We, the rest of the family and Mom, all crowded the windows. Dad was having a lengthy conversation with one of the mob leaders.

After a while, Dad shook hands with several members of the mob. They all turned and walked back across the boulevard into the flames.

I was six years old when JFK was assassinated in 1963. By eleven years old I had gotten a little more observant, a little bit more sophisticated concerning some of the more curious aspects of life. Like the race thing—that I couldn't get. Being black, it seemed to some people, was a really big deal. I found it hard to believe that some people actually hated you for it. By then I'd heard the stories from my parents about the Ku Klux Klan, and all the shit that whites in the South were about.

It was around this time that I first saw the movie *To Kill a Mockingbird*. That film made me conscious of certain realities. Now, in that film, a white-trash chick has the hots for this black field- hand cat, okay? So, she tries to seduce him one day. Her father comes home early and sees through the window his daughter begging this strapping black field hand to bang her. So the black cat sees the father and hauls ass, and the father enters the house and beats the shit out of his daughter. Though you never see this on film. All of this is revealed in the ensuing courtroom drama. See, in order to save face, the father goes and tells all the other crackers in the town that the black cat beat and raped his daughter. And the whole town just knows that he's guilty, but he ain't, see?

What I'm getting at is this. When we lived in the Robert Taylor housing projects on the south side, it was all black. Now that we were living at 2609 West Ogden on the west side, there were a few white people on our block. There was an old Italian couple, Mr. and Mrs. Benno, in the building next door to us on the right. And of course Ann and her son Wayne in the apartment building to our left. At school, although it was predominately Hispanic, there were a few white kids, about just as many whites as blacks. Which wasn't that many. It was a small school, around two hundred kids all told. On field trips we would hold hands and get along just fine. So on one hand, I knew about all that stuff, and on the other hand, my day-to-day experiences didn't jibe. Abstract, the whole thing was abstract. It seemed America had some growing up to do.

America though, at this moment, was in mourning. Black Americans were mourning more. Watching King's funeral on TV was like watching President Kennedy's funeral all over again. Except this time the cast was all black. Jackie Kennedy and King's wife, Coretta King, were interchangeable to me. Kennedy's procession had a horse pulling his coffin; King's was lead by a mule.

The poor people's march on the nation's capital did not cease because of the assassination of Dr. King. America's poor marched on. One of the poor's strongest allies was campaigning for the presidential nomination: John F. Kennedy's younger brother, Senator Robert F. Kennedy. With strong support from black and Hispanic voters, he campaigned against the war in Vietnam. While on the campaign trail, on the night of June 4, 1968, at the Ambassador Hotel in Los Angeles, he too was assassinated.

At this point in my young life, blood had spilled off the television and into our living room so often that now, it was commonplace. Another Kennedy, another funeral procession, Jackie Kennedy mourning, yet again. Americans wept together. We had bestowed our trust in him. We grieved and felt the same pain. The players in this drama were now colorless.

At the time of the assassination, the poor people's march had made its way to the nation's capital. Before being taken to Arlington Cemetery, Robert Kennedy's final resting place, the black funeral car which carried his body made one last stop: in front of the Lincoln Memorial, where all the marchers, now mourners, had gathered on its steps. There they all wept as they sang "The Battle Hymn of the Republic," bidding him one last farewell.

That August, the Democratic National Convention was to be held in Chicago. This convention would not be remembered for its politics, but for its violence, for its televised display of social unrest and national disunity. The country had reached its boiling point. Two

American icons had been assassinated back-to-back. Every day, young American boys were being slaughtered in a land far away, so far away that most Americans before the war would not be able to locate Vietnam on a map.

I remember seeing footage of the war in Vietnam on the evening news. Watching the soldiers wading waist high through the water of the paddy fields with their weapons held above their heads in order to keep them dry. Helicopters, like huge dark dragonflies, hovered dangerously close over the soldiers' heads. The force of the wind emanating from the blades of the helicopters' propellers made the rice shoots bend and sway. Like watching a lethal yet beautiful ballet.

I remember hearing the older boys in the neighborhood, who were approaching the draft age, talk about going down to the draft board and applying for the draft, but not with much enthusiasm. Whenever this subject would come up they'd become glum. I'd already had a cousin die in the war. Some of the older boys, I remember, simply joined up. It was easier than sitting around waiting for the inevitable; waiting to die, I supposed.

Thousands of war protesters prepared to gather in Chicago for the Democratic National Convention.

Chicago Mayor Richard J. Daley was unsympathetic. He posted twelve thousand police officers on the streets and called in the Illinois National Guard. The violence that exploded from the demonstrations was white rage, America's white youth, the flower children, young white Americans who heretofore had not been heard. Or, having been heard, ignored. They were now talking revolution. Drugs, sex, rock and roll, smash the State. The confrontation at the Democratic National Convention in Chicago was the grand climax of this state of mind.

The day after the white riot, as I saw it, was over and its participants gone, my brother Charlie and I rode, with me on the handlebars, his red five-speed bicycle, which also had a banana seat, and a sissy bar, with a fake foxtail attached to it, blowing in the wind. We had decided to journey to Grant Park, which was where the televised battle, had taken place.

Upon arriving we surveyed the terrain. We were the only two people in the park that afternoon. As we rode around slowly, I noticed how worn out it looked, how exhausted. The police barricades, we called them "horses," were still there, tipped over on their sides, and smashed. The glittering fragments of glass, the shards of glass, the blades of grass. Broken glass glimmering, like diamonds along the gutters, the boarded-up windows of the storefronts along Michigan Avenue.

The slight breeze that day carried and tossed old newspapers along the bicycle's path. To my right sat Lake Michigan with sailboats on its horizon. I wondered about the people on those boats—had they heard about the riot? What type of people might they be? What type of home would they return to at the end of their day? Were they rich? Were they famous? Would I ever know people like them? Would I want to?

It was around this time that Black Power kicked in. On my birth certificate, it says "Negro"; on some birth certificates of blacks, it would say "colored." The word "Negro," I thought, was too close to the word "nigger." Some whites pronounced it "Nigra." I remember when white people would prepare to say the word "Negro." That fraction of a second, when a white person's mouth formed, to make the "n" sound, I would hold my breath. Because if someone was about to call me a "nigger," or even say the word period, all hell was gonna break loose. Black Power! Now, black was beautiful! Now, we were black and proud! James Brown sang, "Say it loud, I'm black and I'm proud!" That song was our anthem in the late sixties.

My generation was the first generation of African-Americans that held no fear, whatsoever, of white people.

Before his death, Dr. Martin Luther King had led a nonviolent march through an all-white suburb of Chicago called Cicero. It was said, "Don't let the sun go down on you in Cicero," if you were not white.

On the evening news that day, I watched as Dr. King led the marchers slowly through the streets of Cicero, through jeering mobs of racists. The mobs at first consisted mainly of young men and teenaged boys. I was shocked, because a large number of these hooligans were flying sheets with swastikas crudely painted on them. They had signs which read, "Nigger go home." This, up till now, I had not seen. I'd seen the footage of what had happened in the South, racist police turning fire hoses on school children; I'd seen the battles at the lunch counters. Black college students would sit quietly at the lunch counters, and they would be refused service. Nevertheless, they would sometimes sit there for hours. The restaurants, instead of serving them, would close down altogether. Thus, the college students effectively disrupted service. Soon, whites would, upon hearing that a lunch counter "sit-in," as they came to be known, was to take place, would attack the sitters. The students, being nonviolent, would not fight back. But for me, that was far, far away. This couldn't, I thought, be happening here in Chicago.

As the marchers in Cicero moved along, women began to join the mob. They were coming out of their homes with curlers in their hair and babies on their hips, spewing racist epithets.

I was not intimidated; this did not color my opinion of white people. My own day-to-day experiences at the time did not reflect this. At school, children, being children, would often say mean things to one another out of anger. Sometimes, the words "honky," "nigger," "spic," would be hurled. But, after all was said and done, we remained friends. We were poor people, our fathers worked hard. Our mothers hung out together at PTA meetings, accompanied us on field trips, and participated in after-school programs.

My dad, having grown up in the South a black man, did, I think, have some reservations about white America. My mom did not; she made sure that we were fed, our clothes were clean, and that we studied our lessons. She understood, I believe, that the best revenge against racism was education.

My mother came from a family of twelve, so I had lots of cousins around all the time. We were all very precocious and bookish. My favorite cousin Dorothy (named after my mom) would read to me before I knew how. Once I started school I read voraciously. Stunk at arithmetic, hated it. When I reached junior high I refused to do math entirely. There was a big drama about it. Parent–teacher meetings, threats to hold me back a grade, the whole bit. Somehow the thing resolved itself. How? I forget.

It was around this time my seventh grade teacher gave me the book that would change my life. It was *Manchild in the Promised Land* by Claude Brown. It was about him growing up in Harlem, pulling himself out of the ghetto, and making something of himself. Thus began what was to become my obsession to some day live in New York City. And maybe I'd become a writer.

Then I discovered James Baldwin's *Giovanni's Room*. I read that book over and over. It made me want to see Paris. To travel. It was also the first book I'd read that dealt directly with homosexuality. I read every Baldwin book I could get my hands on. At an early age I knew I was homosexual. I wasn't effeminate. I participated in sports and did all the things young boys did. But I also knew that I liked guys. It was a relief to know there were other homosexuals in the world. Other men that loved men. Reading Baldwin helped me realize I wasn't the only one. Growing up I'd see the obviously effeminate boys, or boys that flat-out acted like girls. I had no desire to be female.

Baldwin led to Jean Genet, which coincided with my growing interest in gangs. I had joined my first gang officially when I was fifteen, and gangs were a major topic for Genet.

The city of Chicago was and still is rife with gangs. When I was growing up, it was almost an impossibility not to be connected with a gang in some form or fashion. That's pretty much what one did upon entering puberty. You joined a gang. The neighborhood that I grew up in was called Pilsen. It's on the southwest side of Chicago. It was a Hispanic neighborhood: Puerto Rican, some Cubans, but predominately Mexican. Before that it was Polish and Irish. The whites that were still there were so ghetto they weren't like white people. Most of them spoke some Spanish, the blacks as well. We all had a handle on Spanish.

Pilsen was separated to the north at Sixteenth Street by a viaduct. The boundaries were from Halsted Street then west to Western Avenue, then south to Cermack Road, or to some, Twenty-second Street, which was roughly a two-mile radius. There were around nine or ten gangs within that boundary. So shit was happening all the time.

I gravitated toward gangs with an almost romantic sense. Even their names seemed romantic to me. The Artistics. The feared Spartans, led by Crazy Clarence, was one of the most violent gangs around. The legendary Chancellors had only ten members, but they got lots of respect. All of them had scandalous reputations.

The Goon Squad was a renegade bunch of marauding thugs, notorious for doing drive bys on bicycles. The Bishops, a bunch of young upstarts, is still around today raising hell. The Almighty Latin

Kings branched out all over the country, today a force in New York City. The Latin Counts was led by Mr. Shy, known for his impeccable wardrobe and the way he held his head. Cocked slightly to the side. His crooked smile. My cousin, Micky Jones was in the Vice Lords. It was an all-black gang that operated out of the Cabrini Green Housing Projects on the north side. Another north-side gang, the Latin Eagles, was run by the Rosario brothers. My cousin Isaac Lee ran the Gypsy Cobras. The Unknown Gangsters and the Insane Unknowns were two other north-side gangs that I didn't know too much about.

Each gang had a female counterpart: the Valkyries, from the Italian neighborhood of Bridgeport, located on the near south side; the Spartanettes, the sister gang of the feared Spartans; the Hell Cats, sister gang of the Goon Squad; the Don Jaunettes, the Duprees, and on and on.

The gang I admired most was an all-black gay gang from the far south side, the Supremes. It was notorious, first for being all gay, second, for not taking shit from anyone. Most gangs were confined to a certain area, or turf. The Supremes could go to any neighborhood. Even the baddest of gangbangers never fucked with the Supremes.

Those faggots knew how to make an entrance (think Little Richard). They would walk into the youth-center dances and all action would stop. I think even the music would stop. And for some reason they always had the coolest chicks hanging out with them. Of course they were the best dancers. Even today I wish that I'd had the nerve to be a Supreme.

The gang I chose to be in was called the Almighty Morgan Deuces. The Deuces had been around since the late fifties. Originating on Eighteenth and Morgan, hence the name.

I went to Edward Tilden High School. During my freshman year met this heavyset black kid named Joel Scott a.k.a., Spooky. He had a pick with a fist stuck in his Afro. He was the president of the Midget Morgan Deuces. You didn't want to upset him. He could kick ass fierce. See, gangs then—I don't know about now—were divided into groups. Usually according to age. There'd be the Peewee division (ages ten to thirteen), the Midgets (fourteen to sisteen), the Littles (seventeen to nineteen), the Juniors (twenty to twenty-one), then the Seniors (twenty-one to infinity).

I'd hang out with Spooky in study hall. We'd talk about all the gangs, talk about who did what to whom. Who was about to go to war. About which gang was showing weak spots. Important stuff. It was all about image. I had been in a gang before, I'd been a Peewee Satan's Disciple, sort of by default. My oldest brother Charlie was a member of the Satan's Disciples, so it was automatically assumed I'd join. But I had plans of my own. Now the Deuces and the Disciples were arch rivals, so when I joined the Deuces, there was occasionally a little static on the home front, since Charlie and I both still lived at home. I'd show up at the house with one of my boys, and my little brother would come to the door, giving us a look that said, "Don't go in," which meant that the Disciples were in the house. We'd go around to the back and wait until they left. They'd leave out the front door, and we'd enter through the back. My mom would be clearing away their dishes. Then she'd feed us. The funny thing was, Charlie and I really loved one another, even though the Deuces and the Disciples were rivals. The reason things never really escalated between both gangs was because Charlie and I, at home at night, squashed any beef that came up between members of our units.

My nickname was Hi-fi. Just about everyone in the neighborhood had a nickname. When I would spray paint my gang's name on the side of a garage or a school building, I couldn't use my real name. So I called myself Hi-fi. No one gave me that name. At around thirteen, when someone asked me what my name was, I said Hi-fi. When I go back to Chicago now people still call me Hi-fi.

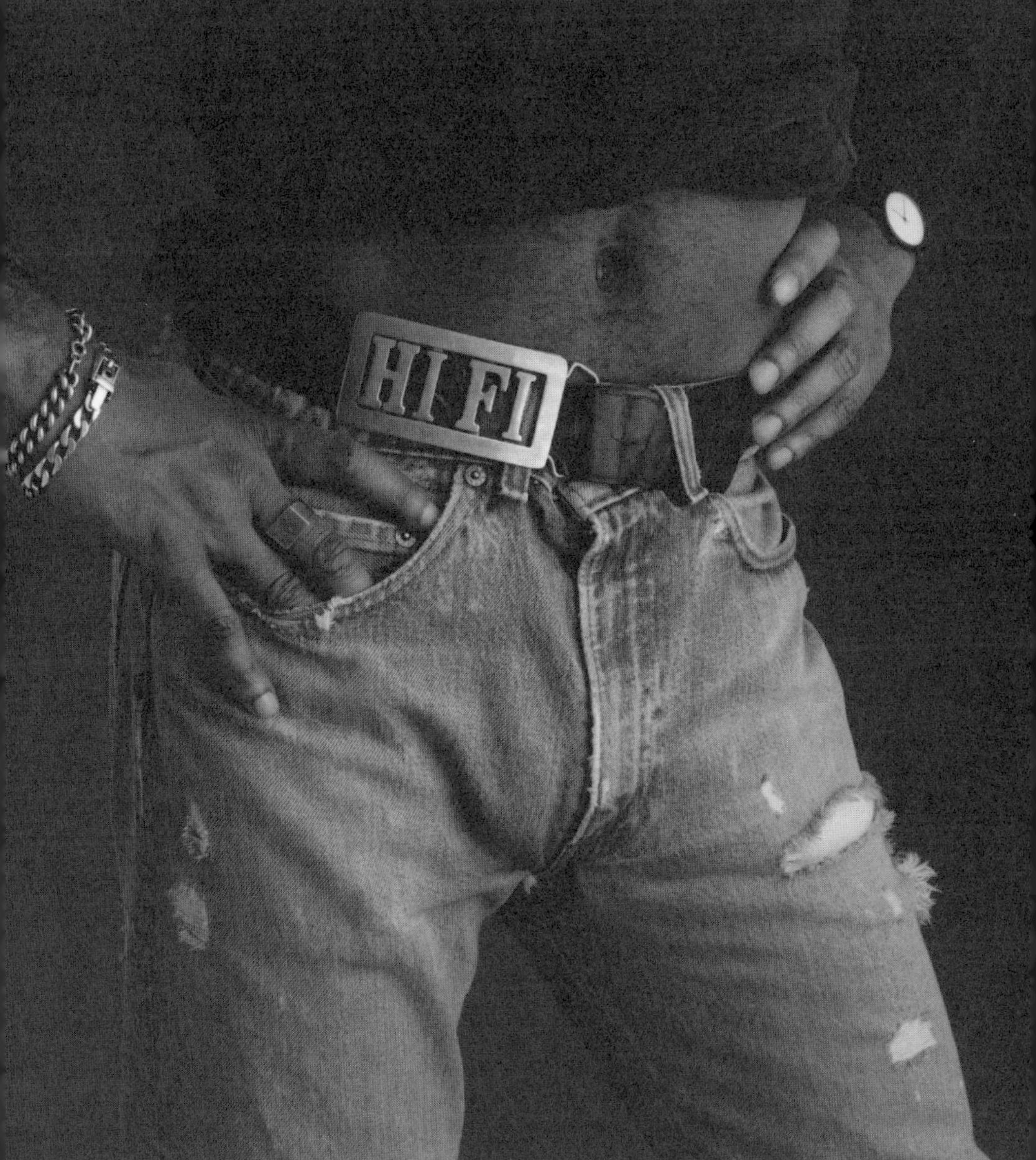
HI FI

Photo: Brian English

LETTERS*

*There are no letters on this page because we did not receive any letters. This is, perhaps, a good thing, as the urge to write a letter to the editor is usually because someone has become annoyed, wants to make a correction, refine a point, object, heckle, et cetera. But this is also a bad thing, because letters make you feel that there is someone out there. So please write a letter and if you have nothing to correct or complain about, perhaps you can nit-pick or make tiny suggestions. The first three letter writers will receive a special prize.

The Editors, Open City, 225 Lafayette Street, Suite 1114, New York, NY 10012. Or editors@opencity.org.